THE
REVENGE
GAME

THE REVENGE GAME

JORDYN TAYLOR

DELACORTE PRESS

Text copyright © 2023 by Jordyn Taylor
Jacket art and design by Casey Moses
Lips image used under license from Shutterstock.com

All rights reserved. Published in the United States by Delacorte Press, an imprint of Random House Children's Books, a division of Penguin Random House LLC, New York.

Delacorte Press is a registered trademark and the colophon
is a trademark of Penguin Random House LLC.

GetUnderlined.com

Educators and librarians, for a variety of teaching tools,
visit us at RHTeachersLibrarians.com

Library of Congress Cataloging-in-Publication Data is available upon request.
ISBN 978-0-593-56364-9 (hardcover) — ISBN 978-0-593-56366-3 (ebook) —
ISBN 978-0-593-70996-2 (int'l. ed.)

The text of this book is set in 10.5-point Chronicle Text.
Interior design by Ken Crossland

Printed in the United States of America
10 9 8 7 6 5 4 3 2 1
First Edition

For Eileen,
who helped me finish the story

Men are afraid women will laugh at them.

Women are afraid men will kill them.

—Margaret Atwood

Adirondack Daily Enterprise

Prep School Lacrosse Captain Missing Since Prom Night
*Police search still underway,
cause of disappearance remains unknown.*

BY GERALDINE JOHNSON, STAFF REPORTER

Authorities are investigating the mysterious disappearance of a star athlete at Sullivan-Stewart Preparatory School who vanished after prom on Saturday evening.

Brenton Riggs Jr., 18, a boarder at the prestigious Lake Placid private school, was reported missing by his lacrosse coach when he didn't show up to practice Monday morning.

1

"At first, I figured he was just running late—probably still tired from prom, you know?" Coach Bradley Pierce said by phone. "I called him a bunch of times, no answer. That was weird. And then his buddies told me they hadn't heard from him since the night before."

The dance took place at the Sentinel Lodge, a hotel in the mountains near Wilmington. School administrators said they knew Riggs would not be returning to campus immediately after the event, and therefore had no cause for concern when he didn't swipe back into his dormitory.

"Brenton followed the proper procedure for notifying us that he'd be spending the night away from school," a Sullivan-Stewart spokesperson said in an email, adding that it's common for boarding students to use their days off to visit friends and family. "We are deeply concerned for Brenton's safety, especially given the weather conditions."

A record-shattering April nor'easter dumped up to 23 inches of snow on the Adirondack region on the night of Riggs's disappearance, resulting in the deaths of at least two people and leaving many residents without power. Lake Placid, Wilmington, and other parts of Essex County recorded the heaviest snowfall.

Riggs, who is 6'3" with curly blond hair, blue eyes, and a muscular build, was last seen wearing a light gray suit with brown dress shoes. Lake

Placid Police chief Ralph Nostrand says a search for the missing teen is currently underway, and it's too soon to make any determinations about his current whereabouts or what may have led to his disappearance. Nostrand also confirmed that investigators are in communication with the student's family in Manhattan.

Riggs is slated to start his freshman year at Duke University this fall, where he'll be continuing his lacrosse career, according to his coach.

"He's a promising kid with a bright future," Pierce said. "Smart. Athletic. A real leader. I really can't put into words how much he brings to the school community. Come on home, Riggs."

CHAPTER 1

September, Seven Months Earlier

I spend a lot of time wondering which of the boys in my immediate vicinity will be the one who finally falls in love with me. For all I know, it could be someone in this AP English Literature class: the guy with glasses in the second row who nodded along as I defined "juxtaposition" a few minutes ago, or maybe the bored-looking kid sitting sideways in the seat in front of me, the tip of his elbow grazing my desk. I steal a glance away from the projector screen to survey the rest of my dozen or so possibilities. I don't know if it's the sexy maroon blazers or my sorry excuse for a love life—it's a hundred percent both—but I'm ready and willing to be swept off my feet by any one of them.

As my eyes dart from one potential suitor to the next, I accidentally tune out Mr. MacMillan as he scrolls through examples of short-story projects his students have done in the past, but that's all right. The assignment seems easy enough: pick a theme; find three short stories that fit said theme; write a paper comparing and contrasting said stories. It's the kind of thing I'd probably do for fun in my spare time, which is why I'm the lone junior in this college-level class.

Mr. MacMillan's next words make me snap back to attention. "In the spirit of you all getting to know each other"—a few people visibly perk up in their chairs, myself included—"I'm going to randomly divide you into pairs. Over the next few class periods, I'll give you time to choose your stories, analyze them, and write your essays together."

Oh my God. Oh-my-*freaking*-God. My chair feels like a roller-coaster car that just left the station, and my blood pumps like I'm chugging up the first big hill. If the point of the group project is everyone "getting to know each other," then that must mean . . .

I'm going to be matched with a guy.

Now that I'm almost seventeen, "possible conversation with boy" shouldn't feel like such a momentous occasion, but this is a big deal for me, pathetic as that may sound. Our private school, Sullivan-Stewart Prep, has been coed for all of a week. Before, we were two separate schools: the all-boys Sullivan School in Lake Placid and the all-girls Stewart Academy in Saranac Lake, a cozier, less-tourist-packed town about fifteen minutes away. They bussed us back and forth for a dance here and there, a rare chance for those who liked guys to gain some semblance of sexual experience. We'd spend hours scurrying between dorm rooms to focus-group potential looks, all for a shot at a dance-floor make-out.

This getting-ready ritual always paid off for a handful of girls, and we'd analyze their exploits on the bus ride home. Sometimes they'd gush about a guy being good with his tongue;

other times, they'd shudder about too much teeth or spit. Frankly, I would have taken either option. They were both more appealing than what I was getting, which was nothing. My most common achievement was embarrassing myself with my overeagerness, like when I tried to make conversation over the music with a guy who'd come up behind me and started grinding, and he yelled in my ear—as politely as possible—that I was supposed to stay facing away from him, like the other couples. If I hadn't maintained a steady diet of romance novels all this time, I'd probably be as jaded as my mom, who buries herself in work to avoid having time for a love life.

Don't get me wrong, Stewart was great from an academic standpoint: cool feminist teachers; lots of extra help if you needed it; a college advisor who encouraged me to take AP English Lit now so I can have it on my transcript when I apply to my über-hard-to-get-into college writing program next fall. But I wished it were coed, like the school on that sexy Spanish Netflix show *Elite,* where everyone's hot and constantly falling head over heels for each other—except without all the murder. And then it actually happened (the coed thing—not the murder). Last fall, because of some financial something-or-other, Sullivan and Stewart announced they were merging into one unified school on Sullivan's campus. To house us, they built two new dorms from stone and wood in the same Adirondack style as the rest of the buildings. You can tell the buildings are out of place with their fresh coats of blue paint, their soft skin that hasn't seen a frigid mountain winter yet. They stick out just like we do, the Stewart transplants, the ones the teachers keep referring to as the "fresh faces on campus."

The question dances on the tip of my tongue as Mr. Mac-Millan gives way too many details on how we should go about choosing our short stories as a team. I know I shouldn't ask it—that it'll make me sound desperate, which is exactly what I'm trying to avoid, especially after what happened this summer—but there are only two minutes left in the period. I compromise by not *thrusting* my hand in the air, as a desperate person might do, but rather raising it at ear height as though I don't really care if he calls on me or not.

Mr. MacMillan keeps talking. Argh. It's probably hard for him to see me since he dimmed the lights for the projector. Now there's only a minute left; people are closing their books and unzipping their backpacks. Screw it. I go for the full-on hand thrust, fingers waggling in the air.

The teacher looks at me. Thank God. "Alyson?"

"Um . . ." I clear my throat. "I was wondering when we'll find out our partners?" I hear murmurs of agreement from around the room. There—no need to be ashamed. I've done a public service.

Mr. MacMillan chuckles. A sixty-something guy with ruddy skin and long, white sideburns, he's taught at the school formerly known as Sullivan for decades. "I know you're all chomping at the bit. I didn't get a chance to make the list before class, so I'll send it out when we're finished here."

The bell rings, and I've never been so excited to see the end of an English period. Is that pathetic? Maybe. Probably.

Whatever.

When I get outside, I spot my best friend, Jess Quigley, dragging her feet up the wood-chip path. When she sees me—in other words, when she knows she has an audience—she slumps against a column next to the door and throws her forearm over her eyes. "I am weary," she moans.

"Why?" I ask, easing her arm off her face. My other hand clutches my phone, my thumb hovering over the refresh button on my email app. So far, nothing from Mr. MacMillan.

Jess runs her nonregulation magenta fingernails through her dyed-black hair, which pops against her ivory skin. She just had AP Macroeconomics in the building next door, and before that, Accounting. Her goal, she says, is to learn everything there is to know about capitalism so she can dismantle it someday. "The mansplaining," Jess replies, "is going to be the death of me."

"What happened?"

She sighs. "This random guy apparently felt the pressing need to explain GDP to me. Not, like, how it's calculated, or what the data is used for, but, like, literally what the letters mean."

I blink at her. "Um . . . what . . . do the letters mean again?" Jess and I bonded in the eighth grade because we both spent our lunches reading library books for fun, but our areas of expertise couldn't be more different.

"Gross domestic product," she answers. "Much like Mr. Mansplainer himself." She pushes herself off the column, smiling smugly at her own play on words. We start back down the path. "How was English?"

"It was . . ." *The most exhilarating class period I've had all week?* No. I need to control myself, for God's sake. My heart still stings from what happened a few weeks ago with Aiden, the cute guy from my summer job at the bookstore—the one I totally rubbed the wrong way with what I *thought* was a romantic gesture. I make sure my voice stays steady as I continue. "It was fine. We're starting this new group project and our teacher's choosing the partners."

"That would be my literal worst nightmare." Jess kicks a stone and it catapults into the bushes. She was a lot less enthusiastic about the Sullivan-Stewart merger than I was, a firm believer that high school boys lack the emotional maturity and ability to locate the clitoris to make them worthy of our presence. "What if you get paired with some bro who expects you to do all the work?"

"Hmm. I guess that would suck." Honestly, though? I wouldn't mind. It's an English project, meaning I'd do all the work no matter what. "Anyway, cheers to us for making it through the first week."

"Hell yes. Cheers."

"I'm so ready for Tasha's tonight."

Every year since the eighth grade, Tasha Thompson has had a party the first weekend of the school year. She's a day student like Jess, whose family lives in one of the giant homes on the shorelines of Mirror Lake—now walking distance from school. Her parents always have some work conference or event on the weekends, leaving Tasha with a lakeside mansion all to herself. There typically aren't boys at the parties, but when I ran into Tasha in the bathroom, she said she'd opened it up to the whole school. "The more, the merrier, right?" she chirped.

Jess and I follow the path to the sprawling main green, where a few fall sports teams are getting ready to practice. The Sullivan-Stewart campus is a giant grassy oval ringed by dense trees, with the academic and athletic buildings on one end and the dorms, dining hall, and student services center on the other.

There's a main road that leads west down to Mirror Lake and the town of Lake Placid, as well as a network of skinnier trails that snake through the woods. Because it's the Adirondacks, there are mountains in every direction, where people way fitter and braver than me spend their summers hiking and their winters skiing and snowboarding. (I agree to exactly one High Peaks hike per year with Jess—our tradition on the last weekend of spring semester—but I'd generally rather head to Main Street for the indie bookstore and maple cream soft serve, no matter the season.) To the west there's the Sentinel Range, and farther off to the northeast is Whiteface, with its impossibly high peak that's usually capped with snow. The blankets of trees draped over the rocky slopes and cliffs are still green, but soon they'll be burning up with all kinds of reds, oranges, and yellows.

I skied at Whiteface once with Jess's family. They moved to the Adirondacks, like so many others, for access to the mountains after city life sapped them of joy. The Quigleys live in Saranac Lake, where Stewart used to be, so Jess has been grumbling about her slightly longer drive to school now. I miss the place, too—not just because it felt more down-to-earth than Lake Placid, but also, randomly, because of its Jewish history. My grandparents, who grew up vacationing there, told me the story one Friday night when Mom and I were at their place for Shabbat dinner: In the late 1800s and 1900s, lots of Jewish travelers went to the "Borscht Belt" in the Catskills, but some bold mountaineers pushed on to the Adirondacks. Many anti-semitic vacation spots said Jews weren't allowed, including this famous social club called the Lake Placid Club. So Jewish people decided to chill around the Saranac Chain of Lakes instead.

Knowing the history made me feel strangely at home there, even though I'm not religious. I'm still *Jewish,* and I would have been banned from the stupid Lake Placid Club all the same.

As we walk the perimeter of the oval, I alternate between checking my inbox and checking out the boys on the cross-country team in their T-shirts and mesh shorts. One of them raises his arms in a triceps stretch, revealing a trail of black hair poking out above his waistband.

Jess pokes me in the shoulder. "Earth to Alyson Benowitz."

"What?"

"You're, ah, very obviously staring at that dude's pelvic region."

Well, that's embarrassing. "How do you know I wasn't contemplating trying out for the team next year?"

"Because you'd literally break your boobs if you ran cross-country."

We both snort-laugh. She has a point: I started on the pill last year because I kept getting these painful ovarian cysts, and seemingly overnight, my Bs turned into Ds. Besides the fact that physical activity requires an industrial-strength sports bra, I'm now self-conscious that anything I wear with the slightest hint of cleavage makes me look like a porn star. Not that there's anything wrong with being a porn star, obviously—I personally enjoy their work on occasion. It's just not necessarily the vibe I'm going for at, say, my cousin Jeremy's bar mitzvah.

We pull open the heavy door to the dining hall, the place on campus where I feel most like a visitor. Beneath the vaulted ceiling with its gnarled horizontal beams, nearly everything's made from dark-brown wood, and the walls are hung with antique topographical maps, snowshoes, fishing rods, and bear traps. Joe, the last guy my mom dated—before she gave up on love and married her work laptop instead—used to soak himself in tobacco-scented cologne, and that's what I half expect the air in here to smell like. The dining hall probably hasn't changed since Sullivan School was founded in the 1930s, except for maybe the sushi station, paninis, and the presence of quinoa in the salad bar.

"You wanna eat outside?" Jess asks as we wait in line for the aforementioned paninis. She winces as a nearby table of boys erupts in raucous laughter, their guffaws reverberating around the echoey space. I recognize a few of them from class, and of course, part of me wishes we'd just waltz over and join them.

But I'm haunted again by the ghost of Bookstore Aiden and the traumatizing thing he said about me when he thought I wasn't listening.

"Yeah, I guess that's fine."

We pay for our sandwiches and carry our plates to the grass outside, where Jess leads the way to a shady spot under a maple tree. Before I get my hands all greasy with melted local cheddar, I refresh my inbox for the four hundred and sixteenth time.

"Why do you keep checking your email?"

Caught red-handed again. Why is it that as hard as I try to control my worst impulses, they always find a way to wriggle free? I'm supposed to be acting chill. Not desperate. "I'm . . ." There's no point in lying to Jess; she knows me too well. "I'm waiting for the English teacher to send out the partners for that group project. He said he was going to do it after class."

She smacks her bare knee. "Aha! I had a feeling you were secretly way more excited about that than you were letting on. You changed the subject to Tasha's party almost immediately."

"Well, this year, I'm trying to be less . . . thirsty-seeming."

"In theory, I approve of that, because these boys are scientifically not at our level of maturity. . . ."

"Why do I sense a 'but' coming?"

"Because I don't love that you're doing it in direct response to what happened with Book Boy. You're still indirectly letting him control you. If you wanna be thirsty, be thirsty!"

"Ideally, what I want is for a guy to pick *me*."

"Ugh, this is *totally* because of Aiden, isn't it?"

I twirl a lock of my long chestnut hair around my finger. We both know she's right. "Jess, c'mon. If it happened to you, you'd be embarrassed, too."

"If it happened to me, I'd tell him he wasn't worthy of all this anyway." She gestures at her curves. I roll my eyes.

Aiden was my ridiculously cute coworker at the Reading Corner in Albany over the summer. His aunt and uncle owned the shop and he'd worked there for a while already, so he was in charge of training me. He was totally my type, which is to say, he loved books. While we stocked shelves together, he tried to sell me on his favorite sci-fi authors, while I made my case for why the romance genre—my personal favorite—deserved more respect. He loved to debate me on that point, which I took to be his way of flirting; I mean, I'd read enough "enemies-to-lovers" plotlines to know that guys often teased you when they secretly liked you. I attempted to flirt back, leaving copies of my favorite steamy novels in Aiden's staff mailbox. In time, I imagined he would push me up against the bookshelves after hours and kiss the living daylights out of me.

By mid-August, he hadn't made a move, but since he still

insisted on critiquing my reading material, I figured our spark was alive. Maybe it was up to me; maybe *I* could be the one to power our plotline forward.

Then, one morning, I saw online that Aiden's all-time favorite sci-fi writer had made an incognito visit to the Barnes & Noble in Saratoga Springs to sign copies of his latest book. It was only an hour away, and I didn't have to be at work until noon, so I jumped out of bed, threw on some random clothes, dragged a brush through my hair, and drove all the way there in time to snag the last autographed copy. Racing to work, I felt like the heroine of my own epic love story. I slid the book, cover lying open, into Aiden's mailbox. Then I hid around the corner from the staff room, my body buzzing with the anticipation of peering through the door and watching him discover my gift.

He ambled into the store with his cousin Malcom, the owners' son. From my hiding spot, I watched them enter the staff room; then I crept closer so I could see inside.

"What's this?" Malcom asked, grabbing the book.

Aiden pushed his black-rimmed glasses up his nose and furrowed his brow. "Whoa. What the fuck?"

My heart hammered with excitement. I'd left him such an incredible surprise that his brain couldn't comprehend it.

"Who do you think left it here?"

Realization dawned on Aiden's face. This was it; he would see that I was serious about us. He'd probably come and find me to say thank you. Would he kiss me? I licked my lips to make sure they weren't chapped. I was in the clear.

The next thing he said to Malcom hit me like a punch in the stomach. "Oh God. I bet it's that girl who works here."

"Alyson? She's into you?"

"Yeah. She does shit like this, leaving books in my mailbox. It's awkward. I think she's kinda desperate."

They both laughed as my face went numb and tears filled my eyes. I walked to the back of the store and pretended to organize cookbooks for the next hour, until I peered at myself in my phone's camera mode and confirmed my cheeks weren't splotchy anymore. I never took ownership for the anonymous gift, and I never left a book in Aiden's mailbox again.

Jess sighs. "I don't get why you're acting like it's *your* fault. When guys do shitty stuff to Tamar"—we always refer to our moms by their first names, because it's funny—"you go into vigilante justice mode."

"First of all, I haven't done anything like that since Joe, which was like three years ago at this point. Second, Tamar's ex-boyfriends totally deserved it, since they were all piles of trash." Things didn't work out between my mom and dad, either, but not for pile-of-trash reasons. My parents got divorced when I was nine because my dad came out, and now he lives with his delightful husband and their two dachshunds in a Philadelphia brownstone.

"Book Boy was a pile of trash!" Jess exclaims, flinging a hand in the air to emphasize her point. "He deserves to have eggs thrown at him just as much as Cologne Joe did."

"For the record, I threw eggs at Joe's *house,* not his body."

"You're derailing."

"Joe ghosted Tamar the week of her birthday. And the guy before that—remember Ray?—he had not one, but *two* secret girlfriends. They deserved to be punished!" When it came to dealing with Ray, it hadn't taken me long to find the aforementioned secret girlfriends on social media, make an anonymous account, and tip them off to Ray's cheating ways. I never told my mom what I'd done, though. I was scared she'd get mad at me.

"And Book Boy? Why doesn't he deserve it, too?"

She's being impossible. I wish she would let it go and let me blame myself in peace. "I just feel like *I* messed up with Aiden."

My phone, lying in the grass between me and Jess, lights up with a notification. It's a new email—from one john.macmillan @sullivanstewart.edu. Subject line: Partners.

We both see it at the same time.

"Are you gonna look?" Jess asks.

Resisting the urge to lunge for the phone, I pick up my panini. I'm an independent woman who doesn't care about that list one bit. "Nah, I'll just check it after."

"Al, if you want to check it now, check it now! Live your damn life."

"I really don't mind waiting. I told you, I'm chill." Except the adrenaline coursing through my veins is refusing to die down.

"You're not chill, babe. You look like you're going to implode at any second. Here, I'll do it for you." And before I can protest, she swipes the phone, unlocks it—the password is my birthday—and scans what I can only assume is a list of names. She raises her eyebrows. "Oh! This is interesting."

I drop my panini. Screw trying to be chill. "Is it someone you know?"

"Not actually, but I recognize the name. I'm almost positive he dated Chrissy Lin last year." Chrissy's a popular lacrosse player in the grade above us. Our social circles have never come close to overlapping, but she seems cool; I always admired her confidence when she strutted onstage at Stewart assemblies to announce her team's latest victories with a huge smile on her face. "I'm pretty sure they're not together anymore, because she hasn't posted any couple-y pics in a few weeks," Jess adds.

There's a fluttery feeling in my stomach. Whoever the guy is, he's probably single. "What's his name?"

"Oh my God, it's *so* preppy. You're gonna laugh when I tell you."

"Tell me."

Jess snorts. "Brenton ... Riggs ... Junior."

CHAPTER 2

I already feel tipsy as I walk up Tasha's driveway, and I haven't had a single sip of alcohol yet. It's my first parent-free house party with boys, and it's taking everything in my power not to sprint across the pavement and burst through the wall, Kool-Aid Man style.

Matching Jess's pace feels like wading through molasses, but I'm trying to play it cool. "I'm so curious which guys are going to be here tonight."

"I'm aware." Jess flicks my bare arm. I'm in a black tank top tucked into high-waisted jeans; she's wearing a gray vintage T-shirt that says *Smash the Patriarchy* in slanted bold font. "You mentioned it a couple of times when we were getting ready."

Great. Way to be casual, Alyson. "Did I really?"

"You did, and I said I didn't know. You might be better off just following him already."

I flick her back. "Jess, *no*! Oh my God, I would never. I don't even know him yet." I decline to mention that I sat on the toilet in the dorm bathroom for five minutes searching for his name on Instagram and daring myself to tap the follow button. In the end, I didn't do it; it seemed contrary to Operation: Don't Be a Desperate Weirdo.

"I'm just *saying,* if you want to know what Brenton is up to tonight—"

"I don't! I'm here to hang out with our friends." Translation: I *so* want to know what Brenton is up to tonight. And more specifically, if he's planning on coming to Tasha's.

As soon as Jess read me his name off the email, I knew exactly who he was. Brenton Riggs Jr., or Riggs, as everyone calls him, is the six-foot-something lacrosse player who sits at the back of the room and looks like a Marvel superhero in training. I know he plays lacrosse because he brings the stick with him to class, carries it like a king wielding a scepter. I've never talked to him, and he's never participated in class, but I am very familiar with the way he slouches back in his chair, his muscular thighs manspreading in a way that somehow isn't repulsive. It's hot as hell. The way his quads fill out those charcoal-gray uniform pants . . .

Sitting there in the grass under the maple tree, I pictured me and Riggs together, the two of us writing the spectacular kind of love story I've only ever read about but long to experience for real.

I've always tried to keep an open mind about who I'll end up falling for, but honestly, I never thought it'd be a *lacrosse* player. Badminton, maybe. Or, I dunno, diving. In my mind, the more popular sports—the ones with lots of violent body-slamming, like lacrosse, football, and hockey—breed the worst of the bros.

The kind who think hazing is cool, and who say stuff like "No means yes, and yes means anal." *Gag.* But maybe Riggs will turn out to be different. Statistically, there have to be a few good lax bros out there, right?

Tasha's front door is open. Her house is unbelievable—it's like the "after" shot from an HGTV home makeover show, but with local touches, like wooden accent walls and giant antler chandeliers. There's a K-pop song blaring from the kitchen, the catchy music accompanied by a bunch of off-key voices scream-singing along. Tasha's the star of every school musical, so it's no surprise her parties often turn into sing-alongs and dance-offs. Last year, I watched her take three tequila shots before climbing up on the kitchen island and performing flawless renditions of some of her favorite Broadway bangers.

My heart leaps at another sound coming from somewhere inside the house. Boys' laughter.

Sure enough, in the open-concept kitchen, a dozen people dance on the massive—and I mean *massive*—kitchen island, their red plastic cups held high in the air. Tasha's up there rocking out in a purple sequined suit, her long coppery box braids swinging this way and that. The dining room table holds a feast of pizza boxes from one of the Italian places on Main Street, plastic handles of vodka, cartons of orange juice and lemonade, and cases of Keystone Light. The room is crowded with people singing, shrieking, laughing, taking selfies, and otherwise letting loose after a long first week back. There are also boys. Everywhere. Idling around the pizza; sitting on the sectional in the adjoining family room and playing drinking games; filming each other doing random stupid stuff. I thought the maroon blazers were sexy, but seeing them out of their stiff uniforms and wearing soft cotton T-shirts feels surprisingly intimate. I'm in heaven.

"AL! JESS!" Tasha screams our names and waves for us to come join her. "GET UP HERE, ANGELS!" Tasha's an outgoing theater kid who's friends with just about everyone: the athletes; the activists; the artists; the outdoorsy hikers constantly comparing how many of the forty-six High Peaks they've scaled; the academic bookworms, like me and Jess. I want to take Tasha up on her invitation, only . . .

I wave back to Tasha before subtly scanning the room for Riggs's sandy curls, chiseled cheekbones, and cleft chin. There's no immediate sign of him, but that doesn't mean he isn't here. He could be in the bathroom, or hanging out in another part of the house.

"I'm gonna grab a drink first," I tell Jess.

I gasp. Two beefy hands just clamped down on my shoulders and started kneading the space between my shoulder blades.

"Lemme join you!"

I twist my neck as far as I can, catching a glimpse of white-blond hair. "Who is that? Riley?"

He releases me with a final squeeze, and I spin all the way around. I was right: it's Riley Prentiss, the guy who sits next to me in French. He has a broad, pale face that reminds me of a scarecrow for some reason. Maybe it's the thin lips and the wispy eyebrows. His shaggy flaxen bangs fall naturally over his eyes, meaning that every couple of minutes, he jerks his head to flick them out of the way. He isn't unattractive, physically speaking, but I always cringe at the way he treats his books, shoving them roughly into his backpack without caring about their pages folding and tearing. Once I saw him tear a corner out of *Le Petit Prince* so he could spit out his gum before the teacher came in. Writing him off for disrespecting books would be a very Alyson thing to do, and I'm trying to ignore my own romantic instincts for the time being. Besides, he could have surprised-massaged anyone at this party, and he surprise-massaged *me*.

"Heyyy." Riley laughs, and I smell the ghost of a beer. He does one of his hair flicks, this time in the direction of the table. "Grab a drink with me?"

At this point, Jess has turned around, too. She gives Riley a quick once-over before looking at me with her eyebrows raised, and I know she's telepathically repeating what she told me earlier: *If you wanna be thirsty, be thirsty.* I guess part of me has been hoping for a tall drink of Riggs instead—which is a totally inefficient strategy for finding someone to fall in love with me. There's a perfectly fine gentleman standing right here, asking if he can accompany me to the drinks table. I smile at said fine gentleman and tuck my hair behind my ears. "Sure."

"I'll be right over there with Mar," Jess says, nodding to our friend with the bleach-blond pixie cut, Marina Topham, who's hovering by the island and staring at Tasha like a human heart-eye emoji. It's amazing how love can transform a leather-and-fishnet-wearing, don't-mess-with-me badass like my former roommate into a sappy pile of mush. Marina says they started flirting during play rehearsal last fall; Tasha was starring as a pirate captain, and Marina was the assistant stage manager in charge of a complicated entrance involving Tasha descending from the ceiling in a harness and wielding a giant sword. Seeing them around campus holding hands and tracing figure eights on each other's thighs, I'd give *anything* to have what they do.

23

Riley's palm lands on the small of my back. I take a deep breath and let him steer me through the crowd—and maybe toward something magical. Who knows?

"How's your night going so far?" He sort of screams it in my ear, but in his defense, the music is pretty loud.

"Good! We just got here. How about you?"

"It's better now!" He grins, and his cheeks are pink. Is he blushing? When we get to the table, Riley points to the vodka and lemonade, and I give him a thumbs-up. He keeps talking as he pours imprecise amounts of both beverages into a red plastic cup. "We don't really get a chance to talk in class, so I thought we should get to know each other, you know? You're really good at French. Like, whenever you read stuff out loud? You sound like you're actually from French."

I cock an eyebrow as he hands me the drink. "From French?"

Riley smacks his palm against his forehead. "France! Sorry. I'm, ah . . ." A hopeful butterfly beats its wings inside my chest. Is he about to tell me he's nervous around me? Riley shakes his head and chuckles. "I'm a little drunk!"

Oh well. It is a party, after all. I take a sip of the vodka lemonade and wrinkle my nose. I'm not a big drinker, and this is heavy on the vodka. Riley grabs what clearly isn't his first Keystone Light, cracks it open, and takes a swig.

I feel like I could be contributing more to this conversation. "So . . . where are you from?"

Another Riley hair flick. "Troy!"

"No way! I'm from Albany!"

"Oh. Cool!"

I wait for him to put the pieces together that we're basically next-door neighbors, but he just takes another swig of his beer and shifts his body so that he's standing right in front of me. My back is against the table, with chairs to either side of me. "My cousins live in Troy, so we're there all the time!" I tell him. "Have you ever been to the River Fest in the summer?"

"No!" He does a hair flick.

"It's cool! It's like . . . a big outdoor market! With music and stuff!"

"Sounds cool!"

Great. I'm just standing here screaming facts at him. There's an awkward pause as we both presumably search for something to say next, but resort to sipping our drinks instead. Maybe I should go find Jess—that is, if I can figure out a way to extricate myself from the corner Riley's backed me into. Suddenly, he lands on something to say to me. "So what's the deal with your friend's shirt?" He makes air quotes with his free hand. " 'Smash the Patriarchy'?"

"What about it?"

"What's she trying to say? That she hates dudes or something?"

Apparently, the old Sullivan curriculum was missing some pretty basic stuff. "No, she doesn't hate dudes. She just wants everyone to be treated equally."

Riley mulls this over, shifting his weight so he ends up even closer to me somehow. I press myself as hard as I can against the edge of the table to retain some semblance of personal space, but it goes out the window when he leans in to talk in my ear. "Okay, but here's the thing I still don't get. You liked it when I made you a drink, right?"

What I'd *like* is for Riley to back up a bit. "Hey, do you mind if I squeeze out?"

"But you didn't answer my question."

"What was it again?"

"Well, what I was basically getting at is, am I 'problematic' now"—he makes air quotes—"if I do something nice for a girl?"

Code red. Must escape this inane interaction. And if I have to smell one more of the beer burps that he keeps trying to blow out the side of his mouth, I think I might throw up. "Riley, of course not."

"Then explain to me—"

"Riley, I—"

What happens next is so shocking and swift, my brain can hardly process the sequence of events. Someone approaches Riley from behind and sweeps him aside like a curtain. This same person throws a muscular arm around my shoulder, pulls me to their side, and whispers in my ear: *Just go with it.* While Riley sputters and tries to wipe the spilled Keystone Light off his shirt, the same voice exclaims, "ALYSON BENOWITZ! I have been looking everywhere for you." They guide me to the most easily accessible exit: the sliding glass doors to the back deck. The blast of fresh, evergreen-scented air is a gift after what just happened. I inhale it in gulps.

It isn't until we're safely outside, the door sealed shut behind us, that I look up into the face of my rescuer.

My stomach does a somersault.

It's Riggs.

He lets go of me and steps back, stuffing his hands into the pockets of his jeans. He winces. "Hey. Are you okay?"

I don't know what to say because I'm too stunned by (a) that ridiculously smooth rescue and (b) how handsome he is up close. He has warm peach skin, very long eyelashes, and soft-looking lips. Instead of formulating words, I'd like to chuck my disgusting drink into the lake, launch myself into Riggs's arms, and bury my face in his neck. Of course, that would be a little much. "I totally wasn't, but I am now, so . . . thank you."

"Anytime. What was he saying? You looked like you wanted to punch him."

"I almost considered it," I admit. "He was asking about my friend's *Smash the Patriarchy* T-shirt, and I told him it stands for equality. Then he asked if it's technically sexist to treat women with respect."

Riggs closes his eyes and pinches the bridge of his nose. "Jesus Christ, Prentiss."

"Bad, right?"

"How hard is it to understand that *everyone* should just treat *everyone* with respect?"

Wow. What if he *is* one of the good lax bros? Riggs drops his hand and shakes his head. "For the record, I didn't swoop in there because you're a girl. I did it because I know Riley Prentiss from lacrosse, and I can spot him being an ignorant dickwad from a mile away."

I haven't heard the word "dickwad" since I was about six, and the seriousness in Riggs's voice as he utters it makes me burst out laughing. Riggs laughs, too. He leans an elbow against the railing. Behind him, the golden lights from Main Street reflect in the glassy black water, and a silver blanket of stars twinkles overhead, but all I want to do is gaze into his light-blue eyes. Not in an overwhelming, staring way—just, like, a normal human amount of eye contact. In romance novels, there's always a key moment when the soon-to-be lovers meet, and even though *they* don't know it yet, there's something significant enough about their connection that *you,* the reader, can tell sparks are gonna fly. What if this is *our* meeting?

"So anyway . . ." Riggs smiles sheepishly. Of *course* he has dimples. "I guess we're English partners, huh?"

I have to play it cool as a freaking cucumber. He can't know I sat on the toilet with my thumb hovering over his profile for as long as I did—or at all, for that matter. "Oh, yeah." I shrug. "I guess we are."

"This is a warning that English isn't my best subject, but I still promise to be as much of a help as possible. Not that you need it."

"Why do you say that?"

"Because you're obviously the smartest person in the class." It doesn't come out as an accusation—just a statement of fact. "And you're a junior, so that's extra impressive. How do you know so much about everything already?"

I look at my feet, my cheeks on fire. My whole body is on fire. "Thanks. Um . . . I just really like books, I guess? I want to be a writer eventually, so . . ."

"Oh yeah? What do you wanna write?"

I swallow. My answer is going to come off as a little forward, but it is what it is—there's no getting around it. "Romance novels."

The first time—no, *every* time—I told Aiden how much I loved the romance genre, he gave me a stern lecture about broadening my horizons. But Riggs nods his head encouragingly. "That's super cool. How'd you get into romance?"

I imagine giving him the real answer: that if I don't keep believing in love, I'm scared I'll end up cold and closed off like my mom, who takes on more cases than any one lawyer should physically be able to handle, because it's easier than confronting her own loneliness. Talk about a mood killer. I'll wait 'til Riggs and I are at the gazing-into-each-other's-eyes-and-baring-our-souls stage of the relationship to get into that. For now, I shrug and reply, "I just think it's the most fun."

"I can't say I've read any romance novels, but they sound way more fun than fuckin' . . . What was that dog book from last year? Something with 'wild'?"

"*Call of the Wild*?"

"Yeah! Damn, that book was boring. *Definitely* could have used some more hookups."

"On the dogsled, do you think?"

"Oh yes. Absolutely. While the sled dogs just sit there and watch."

"*Yes*. I love it." But really, I love *this*. We're bantering. After everything that happened with Aiden, it feels like a high to have a smart, funny, *extremely hot* guy go out of his way to keep talking to me. For I don't know exactly how long, we go back and forth adding sex scenes to the classic novels we've read in English class. Soon we're laughing so hard I have to clutch the railing for support, at which point I accidentally knock my drink into the bushes directly below us, which makes us laugh even harder.

"Okay, okay, I totally got us off topic." Riggs wipes tears—*tears*—from his eyes. "I think my initial point was that it's awesome you want to write romance, Alyson."

Well, there you have it. I'm now a five-foot-seven pile of hot goo. Take me, Brenton Riggs Jr. Scoop me up in your arms and kiss me before I melt through the slats of the deck. "Why, thank you."

"You're welcome." He runs his fingers through his curls; it's *so* much sexier than the Riley Hair Flick. "Hey. I just had a thought." He pauses. "You know the Fall Festival coming up?"

Of course I do. We all got the campus-wide email with the Fall Semester Special Events Calendar, which included the Fall Festival in October, some scary-sounding mandatory camping trip in November, and a semiformal in December. Oh my God . . . Is Riggs about to ask what I *think* he's about to ask, or am I getting ahead of myself, as usual?

Past evidence points to the latter.

"Um . . . yeah?"

"Well, I know it's still a couple of weeks away and everything, but, um . . ."

My heart pounds like a kettledrum in my ears.

"It sounds like some people are planning on taking dates"— *oh my God oh my God oh my God*—"and there's absolutely no pressure to say yes"—*YES YES YES YES YES*—"but I was wondering if you might want to go with me?"

"Yes!" It comes out a little loud, and not very cool-as-a-cucumber, but I don't care. I want to scream it from the top of Whiteface.

His face splits into a grin. "Really?"

"Yes, really!"

He lets out a sigh of relief. "Okay. Awesome."

All of a sudden, the glass door slides open. We both turn our heads to the source of the noise. "Alyson? Are you out here?" It's Jess—and there's a note of concern in her voice.

"Over here!" I wave to her through the darkness.

"Oh, thank God. I looked over to where the drinks were and you were gone and . . . Oh!" She suddenly registers Riggs's presence. "Do you want me to leave you guys alone?"

"Actually, I should probably go in and find my friends," Riggs says to us. He turns back to me. "If I don't see you inside, see you in English on Monday?"

Under normal circumstances, I'd be gutted by his departure, but this isn't the end for us; it's just the beginning. I smile at him. "Yeah. Sounds good. Thanks again for saving me."

"It was my pleasure."

Swoon.

As I watch him stroll back across the deck, I notice specks of neon green dancing in the air between us. Fireflies. I'm one of them, too: a glowing ball of light with wings. Riggs just asked me to the Fall Festival, and I said yes. What'll happen from here? Will he kiss me someday? Will he *more-than-kiss* me? Will he fall in love with me and decide he wants to live happily ever after by my side? I feel like I'm flying, the beautiful possibilities blooming beneath me in colors I've never even seen before.

Whoa. I need to pump the brakes and remember that's all they are right now: possibilities. There's still a chance I could scare him away if I get too clingy. Too . . . Alyson.

I take a deep breath and drag myself back to the present moment, which I gotta say is pretty fantastic on its own. As I beckon Jess over to tell her what happened, it's not just the thought of the Fall Festival that keeps the smile plastered to my face. After all the energy I've wasted chasing boys who don't want to be caught, it's also the thrill—the *relief*—of finally having someone choose me.

WEDNESDAY, APRIL 26

Channel 5 News, Lake Placid

ISABELLE PARK: Welcome back to Channel 5 News. I'm
Isabelle Park. As you know, we've been closely
following the story of a lacrosse player from
Sullivan-Stewart Prep School who hasn't been seen
since prom last weekend. Well, this afternoon,
we're going live to Wilmington, where the search is
underway for eighteen-year-old Brenton Riggs Jr.
Our reporter, Doug Higginbotham, is there on the
scene. Doug?

DOUG HIGGINBOTHAM: Hi, Isabelle.

ISABELLE: Doug, tell us where you are and what's
going on.

DOUG: Isabelle, I'm here at the Sentinel Lodge, a hotel with the dramatic mountain views you can see behind me. It also happens to be the last place anyone saw Brenton Riggs Jr., the missing lacrosse captain from Sullivan-Stewart Prep School. A search party comprised mostly of volunteers has been combing these woods since this morning, but as of yet, there's unfortunately been no sign of the teenager. Here with me are Bradley Pierce and Marissa Cole, two Sullivan-Stewart staff members who came out of the trees just a few short moments ago. Bradley, Marissa, I know you're both freezing, but can you tell us what it was like to be in the search party?

MARISSA COLE: It was . . . um . . . S-sorry, it's s-s-so h-hard t-to t-talk without my t-t-teeth chattering. W-we were out there f-for a while.

BRADLEY PIERCE: I got this, Marissa. You go grab some tea. Doug, I gotta say, it's slow going out there. Every path is basically a skating rink at this point. A lot of them we can't even try because it's too dangerous. You know, one wrong step . . .

DOUG: Do you have any thoughts on where Brenton might be?

BRADLEY: No, but, Lord, I wish I did. It kills me to think he could be out there needing our help . . . Sorry . . .

DOUG: No problem. I know this is hard.

BRADLEY: We don't know for sure that he's even in the mountains. He could be anywhere at this point.

DOUG: Bradley, thank you so much for your time. Now, if you don't mind, I'm going to walk with you over here to the warming tent, so we can speak to a few more people who know Brenton.

[DOUG enters the warming tent and approaches DEVON AARONS, who hands BRADLEY a cup of coffee.]

Devon, can you tell us what's going on in here?

DEVON AARONS: Hey, Doug. Um, yeah, some guys from the team came over as soon as our classes were done for the day. We really wanted to support everyone searching for our buddy Riggs, so we picked up some handwarmers and footwarmers and coffee and tea and stuff, and we've been passing them out to people.

DOUG: You mentioned your friendship with Brenton. This must be so difficult. You've known him since the ninth grade, is that right?

DEVON: Yup—since I started at Sullivan. Riggs has always been the shit— Oh shit, can I say that?

DOUG: You're fine.

DEVON: Sorry. Anyway, Riggs is the best, man. Everyone loves him: the whole team, the whole school.

[Devon looks into the camera.]

Riggs, if you're watching this: I love you, buddy.

DOUG: Brenton sounds like a popular guy.

[Doug turns to RILEY PRENTISS, who sits with a box of handwarmers in his lap.]

Would you agree with that, Riley? I understand you and Brenton have known each other since the fifth grade.

RILEY: Yup. He's popular.

DOUG: Any special memories with Brenton that you'd like to tell us about?

RILEY: Uh, yeah. We played lacrosse.

DOUG: Er, thank you for sharing. Well, Isabelle, as you can see, Brenton is a very valued member of the school community. Here's hoping they find him soon. Back to you.

CHAPTER 3

October, Six Months Earlier

Mr. MacMillan slides the paper facedown onto my desk. I glance up at him, hoping to catch a smile or a wink like I often do from my other teachers, but his stony expression gives nothing away.

Across the room, there's a range of reactions as people flip over their rubrics and find out their grades on the short-story project. Maggie squeals and bounces in her chair before high-fiving her partner, Hudson; Dorian, the perpetually bored-looking kid who sits in front of me, wads up his paper and crams it in his backpack, while his partner, Celeste, shoots daggers at him from a few rows over.

I toy with the corner of the sheet, tempted to peek like a poker player analyzing their hand, but I told him I wouldn't look, not until we were alone together. *I wanna be able to properly celebrate,* Riggs texted me before class. *Assuming we crush it, which we will, because it's you.*

I fold the rubric in quarters and slide it into the pocket of my maroon cardigan.

After the bell, Riggs waits for me outside the classroom. I find him leaning against the wall next to his trusty lacrosse stick and twiddling his rolled-up rubric between his fingers. Why is his brow furrowed? Is he nervous? I doubt he's worried about our grade, given how little it matters for him. The Duke lacrosse team has been wooing Riggs since the start of his junior year, including flying him down to campus to stay with some of the players for a long weekend. The coach has straight up told Riggs he wants him on his roster, so now all he has to do is keep playing well and maintain a halfway-decent average in all his classes. If I didn't have such a massive crush on him, I'd be jealous; my entire future depends on me acing this class, starting with this short-story project.

"All right, you." I poke his shoulder, because shoulder-poking is something we do now. It's amazing how a millisecond of physical contact, and with a *shoulder,* no less, can make my stomach do gymnastics floor routines. "Is it time to open this, or what?"

"Almost." He bites his lip, one of his top three sexiest moves. I've ranked them, obviously: number three is the aforementioned lip bite; number two is when he loosens his tie; and number one, his sexiest move of all, is when he says my name—it makes me feel more alive than I've ever felt. "Alyson, I may or may not have planned something, so if you could do me a favor and wait a *little* longer . . ."

It doesn't take much for me to become putty in Riggs's hands. "Okay." I swallow. "I still have a few minutes before my meeting with Mrs. Cole."

Riggs smiles and loosens his tie. It's like he's reading my romance-charged brain. "I'll walk you there."

At the bottom of the stairs, he holds open the door and we step out into the sunny late morning. After a hot and humid September, there's finally a cool breeze ruffling the grass and nudging the branches of the trees. There's nothing as magical as the scent of ripening leaves on the wind, the way it carries a promise of someone lending you their sweater, or buying you a hot apple cider, or wrapping you in their arms to keep you warm. Of course, none of these things has ever happened to me, but for the first time in my life, by some ridiculous miracle, I feel like they're hovering within the realm of possibility. And I don't want to screw it up.

It still isn't lost on me how lucky I am that Riggs wants to hang out with me. At Sullivan-Stewart, there are two kinds of popular people: the kind who work for it by going out of their way to be nice to everyone—like Tasha, inviting the whole school to her party last month—and the kind who have coolness running through their veins, whether they talk to other people or not. Riggs is in the latter category: elite, just by *being*. He has all the right things going for him: senior; captain of the lacrosse team; legacy student whose dad, I've heard, donates a crap ton of money to the school. Then there's the fact that he's a super-human level of hot. According to every book, TV show, and movie set in a high school, Riggs should be a huge asshole with a résumé like that . . . and yet, he's not. He defies the laws of the universe, but I like him too much to ask any questions. Besides, overthinking is bad, right? I should just go with the flow. Be in the moment.

We amble side by side along the wood-chip path. I catch people staring at Riggs like he's an A-list actor who decided to enroll at our Lake Placid boarding school for some reason. And just like people clamor for details on who their favorite stars are dating, so, too, do they ogle me with squinted eyes, like they're trying to balance the equation of how one hitherto unknown junior equals one *Brenton Riggs Junior*. I try to smile when I catch people gawking because it seems like the polite thing to do, but soon, my cheeks are sore from all the up and down, and I'm worried my grin is so forced that I look like some creepy clown. As we pass a circle of sophomore girls sitting in the grass, I glance at Riggs to see how he handles the attention. He strolls on by like he doesn't even notice them, twirling his lacrosse stick like it's a natural extension of his body.

"So," Riggs finally says, "you may have noticed I've been dragging this out as long as humanly possible."

"I don't mind." I mean, I *do* have to get to my meeting soon, but time with Riggs feels equally important, if not more so.

"Can I tell you why?"

"Is it because I've converted you into a total nerd, and now you're as nervous about seeing this grade as I am?"

"Oh no. Definitely not." Riggs laughs, but his voice hitches. He runs a hand through his hair. "Sorry, uh, I don't usually get awkward like this, but . . ."

I can see his face from the corner of my eye, and something about the way he's blushing makes me forget how to swing my arms while I walk. Now *I'm* the awkward one. Now I feel less like a creepy clown, and more like one of those terrifying animatronic characters at Disney World.

"I may or may not be dragging this out," he continues, "because I . . . uh . . . I don't want the project to end."

Beep, beep, boop. Animatronic Alyson's brain does not

compute. Or it *does,* possibly, but it's scared to jump to conclusions. "Wh-what do you mean?" I ask.

"What I'm basically trying to say is that it's been awesome hanging out with you, even if it's just been, you know, in the library."

Riggs meant it when he promised to help as much as he could with the short-story project. On afternoons when he didn't have lacrosse, and I didn't have peer tutoring or Writing Club, we'd sit in the library and craft our essay together. (Translation: I'd type sentences into our Google Doc, and he'd read them and say, "Whoa, that's freaking genius.") We'd squeeze onto the same overstuffed love seat to see each other's laptop screens, the whole right side of my body on fire simply because it was touching him.

We started texting, too. First about project stuff, then about other stuff: his stress about securing an official offer from Duke; my dreams of getting into Overbrooke College's world-renowned creative writing program; his latest lacrosse victories; my works in progress for Writing Club. Whenever he's bored in some class, he'll stealthily send me a wolf and an eggplant emoji—a reference to our *Call of the Wild* inside joke. And sometimes I'll be in the dining hall, just going about my panini-making, when suddenly I'll feel fingers graze the space between my shoulder blades. I'll look over my shoulder and spot Riggs walking away, a delicious smirk on his face, and every cell in my body will crackle with electricity. Sometimes I'll also spot jealousy on the faces of people around me, as though they'd give anything to have the lacrosse captain flirt with them, too—or just acknowledge their existence.

Which is why there's no question what I'll say back to him now. I'm never letting this guy go—not if I can help it. "It's been awesome hanging out with you, too."

He nudges me with his elbow and says, "I wanted to get you alone so I could tell you . . . I'm pretty sure I like you, Alyson."

And that's when the rest of the world slips away, and the only things I'm sure of are me and Riggs and my thumping heart, my burning cheeks, my shallow breath. We stop near the wildflower garden that separates the student services center from the dining hall. The flowers grow high as my chest, and they wave in the breeze like they're beckoning us closer, away from the kids eating lunch on the grass behind us.

I face him. And try to remember how words work. "I'm pretty sure I like you, too."

Riggs's face splits into a grin, and it sets me ablaze like a match lighting a tinderbox. "Well, that's good to hear. Otherwise, the Fall Festival tomorrow would be really freakin' uncomfortable."

We both burst out laughing, tears springing to my eyes from the holy-crap joy of it all. He likes me. *He likes me.* I've been desperate to know if he feels the same way I do, but given the Bookstore Aiden fiasco, I didn't want to put myself out there and ask him. Much safer to let the other person call all the shots, especially when it's someone like Riggs, who moves through the world surrounded by a red velvet rope, careful about who he lets into his sphere.

"We can look at our grades now, by the way," he says.

"Oh my God. I almost forgot."

We take out our rubrics and open them slowly, savoring the process, neither of us wanting to beat the other. Riggs asks, "What was that weird-ass thing Mr. MacMillan said about refusing to give anyone a hundred?"

I tuck in my chin, lower my voice, and do my best impression of our curmudgeon of an English teacher. " 'Perfection is only found in God and mail-order catalogs.' "

"What does that even mean?" He laughs and shakes his head. "Okay, well, let's look on three. One . . . two . . . *three.*"

I hold my breath and peer at the number in bright-red ink— and then I full-on scream. "Oh my God, Riggs!"

We got 99 percent, aka "perfect" for Mr. MacMillan. Between this and Riggs unclipping his red velvet rope for me, I'm the happiest girl in the land. This is exactly what I hoped to show Mrs. Cole at our college-planning meeting coming up: that I can ace AP English Lit and that I can get invited into Overbrooke's creative writing program, even though she's never had a student get the coveted offer before. Relief floods my veins, followed by fierce determination. When they mix with the giddiness from earlier, I more or less black out.

The next thing I know, Riggs drops his lacrosse stick, lifts me off the ground, and spins me in circles. I don't know how many times we twirl around, but it has to be a lot, because I very much do *not* stick the landing. I'm so dizzy that I stumble as soon as my feet touch the ground, and as Riggs lunges to catch me, I grab a fistful of his blazer and pull.

I let out a bloodcurdling shriek as we both go tumbling into the wildflowers.

Ow. I land hard on my back; Riggs, on his side. A few guys wolf-whistle from over on the grass. Oh no . . . How many people saw what just happened? I want to crawl into a hole and never come out—never face the moment when Riggs realizes he can do so much better than an overeager junior who just dragged him off his feet and into a bush. I bet he's already regretting whisking me away at Tasha's party.

His hand finds my shoulder. Our whole upper bodies are surrounded by stems. "Are you all right?"

I cover my burning face with my hands. Everything was perfect until I went ahead and ruined the moment. "No, no, I'm fine. Oh my God, I'm so sorry. Like, *so* sorry. That was so—"

"Don't be sorry." One at a time, he lifts my hands off my face and gently sets them on my stomach. My searing shame goes away as I process the fact that we're both horizontal. And extremely close to each other. Riggs lowers his voice. "That was actually kind of epic."

I don't know about that. . . . "Epic" is how soft his lips look this close up; it's the way his aquamarine eyes seem to drink me in like he's appreciating a painting in an art gallery. When our eyes lock, something claws so hard at the inside of my chest that it physically aches, and my breathing is shallow, and oh my God, I want to place my thumb on the crease of his chin and my fingers on his jaw and guide his face toward mine.

But that would be too much, especially coming from me. Riggs can kiss me if he wants to—and Lord, I hope he does.

"Alyson." He makes my name sound like warm honey.

"Riggs." I sound breathless, hopefully in a semi-hot way.

"Hey . . ."

"Hey."

We giggle into each other's eyes. The two of us just fell into a flower garden in full view of other people, and somehow, despite it being mortifying, we ended up like this. Staring. Smiling. We *must* be thinking the same thing right now.

And then his lips are moving down, and his eyes are starting to close, and my chest feels like a door bursting open to set the clawing thing free. This is it. I close my eyes.

"Excuse me?! What's going on in there?"

The woman's voice is like truck tires crunching over gravel, and it can only belong to one person—the very person I'm supposed to be meeting with in T-minus *very soon*. Shoot!

It's the feeling of the lights coming on at the end of a school dance: magic over; time to feel like awkward weirdos again. I spring to standing and feverishly brush off my kilt as Mrs. Cole, my college advisor, needles me with her sharp eyes. She's a middle-aged white woman, who today wears pointed leather boots, a flowy black blazer that skims the ground, and her silver ringlets piled high in a grapefruit-sized bun. Back at Stewart, she was known among students as the Sorceress, both because of her knack for helping people get into their first-choice schools and because, well, she's kind of terrifying.

"Nothing was going on!" I squeak as Riggs clambers to his feet next to me. "Seriously, nothing." *It could have been something if you hadn't interrupted.* "We literally fell into the bushes. I'm not even kidding. We were—"

"Alyson, aren't you my next meeting?" She checks her watch. "In two minutes?"

"Yes! Absolutely! I was just about to come over!" My voice is seven octaves too high, my delivery about as smooth as a bike ride through potholes. So much for looking forward to this check-in. Now, instead of impressing the Sorceress with my latest grades, I'm going to be digging myself out of this PDA hole—and the tragic part is, we didn't even *do* anything. It wouldn't have been my first kiss—there were a handful of rushed pecks and way-too-wet French kisses during games of Truth or Dare at sleepaway camp—but it would have been the most romantic, and the first one I'd actually enjoyed. I feel robbed. When will we have the chance to do that again?

I flash Riggs one last helpless look and wave goodbye. As if he's thinking the same thing I am, he smiles and mouths one word: *Tomorrow.*

Tomorrow.

Of course.

The Fall Festival.

My heart hammers as I follow Mrs. Cole to her office. The room is gloomy; a set of gauzy crimson curtains turns the sunlight dark as it attempts to shine through the window. Behind the mahogany desk, Mrs. Cole pulls up my file on her computer, her fingers slamming the keys with so much force that her curls seem to tremble with fear. At Stewart, everyone had their first college-planning meeting in the spring semester of tenth grade. I remember mine, last April, when I told Mrs. Cole about my dream to go to Overbrooke and eventually become a writer. "It's going to take everything you've got," she replied with the gentleness of a rusty hammer. Afterward, I stress-cried in the bathroom for a half hour, until a rousing pep talk from Jess helped me find my determination again.

"So," Mrs. Cole begins, "tell me how your semester's going."

"It's going great!" I need to get back in her good graces, so I pull out the rubric from Mr. MacMillan. "My partner and I— that guy I was just with—we got ninety-nine on this huge short-story project in AP English Lit, the class you told me to take. . . ."

"Hmmm." With two of her ringed fingers, she drags the paper across the desk. I sit there clutching my backpack to my chest like a shield as she surveys it for a while—a long while. I study the dust motes dancing in the air by the window to pass the time. Finally, she says, "This is excellent, Alyson." Relieved, I ever so slightly release my death grip on the backpack. "But . . ."

Did she just say "but"? As if ninety-nine isn't good enough? Mr. MacMillan literally doesn't give one hundreds!

"I know how important Overbrooke is to you, and it's going to take a hell of a lot of work to even have a shot at getting into that program. As I told you in April, I've never had a student pull it off before." Mrs. Cole drums her fingernails against the paper. "These are the kinds of grades you'll have to keep up all year, and I don't want to see you potentially jeopardizing your success. I've had plenty of experience around Sullivan boys . . ."

Did Mrs. Cole used to work at Sullivan?

". . . and I'm worried about how certain . . . distractions . . . could affect you."

I'd like to be sucked into a hole in the hideous brown carpet. I don't need AP English Lit to read between the lines and know that by "distractions," she means "boys." She means *Riggs*. I'm not just embarrassed that my college advisor is all up in my love life; I'm also mad that she's implying I can't roll around in the wildflowers with a super-hot guy *and* get in to a super-selective undergrad program. My inner righteous feminist ignores the part of me that feels proud of how palpable my connection with Riggs clearly is—enough that Mrs. Cole, with her antiquated views, has made it the subject of our conversation thus far.

"I promise I'm not distracted, and I'll stay totally focused. I want to get in to Overbrooke so badly."

"All right," Mrs. Cole concedes, sliding the paper back across the desk. She offers me a smile so tight, I can't help but wonder when the last time the Sorceress felt joy was. "To be clear, I'm just looking out for you, Alyson."

If I were less of a teacher's pet and more brazen, like Jess, I might say something like *"To be clear,* you sound like you're trying to shame me for being a human girl with a sex drive." God forbid Mrs. Cole got a look at my romance novel collection. Or my browser history. (All I can say is, it's a good thing juniors and seniors can opt for single rooms here.) Instead, I take the path of least resistance and give her a double thumbs-up. "I won't let you down. I've got this. I promise."

For the remaining twenty minutes, Mrs. Cole goes on and on about how hard I'll have to work this semester. As if I didn't already know this—as if I'm not already so stressed about getting into Overbrooke, I'm routinely waking up in cold sweats from anxiety dreams where I can't find a computer to send in my application. At the end of the meeting, she warns me *again* about "distractions." I feel like I'm at a school where people with boobs get sent home for wearing spaghetti-strap tank tops.

It's a relief when Mrs. Cole's next victim arrives and I can leave her gloomy lair of sex negativity. After saying goodbye and promising for the zillionth time to stay focused, I walk back through the student services center, past the nurse's office and the bookstore with all the newly designed Sullivan-Stewart apparel in the window. All the while, I clutch the piece of paper Mr. MacMillan slid onto my desk today. This rubric—that bright-red 99, aka 100—is all the proof I need that I *can* chase two dreams at once, the Sorceress's puritanical warnings be damned. I leave the student services center and hurry to grab lunch, past the wildflower garden where Riggs and I came *this* close to kissing.

Tomorrow, he'd mouthed before I left him.

The leaf-scented breeze still dances around me. I breathe it in deep, filling my lungs with its promises.

CHAPTER 4

When I told myself that I was a multitasker, that I could focus on Riggs and school at the same time, I didn't account for how it would feel to sit through class after class on Friday as the Fall Festival comes together on the oval. There are kiosks for activities, like ring toss and pumpkin carving; a contraption for making apple cider doughnuts; an axe-throwing lane; and a petting zoo with sheep, goats, and alpacas—thankfully, far from the axes. I can't focus for more than forty-five seconds before my mind wanders to tonight—to where and when Riggs might finally kiss me, and what it'll feel like, and how good I'll be at kissing him back.

When classes are finally over, Jess and I go to Marina's dorm room to get ready for tonight. Marina, an international student from London, England, was my roommate back at Stewart; then she and Jess got close through Gender-Sexuality Alliance stuff, since they both came out—Marina as a lesbian and Jess as bi—around the same time in seventh grade. We've seen less of

Marina since she and Tasha became a thing at the end of last year, and even though I miss sitting on her bed watching her favorite BBC crime dramas and eating the Cadbury's Dairy Milk Buttons and Digestive cookies her parents sent over from England, I'm mostly just happy to see her in love. Tasha's also here with her best friends, Tori and Raquelle, who I'm sort of friendly with. Marina's eighties punk music blares from a Bluetooth speaker, and the smells of burned hair and body spray permeate the air.

From her perch on Marina's lap, Tasha demands I recount the full story of my romp in the wildflowers yesterday. When I'm done, she declares, "You're a *hundred* percent kissing that boy tonight."

Tori, who has her auburn hair pulled up in a messy bun so she can practice her smoky-eye skills on Raquelle, chimes in to agree. Jess sits cross-legged on the floor, engrossed in something on her phone, but I know she thinks so, too.

"Are you *so* excited?" asks Raquelle, who claps and bounces on the edge of Marina's bed.

"Don't move," Tori hisses, placing a palm on top of her friend's red curls.

"Oops, sorry."

A kaleidoscope of butterflies comes to life in my chest. "Yeah. And nervous." It's a little embarrassing to admit how inexperienced I am, especially in front of people I'm pretty sure have had sex already, but on the flip side, maybe this is my chance to do some research. "I've actually, uh, never made out with anyone before? I'm scared I don't know what I'm doing."

"Oh my God!'"

"*Raquelle!* No moving!"

"Sorry! Okay, Alyson, don't be like the guy I kissed in July, who came at me with his mouth already wide open. I'm pretty sure I could see his molars."

"Ew, what did you do?" Marina shrieks.

"Well I had to mirror him, right?" She tilts her head to the side and opens her mouth, demonstrating. Tori groans in frustration. "Otherwise my mouth would've ended up inside of his. Antoine is a *much* better kisser," she adds with a giggle, referring to the Parisian exchange student she's been casually hooking up with. "And he whispers stuff in French while we're making out. It's *so* hot."

"The point is, better to start with your mouths closed, then *gradually* open them," Tasha summarizes.

"Okay . . ." I'll file that one away for later, hopefully. "And what about tongues?" I ask. "When do they come in?"

"Once your mouths are open," Raquelle explains. "You give each other, like, a little tongue massage."

"Whatever you do, do *not* jab in and out," Tori adds. "You are not a lizard. Or a guinea pig drinking from a water bottle."

Raquelle, Tasha, and Marina burst out laughing, while I make a few more hurried mental notes. Jess is still lost in phone land.

"How do you all feel about lip sucking? And lip biting? Do people actually like that stuff, or do they only do it in movies?"

"I'd say a little goes a long way," says Tasha, patting her girlfriend's knee in a knowing way.

"Is it weird that I like biting so much?" Marina asks. She nips at Tasha's tawny brown skin peeking out from her off-the-shoulder sweater. Tasha shivers.

"It's not weird at *all*," Tori answers. "A little pain can feel good when you're really into it."

Now my head is spinning. I want to do a good job and make it seem like I've done this before, but I'm worried I won't be able to keep track of all these rules in the heat of the moment. I think I need my best friend to weigh in. She hooked up with this girl Sierra at her restaurant job all summer. "Jess? What do you think?"

For the first time in the conversation, Jess looks up from her phone. She seems a little surprised to find herself in Marina's dorm room. "Sorry, what do I think about what?"

I peek at her screen and spot a video of a guy with dark wavy hair, circular glasses, and an olive-green beanie. He looks kind of familiar.

"Who is that?"

"Oh." She blushes and flips her phone over. "This guy I started talking to in econ yesterday. Sam Young."

"I thought all the guys in your econ class were wankers," Marina says.

"*Almost* all of them," Jess corrects. "He's the *one* who doesn't make me want to scream on a regular basis. He's . . . actually kinda cool," Jess goes on, shrugging. "He makes these surprisingly hilarious videos about his anxiety and stuff."

I know Jess. If she's shrugging and calling Sam "kinda cool," she must be pretty into him. "Do you know if he has a date tonight?" I ask.

She sighs. "No idea."

"Don't worry," Tasha says, "you can always hang with us while Alyson gets it on with Riggs."

I gaze at my pink-cheeked reflection in the full-length mirror on the back of Marina's door. Tori, an aspiring stylist, was nice enough to weave my hair into braids that wrap around my head like a halo, with a few pieces hanging loose "for added sexi-ness," as she put it. I barely recognize myself, and it's not just because I'm used to wearing my hair down. I think I'm seeing myself through Riggs's eyes, imagining what it'd be like to, well, make out with myself. Is that weird? I don't know. The point is, I look good. I feel excited, albeit anxious that I might accidentally kiss him like a guinea pig. As everyone else admires Tori's com-pleted masterpiece on Raquelle's face, I give myself the tiniest of nods in the mirror. *We got this.*

Riggs and I agreed to meet by the moss-covered fountain where the paths to each dorm intersect. When my friends and I emerge from the trees and into the clearing, he's already perched on the wide stone rim, dressed in jeans and a gray Hen-ley and manspreading in that way that makes me feel like a bad feminist for finding it hot. His tanned skin has cute touches of sunburn underneath his eyes and on the tip of his nose. He was off-campus for a lacrosse tournament all day, so we haven't laid eyes on each other since the almost-kiss.

Riggs smiles easily. "Hey, you."

My heart does a backflip as I jog over to him. "Hey! You're early."

"Couldn't help it. I was excited."

Literally how is this guy so earnest and a lax bro at the same time? Riggs should be studied in a lab. He opens his arms like an eagle spreading its wings, and for the first time ever, we hug. He squeezes me tight, and since I'm roughly as tall as his shoulder, my nose gets buried in his pec muscle, and I can smell whatever musky boy-cologne he's currently wearing. I swear there's some kind of pheromone in there that makes me want to drag him to the nearest tree and reenact the scene I read in my book this morning, where this princess shows a sexy stable boy how to slide his hand beneath her corset. *Hot.* It's a good thing it's too chilly for mosquitoes this time of year, because otherwise, we would both reek of bug spray instead. Who am I kidding? As if *that* would have kept me away from this boy.

Riggs releases me and takes in my new hairstyle. "Whoa. You look amazing, Alyson." He squints at both sides of my head. "How did you even do that? Where did you put all your hair?"

"Tori Rivera did it. She's a magician. It's all wrapped up in there somewhere. I'm a little scared to touch it, to be honest." I point to where the girls are standing and ogling us. "Do you wanna come meet my friends?"

As soon as the words leave my mouth, I regret them. Riggs's smile falters. Of course he doesn't want to meet my friends yet; at boarding school, that's the equivalent of asking a guy to meet your parents before you've gone on a first date. It's a big step, and in classic Alyson fashion, I just launched us across it.

"Uh, sure," Riggs says. I can tell he's being polite.

My cheeks burning, I lead him over to my friends and speed through the introductions. I was worried he'd be awkward when forced to interact with so many strangers, so I'm relieved when he turns on the charm like a celebrity signing autographs for fans.

"So you're the famous Jess," he says, holding out a hand to my best friend. "Alyson's told me all about you—good things, obviously."

She returns the gesture and looks straight into Riggs's eyes. If my dad were one of those guys who jokes about dusting off a shotgun to meet his daughter's boyfriend—and not, you know, a liberal dentist who takes portraits of his dachshunds in his spare time—I think I'd *still* be more nervous introducing Riggs to Jess. I know I don't *need* Jess's approval—or anyone's approval—but she and I agree on practically everything, and I'm scared of what it would mean if she didn't like him. "She's told me good things about you, too." She smiles, but she holds his gaze in a way that warns: *Don't prove her wrong.*

Riggs lets go of Jess's hand and puts his arm around my shoulder. "Thanks for letting me steal her away tonight."

My face gets even hotter. Most people wouldn't think twice about that line, but I know by the twitch of her eyebrows that Jess is inwardly cringing at the implication that I'm some piece of property. "You don't need to thank *me,*" she says.

Does she have to be so politically correct all the time? Oh God, what's gotten into me? I sound like some right-wing podcast host.

Before I can jump in to defuse the tension, Riggs ekes out a smooth recovery. "Good point. Apparently, I say dumb stuff when I'm nervous. Alyson, thank *you* for hanging with me tonight."

"You're welcome!" I look at Jess. *See? He's not problematic!*

"Better," she concedes.

We should quit while we're ahead. I wave to all my friends. "All right, well, I hope you guys have the best time tonight!"

"Text me later," Jess says.

After everyone says goodbye, I thrust my hand in the crook of Riggs's arm and steer him away from the group. My fingers cling to the fabric of his Henley like they're holding on for dear life.

Once we're out of the girls' earshot, I mumble, "I'm sorry Jess was kind of intense."

"Intense?" Riggs asks. "I just thought she seemed super smart, like you. I can see why you guys are friends. Don't worry." He squeezes me with the arm that's still draped over my shoulder. Now I feel guilty for throwing Jess under the bus the minute we walked away from her. Clearly Riggs isn't problematic, but maybe *I* am.

As we walk into the Fall Festival, Riggs and I turn heads, which pulls me out of my own. As usual, I struggle with where to look, who to smile at, what to do with my face, but Riggs strides along in the golden light of the early evening like he's out for a casual walk.

He moves his hand down to my lower back, his pinky finger making definite top-of-butt contact. "Should we hit up some of the games first?" he suggests. "Not to brag, but I'm freakishly good at ring toss."

"That's the real reason Duke is recruiting you, isn't it?"

"Damn. The secret's out."

"Remember me when you go pro, okay?"

"How could I forget you?" He tickles my back, and chills shoot up my spine to the top of my head. I almost feel dizzy.

As Riggs steers me to the kiosk containing the sea of green bottles, a trio of guys who sit with him in the back of AP English Lit call out his name. When we both look over, they make a show of checking me out and flashing Riggs a thumbs-up. I'm pretty sure this is the *definition* of objectification and that Jess would have a field day tearing the dudes to shreds, but there's also something strangely satisfying about the attention, like when Mrs. Cole first mentioned her concerns about "distractions."

I kind of like that people are noticing me on Riggs's arm; it reminds me this fairy tale is actually happening to me.

Riggs is indeed freakishly good at ring toss, not that I would have doubted his hand-eye coordination. He's good at axe-throwing and archery, too. With the bow and arrow, he lands a bull's-eye, earning himself the grand prize of a maroon and navy Sullivan-Stewart scarf, which he promptly drapes around my neck.

"For me?"

"It looks way better on you."

He plays around with how I should wear it, first wrapping it three times around, then unwinding it and tying a knot. We start laughing as it dawns on us how little Riggs knows about scarf styling, but then I glance over his shoulder and notice the group of girls standing in a tight circle. The tall, pretty senior with elbow-length black hair is Chrissy Lin, the lacrosse player who apparently dated Riggs last year. Now that I see her, it hits me that she hasn't been making her usual assembly announcements this year. The red-haired girl standing next to her, Cassandra, has been doing them instead. I *did* see Chrissy hunched over her laptop in the library the other day, at the same time when teams generally practiced. Maybe she stepped back from lacrosse this semester to focus on college applications? But that doesn't make much sense—colleges *love* extracurriculars.

Chrissy crosses her arms in her oversized flannel shirt, and the next thing I know, *she's looking at me.* I avert my eyes, but not fast enough. She must have caught me glancing at her, because the expression I could make out between her dark curtains of hair was . . . pissed.

I hope she doesn't think I was trying to catch her eye and

gloat that I'm here with her ex. As I tie my scarf for real this time, I steal another glance in Chrissy's direction, just to make sure she isn't, like, fuming at me. Update: she isn't, but she *is* huddled against Cassandra's side, the redhead's arm draped around her shoulders.

"Should we go get some apple cider doughnuts?" asks Riggs, oblivious to the unsettling exchange I just had with his ex.

"Yeah, let's go." I smile, trying to forget the sting of her narrowed eyes. "I'm starving, actually."

We grab a spot in line underneath the twinkling string lights. As tends to happen when fried dough is being offered up for free, a queue of at least twenty people snakes across the grass. Riggs offers to get some hot apple cider for us to drink while we wait, so I stay here to hold our spot.

As soon as he's gone, I scan the oval in search of my crew from the dorm. At the axe-throwing lane, Marina and Tasha are doubled over laughing; at the petting zoo, Tori and her date, Karl, take a selfie with a sheep. Raquelle and Antoine are carving a pumpkin; and Jess . . . It takes me a minute to spot her, because she's way off on a bale of hay, deep in conversation with a lanky, olive-skinned guy in a forest-green beanie, who looks just like the person I saw on her phone: Sam. My heart glows for her.

"Hey."

A hard tap on my shoulder startles me, but it's nothing compared to my shock when I turn around and see the same face that caught me staring a few minutes ago.

"I'm Chrissy," she says, without any hint of the smile I've seen her wear before. Even when she had to report a crushing defeat at assembly, she'd find a way to put a positive spin on it, like "But it only made us stronger as a team!" or "Now we know exactly what to work on in practice this week!" Apparently, there's no positive spin she wants to put on me being at the Fall Festival with her ex-boyfriend.

What am I supposed to say right now? "Sorry I'm on a date with your ex"? "I'm sure the breakup wasn't you; it was him"? There's no way I'm bold enough to pull anything like that, and I'd like to avoid a fight.

"H-hey," I stammer. "I'm Alyson. I've obviously, um, seen you around school, back at Stewart and everything, so it's nice to finally—"

She cuts me off in a clipped tone. "Are you Riggs's date?"

I'd like to be launched into the sun. I guess I'll lean in to my killing-with-kindness strategy. "Um, yep! He, um, he asked me a little while ago!"

Chrissy's eyes flit to her right, and I follow them to where—thank sweet baby Jesus—Riggs is walking back with a steaming drink in each hand. Feigning a smile, I wave to him in a subtle *Please get over here ASAP* kind of way. He grimaces. Even with his athletic skills, I guess he can move only so fast while carrying two paper cups of scalding-hot liquid.

Chrissy startles me again by grabbing my wrist. Instinct makes me jerk it away, but she holds on tight, her nails digging into my skin.

"Hey, could you—"

She squeezes even tighter.

"Ow!"

"Watch out," she snaps.

"Are you *threatening* her?" Finally, Riggs is at my side. "Chrissy, let go of her wrist, for God's sake."

Chrissy drops my arm, and I rub the spot where her nails

nearly cut me. She looks up at Riggs, her deep brown eyes welling with tears, before turning on her heel and storming away through the crowd. I watch her green-and-black flannel disappear among the chunky fall sweaters, while I massage my sore wrist and wonder what the hell happened—not just between me and Chrissy, but also between Chrissy and Riggs. Her threat made it seem like she wanted me out of the way—like she was planning, maybe, on getting him back. Panic ricochets like a metal pinball around the inside of my chest, each strike making it harder and harder for me to stay upright and fight the urge to crouch on the ground with my hands over my head.

"Alyson," Riggs says. "I'm so, so sorry. Ugh. Are you okay?"

No, I am not okay. My perfect love story is veering way too close to the danger zone. I don't know how to answer his question without word-vomiting my entire tragic romantic history, from watching my mom go through one brutal breakup after another, to Bookstore Aiden, to how badly I want whatever Riggs and I have to work out. Just thinking about it all makes my bottom lip tremble. I shake my head no.

"Here, have this, at least." Riggs puts one of the paper cups in my hands. I know the sweet, spicy aroma should comfort me, but instead I feel sick. He takes my shoulder and guides me into his chest, his hand sliding over to knead the back of my neck. "Do you want to go sit somewhere and talk?"

Getting as far away from Chrissy as possible sounds like a solid idea to me. My voice is weak and flimsy when I reply, "Let's go."

The next thing I know, Riggs takes the hand not holding a cup and guides me on a winding escape route, past the other food stalls and games kiosks and the wooden stage where the

Sullivan-Stewart String Quartet is playing a set. It's not until the bodies and sounds are safely behind us that I realize he's steered us back to the wildflower garden.

"Maybe we could try the bench this time," he says.

"The bench?"

"Come, I'll show you."

I've never clocked it before, but there's a gap at the edge of the garden where a very narrow grass trail cuts a path through the foliage. Riggs leads me down it, his strong grip on my hand never faltering, until we arrive in a tiny clearing just big enough for one stone bench. Wonder courses through me, as though we've stumbled on an ancient ruin—a small, secret world that belongs only to us.

"How'd you figure out this was here?" I ask.

He points to a gold plaque on the backrest: IN LOVING MEMORY OF CROOM RIGGS '52 (1934–2010).

"My dad actually donated it. He had it dedicated to my grandpa."

I look at the numbers next to Croom's name. "Your grandpa went here?"

"Yup. Three generations of Duke lacrosse players, too." This time, when he chuckles, there's something off about it— a twinge of darkness, maybe.

It distracts me from what we actually came here to talk about. "Wow. What's *that* like?"

Riggs lets out a long sigh. "Can I be honest?"

"Of course," I answer immediately. Riggs barely *looks* at other people around campus, so I doubt he's having heart-to-heart conversations with many of them. I'm honored he's willing to do it with me.

"It's stressful as *fuck*," he says.

"Oh no, I'm sorry. Is your dad pressuring you to follow in his footsteps or something?" Maybe the reason Riggs is so un-bro-like is that he never wanted to play lacrosse to begin with.

"Nah, it's not like that. Honestly, I *wanna* follow in my dad's footsteps. Anyone would. He played lacrosse at Duke and stayed on for business school. Now he's the CEO of a company, has a sick apartment on the Upper West Side, plus a place in the Hamptons..."

"So you're stressed because...?"

"Because it'll be so fucking embarrassing if I fail. Coach Pierce and the guys at Duke can say whatever they want, but you know nothing's official until I actually get that offer letter."

"You're gonna get it, Riggs."

He pulls me to the bench and we both sit down, cups in our laps. Riggs scoots over so our arms and legs can touch. It's like we're back on our love seat in the library: close; comfortable, the way we were meant to be together.

"I fuckin' hope so. Anyway, enough about that. Are you okay? What happened back there?"

What was I so worried about a few minutes ago? Oh, that's right. The reason my wrist still stings.

"Chrissy warned me to watch out."

He slowly swallows a mouthful of cider. "What exactly did she say?"

"Just that. She literally said, 'Watch out.' And she grabbed my wrist really hard."

"She didn't say anything else?"

"Nothing else, no, but..." I'm scared to say it because I don't want to put the idea in his head, and I *definitely* don't want to sound like a jealous girlfriend—especially since this is only our first date. At the same time, I'd rather tell him my suspicions so at least he can quash them. ". . . I feel like Chrissy might still be into you."

"Well, I'm not into her, so . . ."

I know I'm about to violate the first commandment of dating, which is Thou Shall Not Grill the Other Person on Their Past Relationships, but I can't help it; I want their whole history so I can be *sure* of how he feels about her. "How did you guys meet?"

"Sullivan and Stewart's lacrosse teams used to travel to away games together sometimes." He shakes his head. "One day last spring, we had this long-ass bus ride somewhere, and the girls made us play this game where we had to pick our seat partner out of a hat. I picked Chrissy. She actually seemed cool at first."

Chrissy *did* seem cool. Back at Stewart, I sometimes did my homework in this shady spot near one of the athletics fields. Once or twice, I was there during lacrosse practice, and I distinctly remember Chrissy's upbeat voice as she led her team through warmup drills. The slaps of high-fives. On the field and at assembly, she came off as being sweet and badass at the same time—but then again, I didn't actually know her at all.

"So she ended up being . . . not cool? When did you guys break up?"

"Yeah." Riggs sighs. "I ended things over the summer. I knew I'd have so much college shit to worry about this semester, and I didn't know if I could handle us being on campus together on top of it. Chrissy does her whole 'nice girl' persona, but I'm telling you, she's nuts. She snaps like *that*." He snaps his fingers. "I guess you just saw it for yourself, huh?"

"Um, yeah. No kidding." I'd normally be skeptical of anyone who rants about their "crazy ex-girlfriend," but Chrissy *did* just threaten me using physical force. Riggs's answer makes me feel a lot better.

"Can I say something totally cheesy that's gonna sound like a line in one of those romantic movies?" he asks.

"I love romantic movies."

He lets his hand drop onto my thigh, light as a bird. "She never made me laugh like you do, Alyson."

Even though, yes, it *was* painfully cheesy, neither of us reacts to it. That's because his hand slides up my thigh until his pinkie grazes the crease of my hip, and we both end up watching it with bated breath, like it's a thing that's happening *to* us—a magnetic pull we can't deny, as though the universe herself is telling us we're meant to be together.

"When I'm with you, I forget about everything else. You're, like, *exactly* what I need right now. . . ."

What's supposed to happen next? Do I just turn my head, and he'll know I want to kiss? Instead, my traitorous brain decides to say something weird, because of course it does. "Your hand is warm from the cider. I can feel it through my jeans." *Hey, Riggs, I'm a total nerd! Let me tell you more about the science of heat transference!*

But thankfully it doesn't knock him off his game. "Really? Does it feel good?"

"Yeah, I guess it does, actually."

"Okay . . . then let's try this." Using his other hand, Riggs takes a sip of his cider. As he swallows, I remember this thing I read in *Cosmo* once, where a woman said the best hookup she'd ever had was when her partner sipped hot tea before going down on her. Just like that, I feel a telltale ache between my legs. Riggs sets the cup down on the bench with a *thunk* that makes my stomach pulse, and the next thing I know, his hand is on my chin and guiding it toward him, and I don't have to think about anything except remembering *absolutely everything* because I know this is it: I'm about to kiss Riggs. I see an orange butterfly beating her wings and the purple lupines swaying in the breeze; I hear the far-off music of the violins and smell the sweetness and spice of our drinks. When his lips touch mine, they're so warm and soft that it's like kissing sunshine. Then he opens his mouth and his tongue is like fire.

Holy hell. I need more.

I put my cup down somewhere to the right of me, not caring if it spills. Then I twist to the left and lean in to him as we kiss, my tongue exploring deeper, his hand finding its way to the back of my head and pulling me even closer. I feel his fingers working their way into my braids, burrowing there. It's like we've done this a thousand times before; that's how naturally we fit together.

"That stuff you said about me earlier," I whisper between kisses, "it was really nice of you."

"I wasn't trying to be nice," he replies. Suddenly, he drops his hand and pulls back. "Shoot, I'm so sorry!"

Oh no, did he think that I hated the way he nibbled my lip just now? Because I didn't—not remotely. I'm Team Marina when it comes to biting, I think. "What is it?"

"I told myself I wasn't gonna mess up your hair, and then I totally forgot because of how great this is."

"You think I'm worried about my *hair* right now?" I literally pick up his hand and return it to my head.

Riggs grins. "I'm more than happy to continue destroying it if you say so."

I kiss him again. I'm feeling more confident than I've ever felt in my life, and I don't know how I'm going to stop when it's time for curfew. "I most *definitely* say so."

Time moves faster than it ever has in the history of the Earth. When I take out my phone to check the clock, I realize we only have five minutes until curfew. No wonder I can't hear anyone on the oval anymore. Riggs and I just kissed—and talked, and laughed, and traced patterns on the backs of each other's hands—for close to an hour. It doesn't even bother me that we missed a good chunk of the Fall Festival.

Riggs is staying over at a teammate's house and has to race to meet him in the parking lot, so we hug goodbye at the mouth of the trail. From there, I don't *walk* back down the path to the dorms; I glide. Every kiss plays on a loop in my head like the world's most romantic movie, the kind I could watch again and again without it ever getting old. I feel like shouting it from the rooftops that I KISSED BRENTON RIGGS JR., but in the meantime, I'll settle for telling Jess everything. I pull out my phone to text her, only to find she's already sent me a barrage of messages first:

Sam and I hung out the whole time

Omg I'm obsessed with him

I realize this goes against my personal brand

> But

> I HAVE A CRUSH!!! AHHHHH!

> How was Riggs???????

As I start to type a response, I trip over a tree root and come *this* close to my second spectacular fall in a two-day period. On second thought, it's so dark on this tree-lined path that I should probably save the texting for later so I can see where I'm going. Up ahead, I hear the gurgling of the fountain where I met up with Riggs, and a little way behind me, the footsteps and voices of two other last-minute stragglers heading back to the dorms for the night. One of them sounds familiar, actually; it's Hudson Gale, from my AP English Lit class.

"What do you wanna know?" Hudson asks his buddy.

"Did you make out with Maggie?" the friend responds.

I wonder if he means Maggie Finlay, Hudson's partner on the short-story project. I know I shouldn't eavesdrop, but I can't resist a conversation about kissing, especially now that I'm someone who partakes in such a thing.

"Yeah."

"Dude! How was she?"

"Eh, it was all right. She seemed a little nervous."

"Whatever, man. Points are points."

"True. I have a bunch now."

"You should try to get her in your Wilderness Excursion group. Tell her you can keep her warm all night long."

"Hey, Maggie, do you have stage three hypothermia, or are you just taking your clothes off for me?"

The guys erupt with laughter.

My intrigue morphs into skin-crawling revulsion. They're talking about hooking up like it's a sport, and not, you know, something you share with another human being. Now I'm mad at myself for thinking on the first day of class that Hudson was cute.

His buddy laughs. "Damn, I gotta up my King's Cup game. Does Maggie have any hot friends?"

When I reach the fountain, I have no choice but to veer left toward the girls' dorms. There's literally a minute left before curfew, and if I roll in late, our dorm supervisor, Ms. Skidmore, will give me a strike. (Three, and you get suspended.) Hudson's and his friend's voices fade into the ether, although to be honest, I'm not sure if I could stomach much more of that disgusting conversation. Thank the freakin' Lord I didn't go to the Fall Festival with one of those guys.

The rest of the way home, and then as I get ready for bed, I cleanse my brain with blissful memories of me and Riggs in the wildflower garden. My scarf still smells like his sexy boy-cologne, so I end up taking it into bed with me.

I listen for the sound of Ms. Skidmore's footsteps as she makes her final rounds. Then, with the lights off, I close my eyes, nuzzle the fabric, and replay every single moment we shared on that bench. I hear his voice, so experienced and mature-sounding: *Really? Does it feel good? Okay . . . Then let's try this.* I didn't know something that hot could happen to me in real life. I roll onto my bed and let my hand creep down the waistband of my pajama shorts. The memory is too swoon-worthy to sleep on right away.

THURSDAY, APRIL 27

Riley Prentiss @RPlax6000 · 5m

As a member of the Sullivan-Stewart lacrosse team, I'm asking you to please share this:

LINK:

> **Adirondack Daily Enterprise**
> *Prep School Lacrosse Captain Missing Since Prom Night*
> Police search still underway; cause of disappearance remains unknown.
> By Geraldine Johnson, Staff Reporter

Chris Collingwood @thechriscollingwood · 1m

Replying to @RPlax6000

Hey, Riley, I'm Chris Collingwood with the *New York Times*. I'd love to chat with you for a story—what's the best way to get in touch?

FRIDAY, APRIL 28

The New York Times

It Was Supposed to Be the Best Night of Their Lives. Then Their Teammate Disappeared.

A teammate of Brenton Riggs Jr. shares details on the days and weeks leading up to the lacrosse captain's disappearance.

BY CHRIS COLLINGWOOD, STAFF REPORTER

The prom after-party at the Prentiss family lake house was teeming with students from Sullivan-Stewart Preparatory School in Lake Placid, New York. It's unclear whether Brenton Riggs Jr., 18, was among them.

What *is* clear is come Monday morning, after a deadly snowstorm had swept through the

Adirondack region, the popular lacrosse captain was nowhere to be found when his team met for practice in the boarding school's gymnasium.

"Me and the guys didn't know where he was," teammate Riley Prentiss, 18, who hosted the Saturday-night after-party, said in a direct message on social media. "And then we were like, 'Damn. Does anyone remember if he was at the after-party?'"

The resounding answer was no, which raised even more questions about the star athlete's mysterious disappearance and still-unknown whereabouts. As the Lake Placid Police Department continues its search for the missing teen, the *New York Times* has obtained an exclusive interview with Mr. Prentiss about the days and weeks leading up to his friend's disappearance.

"I have no idea what happened to him that night, and I have no idea where he is now," the senior said.

Mr. Prentiss, who has known Mr. Riggs since the fifth grade, described him as "popular" and "the kind of guy where good stuff just happens to him without even trying." Indeed, the photos on Mr. Riggs's public social profiles depict a happy, handsome teenager with plenty of friends and high hopes for his future. To Mr. Prentiss's knowledge, Mr. Riggs had been enjoying his final semester of senior year and looking forward to starting at Duke University in the fall.

"A lot of us would have killed to go to Duke," Mr. Prentiss said. "Riggs was the lucky one who got the spot."

Mr. Riggs's social media indicates he was accepted to Duke and offered a spot on the university's nationally ranked lacrosse team in December. In a caption, the teenager expressed joy that he was following in his father's footsteps, as well as sympathy for his high school teammates who didn't get in.

"That would be me," said Mr. Prentiss, who will be taking his lacrosse talents to Lafayette College in September.

Despite the competition among the young men, Mr. Prentiss said the lacrosse team was a "tight-knit group," which is why they all agreed to attend the prom after-party at his family's vacation home on the southwest shore of Lake Placid. Mr. Prentiss admitted he was intoxicated by the time he and a group of friends took a taxi through the snow to his family's house, and that his memory of the rest of the night is foggy.

"I don't remember seeing Riggs there, but I think I just assumed he went to another party or bailed because of the storm," he said. "I wasn't even there for much of the after-party myself. I passed out not too long after we got back and woke up the next afternoon."

The nor'easter that claimed the lives of two Lake Placid residents—both in vehicle accidents—

reached its peak overnight. By the time Mr. Prentiss woke up midday on Sunday, a bulk of the party guests had already left, he recalled.

Was there a chance Mr. Riggs had been there? "I just don't know," Mr. Prentiss said. "It's like I told the detectives: I was too drunk to remember much of anything that night."

SATURDAY, APRIL 29

From: Philip.wheaton@sullivanstewart.edu
To: student-body@sullivanstewart.edu
Subject: PLEASE READ: Reminder

Dear Sullivan-Stewart Student Body,

I hope this message finds you all supporting one another
amid this uncertain and worrisome time. As the search
for our classmate Brenton continues, I know how
eager we all are to find answers, but I must urge you
to exercise caution in the expression of such impulses.
Many of you are likely aware that the events of the past
week have launched a police investigation and drawn
much media attention to our school. In light of that, I
would like to remind everyone that speaking to members
of the press without the permission of the dean of
students or myself is strictly prohibited, on the grounds

that doing so could reflect negatively on our community, jeopardize the integrity of the investigation, and open yourself up to scrutiny from authorities and the public. I also urge you to exercise caution in what you share on social media.

As a reminder, the counseling center has expanded its hours and staffing to accommodate students 7 days a week, 9 a.m. to 6 p.m. You may book an appointment through the MySSPS Wellness Portal.

I hope to see you all at the candlelight vigil tomorrow at 6 p.m. on the oval.

Sincerely,
Philip Wheaton
Headmaster, Sullivan-Stewart Preparatory School

CHAPTER 5

November, Five Months Earlier

If I got to plan my dream winter weekend, it would involve reading and writing in front of a fire with a mug of tea and various baked goods within reach. It would *not* involve strapping on cross-country skis to schlep a backpack full of camping gear to the middle of the woods and then sleep there for the night.

And yet, here I am.

The November Wilderness Excursion was a decades-old Sullivan School tradition aimed at "building character" and "forging lasting bonds," according to the email our headmaster, Mr. Wheaton, sent to the junior and senior classes. "I am pleased to announce the tradition will live on at Sullivan-Stewart Preparatory School," it continued, much to my dismay. The silver lining was that everyone was allowed to pick one friend—I picked Jess, obviously—and then the school would sort those pairs into groups of ten students each.

Our group packed up and skied out of basecamp about ten minutes ago, and now we're standing in a snowy clearing as our wilderness guide, a bearded mountain man named Jasper, points out our five-mile route on a laminated map. The other kids in our group are Riley Prentiss (barf) and his lax buddy Devon; Kavita and Becca, two popular girls in the grade above us; Erica and Zoë, a pair of outdoorsy skiers in our year; and—this part is truly a miracle—Riggs and his best friend, Cameron. The next time my self-doubt makes me question whether I deserve to be with Riggs, I should remember this: the time the cosmic forces of the universe assigned me to the same group as my boyfriend.

Just thinking the word "boyfriend" makes the wind a little less icy and brings feeling back to my numb toes. Riggs and I made things official precisely two weeks and three days ago. The weather had finally gotten too cold for our bench in the wildflower garden, so we were making out in the back seat of his black Ford Explorer, which felt very grown-up.

As he kissed me, his fingers toyed with a button on my shirt. He pulled away and glanced down. "Do you wanna show me what you're wearing under here?"

Believe me, I wanted to rip off my shirt as fast as possible, except I hadn't known we'd be doing this today, so I'd worn one of my comfy T-shirt bras. It was the exact color of a Band-Aid and not the way I wanted Riggs to meet my boobs for the first time. So I reached for his hand. "I want to, but . . . not today. Can we wait? I'm sorry."

"Don't be sorry. We have all the time in the world." His hand moved to my cheek and he planted a kiss on my nose. "Hey, speaking of which, there's something I've been meaning to ask you."

Riggs pushed himself up and started riffling through his backpack, which was on the floor. He baffled me by taking out his history textbook—did he have a homework question?—but then he opened the front cover and presented me with a hand-drawn card he'd been storing there to keep it flat. On the front, it said:

> To the best English partner, Fall Festival date, writer, and expert on dogsled sex that I've ever met . . .

Giggling, I opened it to read the inside—and gasped.

> . . . will you be my girlfriend?

"Oh my God!" I screamed. Here it was: proof that romance was real, and that it could happen to me. I still didn't understand how I'd gotten so lucky, but I'd resolved not to think too hard about it, the same way I avoided thinking about black holes or what happens after we die. I grinned up at him. "Yes!"

Riggs smiled sheepishly. "Really? You're sure?"

"One hundred and fifty billion percent. *Yes.*"

I'd been waiting for this moment since the Fall Festival, wondering when, and if, it would ever happen. Riggs and I had been talking and texting and making out every lunch period after AP English Lit, but because of his demanding lacrosse schedule—he played for Sullivan-Stewart and another team outside of school—we didn't have time to go on "dates" or anything. I understood, but I also craved a name for whatever we *were*—something that made us real, that proved he wanted to hold on to me. After reading the card, I was so happy that I teared up, and then we both laughed, and then we kissed some more.

I wore my black bra the next time.

"Everyone ready?" Jasper rolls up the map. "I'll take the lead. Remember, if you're not sure which way to go, follow the blue circles nailed to the trees. And if you start to get cold, just work harder." He chuckles. "Got it?" Everyone nods with varying degrees of terror on their faces. "Good."

Erica, Zoë, and Jess, whose parents put her on all kinds of skis as soon as she could walk, go bombing after Jasper. Next, Cameron, Riley, and Devon challenge Becca and Kavita to a race, and the five of them take off down the trail, laughing.

Riggs swats my butt with his ski pole. "You lead the way."

"I thought *you* were Mr. Athlete."

"If I go first, I won't be able to look at you."

Grinning, I make my way down the trail. I've done a lot of downhill skiing in my life, but somehow, despite where I go to school, this is my first time on cross-country skis. The odd thing is, even though we're on relatively flat ground, I feel way less sturdy. Not only are these skis like matchsticks, but also my heels aren't strapped into the binding, so the front of my boots are the only solid points of contact. It's like tiptoeing on ice. At basecamp this morning, they taught us to "shuffle, shuffle, gliiide." It's a lot harder than it sounds.

"You're doing great!" Riggs shouts from somewhere behind me.

A slight dip in the path makes my legs go as wobbly as a baby deer's. "Am I, though?"

"For your first time? Yeah. See if you can do a little less 'shuffle' and a little more 'glide.' "

I peer up the path at Riley, who, in his quest to catch Becca, shoves his buddy Devon into a bush. I glance back down at my cursed skis. "I'm worried I'm going to fall if I push off any harder than I already am."

"Well, you *might*—"

"That doesn't help!"

"—but if you do, I'll help you up. And I'll kiss you."

"Okay, now you're making me *want* to fall!" I exclaim. "Wait, did you do that on purpose? Isn't that some kind of psychological principle—like, once you accept the fact that you might screw up, the more confident you'll be at whatever you're doing, and actually, the more successful you'll be? I think that's a thing, isn't it?"

"I don't know, but I think you're stalling. Shuffle, shuffle, glide."

I squeeze my poles and set my sights on the trail ahead. I can do this. *Shuffle . . . shuffle . . .* God, this is harder than it seems. *Shuffle . . . shuffle . . . shuffle . . .* What's the worst that can happen? I fall, and Riggs kisses me. With a deep breath, I push off, and . . .

"Oh my God, I JUST GLID!"

"Yes, you did!"

"WAIT, 'GLID' ISN'T EVEN A WORD!"

"Alyson, you're a huge nerd."

"WHY DO WE KEEP RHYMING?"

It turns out, cross-country skiing is kind of fun once you get the moves down and learn to trust the equipment. Like magic, the clouds part, and sunlight beams through the trees, and that's when it dawns on me. There's this trope in the romance genre—in rom-com movies, specifically—known as the "falling-in-love montage." It's a collection of short scenes showing the main couple falling deeper and deeper in love over time, while peppy music plays in the background. If there were a falling-in-love montage for me and Riggs, this moment, here in the wilderness of the Adirondacks, would one hundred percent be in it.

"Wait a second," Riggs says minutes later. "What *is* the past tense of 'glide'?"

Oh shoot. I was so distracted thinking about our falling-in-love montage that I just *glided* right over the crest of a steep and narrow slope. Holy crap. I'm gaining speed like a snowball rolling downhill. Shoot, shoot, shoot.

"RIGGS! HOW DO I STOP?!"

"Snowplow!"

"It's not wide enough for snowplow!"

"You have room! I'm behind you!"

I try it but my legs are way wobblier than I'm used to on downhill skis. It doesn't take. The path bends to the right at the bottom of the hill, and I'm scared that if I don't get my skis under control soon, I'm going to career right into a massive pine tree. Why did there have to be so much snow in November this year? Why couldn't we have gotten lucky and had this be a hiking trip instead? I take it all back: Humans were simply not meant to ski on matchsticks. I'm fully screwed. I need to bail. Abandoning everything I learned in today's tutorial, I forgo the snowplow in favor of collapsing like a house of cards. My body crashes to the ground, and I slide the rest of the way down on my side, finally coming to a stop when my skis collide with the very tree my face was formerly aimed at.

Riggs snowplows to a stop beside me, and, after making sure I'm okay, helps me get back onto my feet. I look into his eyes, today the same color as the shards of ice-blue sky visible through the branches overhead, and imagine how it would feel to tell him I'm falling in love with him. My heart wants to do it, but I don't want to scare him away.

"Thanks for helping me up."

"No problem."

"I thought you said you'd kiss me if I fell, too."

"Trust me, I didn't forget," he replies with a smile, his lips already moving toward mine.

We set up camp near a glassy black lake and cook penne with pesto over a fire. It's freezing, especially when the sun starts to go down, and I like it when Riggs warms me up by pulling me into his lap and wrapping his arms around me for everyone to see. After dinner, we go around telling ghost stories, and I won't lie, I pretend to be scared so I have an excuse to curl into Riggs and bury my face in his neck. Then it's time to look up and stargaze, and Jasper makes a pot of hot chocolate, which Riggs and I drink from the same tin cup. I may be on the verge of hypothermia, but this night is still pretty darn close to perfect.

Later, the girls and I are back in our tent—everyone except for Becca, that is, who went off to pee in the woods. We're sitting up in our sleeping bags, analyzing the blocks of lard and chocolate chips that Jasper instructed us to nibble throughout the night in order to replenish all the calories our bodies would burn just trying to keep warm.

Jess contemplates the plastic-wrapped lard block in the beam of her flashlight. "I like outdoors stuff," she says, "but this is some weird-ass, Sullivan-School, *Lord of the Flies* shit."

"I'm gonna try it." I roll back the plastic and take a tiny bite off the corner. "Hmmm." I chew and swallow. "Honestly, it's pretty good. It tastes like a granola bar."

Kavita scoffs. "There's no *way*," she insists, flinging her lard block into the corner of the tent like it's a dirty sock. "You're too optimistic."

"Alyson's in love," Jess interjects. "You'll have to forgive her."

I pick up my feet in my sleeping bag and playfully kick Jess so that she teeters over onto her side. "Okay, Miss I-FaceTime-with-Sam-Young-Like-Seven-Nights-a-Week."

"Hey, it's because we send news stories to each other every day!" she fires back. "We have to discuss them at some point!"

"I rest my case, Quigley."

Just then, the tent's front zipper jerks open. It lets in an icy blast of wind, and with it, Becca, who looks like she's seen one of the ghosts from the stories around the campfire. "You guys," she hisses, "something really messed up just happened."

Kavita holds up her palm. "I swear to God, Becca, if you tell me you saw a bear out there, I will never speak to you again."

"No," Becca snaps, her curt tone wiping the smile off her friend's face. "I . . . Ugh, can someone help me with this stupid thing?"

Erica eases the zipper from Becca's shaking hands and swiftly closes the entrance flap as Becca crawls across our legs to her sleeping bag. Nobody speaks; we don't know what to say. It's only when Becca's wrapped up and sitting with her knees tucked against her chest that Kavita asks, "Bec, what happened?"

Becca looks warily at the four juniors. She has a face like a fox: small, pointed, and pretty, with pinkish skin and big, brown eyes. "You guys can't tell *anyone*."

We shake our heads.

She breathes in and out, then, fidgeting with the tassels hanging off her hat, starts to whisper. "The other night, I snuck into Riley's dorm room so we could hook up—it's been happening for a few weeks now. This last time, we did some stuff I'd never done before, and it was really good. Like, really, really good. I liked him, but now I swear to God I want to *kill* him."

Kavita leans in. "What the hell did that asshole do?"

Becca's whisper is thin and shaky; she sounds like she's panicking and looks like she's going to cry. "I passed the guys' tent, and I overheard Riley telling them everything we'd done. Not just this most recent time, but a bunch of other times, too. And like, I get it, you want to tell your friends about your hookups, but . . . but I'm not exaggerating when I say they *all . . . know . . . everything.* I heard Riley doing an impression of . . . an impression of . . . of the sound I make when I . . . He said I sound like a 'horny mouse'—a fucking 'horny mouse'!" I see the first tears spill from Becca's eyes before she covers them with her mittens. She sobs, "And then Devon was like, 'Get that horny mouse, bro!' And they high-fived."

I feel like I'm going to be sick. The story reminds me of the conversation I overheard between Hudson and his friend after the Fall Festival, when they talked about Maggie like she was just some means to an end—the end being bro-on-bro bragging rights and mean jokes.

Kavita scooches over and puts an arm around her friend. "He can go straight to hell."

We all nod.

"If it makes you feel any better, Riggs has called Riley an 'ignorant dickwad,'" I chime in.

Becca lifts her head off Kavita's shoulder, sniffs, and wipes her eyes. She laughs weakly. "That's the most accurate thing I've ever heard. Especially with what happened next."

"Tell me," Kavita demands.

"He"—Becca sniffs again—"he was talking about each thing we did like there were points attached to it, and he was adding them up. One point for a regular kiss . . . two for a make-out . . . He bragged about how high his score was, thanks to me. It . . . it sounded like they had some kind of sick competition going."

"Wait a second." Hudson and his friend's conversation just came back to me in full. "Becca, did they say anything about"—I make air quotes—" 'the King's Cup'?"

"Yes!" Her eyes go wide. "Wait, how did you know? Have you heard of it?"

Kavita rounds on me. "Does Riggs have something to do with this?"

"No!" I exclaim, horrified. Riggs would never, in a million years, have anything to do with a thing like this. Riggs is the kind of guy who gets love *right*—who made a handwritten card asking me to be his girlfriend. "I overheard Hudson Gale talking about it."

Kavita balks at this information. "*Hudson Gale?* As in the kid who carries his saxophone everywhere?"

"Yeah."

"Well, *that's* not a good sign."

"Why?"

"Because he and Riley are in completely different social circles. I doubt they've ever spoken in their lives. If they're *both* talking about this King's Cup thing, I feel like it's kind of a big deal."

Kavita's words seep through me like ice water. A second ago, it seemed absurd that Riggs could have anything to do with this caveman-like competition. But it also makes sense that if Hudson and Riley are both part of it, then the King's Cup must be pretty widespread. Plus, Riggs has to at least know what it is, if Riley was boasting about it in the tent. So why has he never mentioned it to me?

Probably because he's so far removed from it, it's barely on his radar.

"Oh my God," Kavita continues. "Bec, what if this is why Greg Wyatt randomly slid into my DMs that one time and asked if I'd be down for a threesome?"

Zoë's been quietly listening this whole time, the creases in her medium brown forehead getting deeper and deeper. "Everything with Zeke makes so much sense now," she mutters.

As far as I know, Zoë, like me, never dated anyone when we were at Stewart. Her family's pretty Christian, and apparently, she wasn't allowed to date until she turned seventeen. She marked the occasion at the start of the school year by getting together with Zeke Alonso, another skier in our year.

"Ever since we started dating, Zeke's been obsessed with having sex. Like, he'll tell me which of his friends have done it and how great it was." Zoë wrinkles her nose. "This one time I snuck into his dorm, he even showed me the box of condoms in his drawer. I had to tell him I wasn't ready, and probably wouldn't be for a long time. He claimed it was fine, but now, whenever we hook up, I feel like he's disappointed when I pull his hands away from somewhere, and it's like I've done something wrong. It's this really awkward dynamic. I wonder if King's Cup has anything to do with it."

Erica claps a hand over her mouth. "Zo, remember when Zeke asked me if I'd ever be up for a double date with his friend?"

"And you said no, and he practically begged you?"

"It was so weird at the time. . . ."

"But what if . . ."

"These boys are *all . . . fucking . . . in on it.*" Jess looks furious enough to breathe fire. "And here I was thinking Sam was actually into me. I bet he doesn't give a crap about anything we talk about. He just wants me to like him so I'll let him hook up with me. *Ugh.*"

"It makes you feel disposable, doesn't it?" Becca mumbles.

I don't have a revelatory relationship story to share—other than the fact that I have a boyfriend and I'm pretty sure I'm falling in love with him—but it's breaking my heart to hear my friends sounding similar to how my mom did after Joe. These objectively amazing women shouldn't be questioning their self-worth because of a bunch of loser guys. And that's when it hits me. "I just had a thought," I tell the group. "About how we get revenge."

I smile at Jess specifically, whose eyes widen with excitement. "*Vigilante justice mode.* Oh my God, yes. YES!"

Kavita tilts her head. "Can someone please explain?"

While Jess fills them in on my secret revenge operations— she really is an excellent hype woman—the cogs in my head keep turning. What can we do? How do we hit the boys where it really hurts? Do we orchestrate a sex strike, like in that Greek play *Lysistrata*? I scratch my chin. I feel like it's still not quite there.

"Alyson, what do you think we should do?" asks Zoë.

I start to talk slowly, working it out as I go. "So the King's Cup is about who can do the most stuff with girls, right?" The rest of the group nods. "I feel like on the surface, it's about sex, but on a deeper level, the competition is actually about—"

"Power," Jess breathes. "Who's the manliest of the men."

"Exactly. We need to knock them off their high horse. We

need to— Oh!" It just hit me. "What if we got back at them by intentionally rejecting them in super embarrassing ways?"

"Wait, that's *genius*," Erica says.

"Not kissing a guy is one thing," I continue, "but letting the whole school know you don't find him kissable—"

"—is the chef's kiss of revenge plots," Jess finishes.

I turn to Kavita. "Like, what if you told Greg it would *really* turn you on if he and a friend waited for you in the woods wearing nothing but tighty-whities and holding a rose between their teeth? And then . . . I don't know . . . we all showed up and took pictures of them?"

Everyone forgets about whispering; we explode with shrieks and cackles.

"Girls, lights-out is in five minutes." It's Jasper, crunching around outside in the snow. We all try to suppress our giggles as we switch off our flashlights. "It's time to get some sleep. Remember, if you're cold, doing crunches or sit-ups in your sleeping bag will help generate heat."

We burrow into our makeshift beds in full snow gear. The tent is loud with the *swish-swish* of outerwear rubbing against sleeping bag material as people try to find the most comfortable way to curl up on the ground.

Jess shuffles over to me. "Hello, my genius friend. It's freaking freezing in here. Wanna be little spoon?"

"Yes, please." I flip onto my side, and Jess scoots her body against my back. This is how we lie when we have sleepovers at Jess's house.

"Hmmm . . . Does this feel any warmer to you?"

"Not really," I admit.

"Maybe we need to do some Pilates in here."

We both try and fail to muffle our laughter.

Jess stops laughing first and goes quiet for a few moments. I figure she must be drifting off to sleep, but then she whispers, "So I'm *obsessed* with your revenge plot."

I wasn't expecting the edge to her voice—like there's a "but" coming. "Do you think we should actually do it?" I ask.

"Hell yes. They deserve it." Jess scoots even closer so she can whisper straight into my ear. "But, babe . . . I wanted to talk about Riggs for a sec."

My whole body goes rigid. "What? Why?"

"Well . . . I don't want you to freak out or anything . . . but I overheard something weird in econ the other day."

"Something about *Riggs*?"

"Yeah. It didn't seem worth mentioning at the time, but now I think you might wanna know."

"What was it?" I want to turn around and shake it out of her, just so I can squash it faster.

"These lax bros were talking about Riggs getting a 'huge head start' on something over the summer."

"A huge head start on what?"

"I don't know. I only caught the end of the conversation, 'cause I was sitting near the door, and I could hear them talking as they walked down the hall; they stopped as soon as they got to class."

Okay. Phew. That wasn't necessarily bad, was it? Riggs could have been getting a head start on *anything*. It could have been a college application. "That was literally all you heard?" I ask.

"That was all I heard. I obviously don't know what they were talking about . . ."

My back starts to feel all prickly, and I wriggle an inch forward, so our bodies aren't quite so pressed together. "But you think he's in the King's Cup."

"I didn't say *that*. . . ."

"You didn't *not* say it."

"Al." She closes the gap between us. "I just want you to be careful, okay? Make sure you guys are on the same page with what you're getting out of the relationship."

"Riggs isn't like that." It comes out louder than I meant it to, but I can't have Jess questioning the integrity of my relationship. Like, I obviously thought it was a little random at first that a guy like Riggs would be into me, but I feel like I know him pretty well at this point, and he's just not like the other guys. I believe in what we have. I really do.

"Girls!" It's Jasper again. He must be waiting to make sure we stop talking. "You're going to need the rest for the trek we have tomorrow."

We lie there in silence for another few minutes, until Jasper's boots crunch back to where they came from. When our wilderness guide is far enough way, I ask Jess again in a quiet voice: "Do you think I should ask Riggs about the King's Cup?"

But Jess was going hard on the trail today—I saw her yawn about forty times when we were sitting around the campfire. And skiing or not, she's always been the kind of person who goes unconscious the second their head hits the pillow. My best friend seems to have fallen asleep, so there's no one to hear my question except the dark and frigid night.

CHAPTER 6

As the tent fills with the sounds of soft snores and deep breathing, I lie awake, dwelling on Jess's suggestion that Riggs might be using me in some way. Even though she's my best friend, I wish I could just be mad at her and call it a day. Instead, I'm dealing with something scarier than anger: doubt. Could it be true? Could Riggs be competing in the guys' twisted game and hiding it from me?

It's impossible to imagine him keeping track of our hookups and bragging about the points to his friends. The night we met, Riggs rescued me from Riley and proved he understood at least some basic tenets of feminism. That alone should be proof he'd never stoop to the level of the King's Cup.

But what if Jess is right, and all the guys—at least, all the guys who are into girls—are "fucking in on it"?

Fine! Let's say Riggs *has* been logging the points for each of our hookups. Would that really be so bad? It wouldn't change the fact that we like each other, or that we both want to do stuff together.

Unless he doesn't really like me, and everything he's ever said to me has been an elaborate charade to beat his classmates at some stupid, sexist competition.

What the hell? No one's that good of an actor. And besides, if Riggs were only in it for points, he could easily hook up with most girls on campus. Why pick *me*, of all people?

Riggs is different from the other guys. He and I have something special, and Jess just doesn't get it. She didn't *feel* the falling-in-love montage yesterday, the way I did.

Let's say I *did* just ask Riggs point-blank if he's in the King's Cup; he knows what it is, after all. Wouldn't that be bad for our relationship? He's been nothing but an amazing boyfriend, and I'd essentially be marching up to him and telling him I don't trust him. If I were in his position, I'd be pretty insulted.

It's probably better not to say anything and trust my heart. It knows Riggs better than Jess does, and it wouldn't steer me wrong.

Shortly after sunrise, Jasper takes a lap around camp banging a metal pot to wake us up. It took me hours to fall asleep last night, and I'm really not loving this rude awakening. Inside our sleeping bags, we each take part in the wordless ritual of shimmying out of our snow pants, sweatpants, and leggings, changing our underwear, and then putting all the layers back on. I can't wait to cram all these clothes into a dorm washing machine, take a forty-five-minute hot shower, and then not go outside again for the rest of my life.

Reaching up to maneuver my oily hair into a braid, I catch a whiff of my underarms, and it isn't good. One of my general life principles is that if you can smell yourself, you have a problem—and you especially have a problem if you're about to spend the whole day with the person you like. I plunge my hand into the pocket of my backpack where I stowed my basic toiletries, only to panic when I realize—

"Did you forget deodorant?" Jess asks, reading my mind. Before I can answer her, she tosses some my way. "I gotcha covered, babe."

I catch it and thank her, burying any lingering awkwardness from last night. I know she was just looking out for me, the way she always does, and I'm grateful for that. Even if she is wrong to be worried about Riggs.

Erica pauses with a hand on the tent zipper. "Before we go out there . . . Should we tell the guys we know about the King's Cup?"

"No way," says Becca, who looks considerably more chipper than she did when she came barreling back into the tent last night. She looks at me and grins. "I think we should have a little fun with them before we show our cards."

I'm all for it, obviously. The only catch is that Riggs can't know I'm doing this. I don't want him thinking I'd ever plot revenge on *him.* "We should strategize more when we're back at school and no one can overhear us," I whisper.

We all exchange curt nods before we clamber out into the cold. They made us leave our phones back at basecamp, but I don't need my clock to know it's super early right now. There's a bit of orange sunlight peeking out from behind the silvery, snow-dusted mountains, and the sky above is lavender and deep periwinkle.

The girls are the first to arrive at the campfire down by the lake, where Jasper serves up tin cups of gluey oatmeal, which is excellent because it is hot. Steam rises in front of my friends' faces as they eat, but I can just make out five conspiratorial smirks as the boys crawl out of their tent and amble down to join us on the icy shoreline. Maybe I'm just seeing what my brain wants me to see, but I swear Riley's walking with his chest puffed out and his elbows cocked like some big man on campus. I get a rush knowing he thinks he's *so cool* for secretly getting points off Becca, when really the six of us know all about the King's Cup—and have plans to make him pay.

"Hey, you." Riggs plops down next to me on the log. He wastes no time wrapping an arm around my shoulders, pulling me in to his side and kissing my forehead. I'm no expert, but I'm pretty sure guys in the King's Cup don't *kiss their girlfriends' foreheads.* They'd probably get negative points for extreme cuteness and lovability.

"Hey." I brush aside his curls to peck the warm spot behind his ear. "I missed you."

"I missed you, too." He checks to see where Jasper is before lowering his voice. "Sucks we can't sleep in the same tent, eh?" He squeezes my thigh. "That would be fun."

My blood runs cold at how quickly he just alluded to sleeping together, and once again, Jess's warning plays in my head. I steal a glance toward the other side of the campfire, where my best friend eyes me over the rim of her cup like a mama bear watching her cub. To her left, Becca is more like a spider; she greets Riley with a syrupy-sweet smile and pats the empty space next to her on the log.

I turn back to Riggs and take a deep breath to steady my

pounding heart. I know my own boyfriend better than anyone else here. "That *would* be fun. Instead, I had to make out with my block of lard."

Riggs claps a mitten over his heart and pretends to be offended. "I see how it is, Alyson." I'm already snickering. "You like that block of lard better than me. It was the chocolate chips, wasn't it? I knew this would happen."

"It's true," I joke. "There's something magical between us that I just can't resist."

We stop screwing around and smile at each other, because we both know I was actually talking about my feelings for him.

"Ski with me again today?" he asks.

"Of course."

Jasper stands up and raises a hand to get our attention. "All right, campers!" he announces. "I'm gonna go over the plan for today. Obviously, we're headed back to basecamp, but we're not gonna take the same route we came in on." Jasper unfurls his laminated map and holds it up so everyone can see. "You're all pros at cross-country skiing by now, so we're gonna take this longer, hillier route to test your skills." He gestures to a yellow line that snakes over a lot of close-together black lines, the sign of a steep slope on a topographical map. "When you're done eating, you're gonna make sandwiches to stick in your bags for lunch. Then we'll pack up camp, hop into our skis, and hit the trail. We want to be back at basecamp by midafternoon, because there's snow in the forecast. I'm hoping the worst of it holds off until we're back. Remember, if you get lost, you're following yellow today."

We head off in the same formation as yesterday; the only difference is that this time around, we're all keeping secrets from each other. It's hard not to straight-up ask Riggs if he's in the King's Cup, but if I did it now, I'd not only risk insulting him, I'd also risk him telling the other guys that we know what's up and ruining our chances at a sneak-attack revenge plot.

Thankfully—well, sort of—the grueling trail is a good distraction. Today's route is all up and down, so for three hours straight, I'm either waddling up a seemingly endless incline or hurtling (while screaming) down a slope, which more often than not ends in a crash.

"Should we stop here for lunch?" Riggs suggests. We've just made it to the top of a long, gradual hill and glided onto a bridge that spans a babbling brook.

"Please—I'm starving. And my butt needs a break before I fall again."

Following Riggs's lead, I shrug off my backpack, unclip my boots from the skis, and carry my cream cheese and jam sandwich over to the railing. Riggs looks so handsome and rugged as he leans against the wooden plank, I could melt, which is saying something, given our surroundings. His face is flushed from the cold, and there's frost in his eyebrows and the curls springing out from underneath his hat. His lips are extra pink.

But he also looks kind of forlorn as he gazes out at the water. He tears off pieces of his sandwich and places them in his mouth like a robot.

"Riggs, are you okay?"

He swallows with a grimace. "I fuckin' hate Prentiss."

"Oh!" The answer is so out of nowhere, I can't help but wonder if it was triggered by the conversation in the boys' tent last night. I gently pry for more information. "Why do you hate him so much?"

"A few reasons." This time, he tears off a bite of sandwich with his teeth. "I found out Duke Lacrosse is looking at us for the same spot."

"What? I thought that spot was yours. It was basically a done deal."

"It *was*. But Prentiss has been having a really good season. And then, I swear to God, that fucker sabotaged me at finals."

"Are you serious?"

"I mean, I'm *pretty sure* he did. He checked this massive Hardwick guy for no reason, and the guy crashed into me from the other side, and then I lost my balance and messed up my ankle and couldn't play the rest of the game. We lost, but Prentiss got his chance to show off for the coach without me on the field to compete with him. And I came off like a loser captain who choked in the most important game of the season."

"Could you explain what happened to Duke?"

"No. I'd seem like a wimp, and that would make things even worse. I can't prove what happened, anyway."

"What does it all mean for you?"

"Well, only one of us is gonna get to play for Duke; the other is gonna end up at some sad safety school. And because of that, I had to bust my ass on the application, and my dad had to make a bunch of phone calls to his guys in the alumni office." He squeezes the empty tinfoil into a tight ball. "Asking him to do that for me was so fucking embarrassing."

I assume he means he's ashamed of having pulled strings to get into college, like those rich kids you hear about whose parents conveniently make multimillion-dollar donations right around the time applications are due.

Then he adds, "My dad probably thinks I'm pathetic."

Well, okay, then. That's an icky side of Riggs I haven't seen before. I wince as the thought crosses my mind that there could be *other* sides to Riggs I haven't seen before. I know I should politely remind him to check his privilege, but . . . well . . . maybe I don't want to know how he'd respond to that. "I'm sure your dad's still proud of you," I tell him.

"I doubt it."

I slide closer to him and rest my head on his shoulder. "If he's not, then he's an idiot. I'll tell you that much."

"Why?"

"Because I think you're perfect."

That's when the snow begins to fall: tiny, perfect flakes that dance in the air like magic.

Is this for real? Is this why people like Christmas movies? As snowflakes land on our eyelashes and we smile at each other, it's like the past conversation and Jess's warning never happened, and I'm back in the rom-com starring us. A flame in my core lights me on fire from the inside. I turn to him, and he does the same to me; it's like our bodies are speaking their own secret language. And mine needs to touch his. Now.

This will *not* be a G-rated Christmas-movie kiss. I throw my arms around his neck and our mouths collide, ice cold and then blazing hot. I want him to kiss me deeper, as deep as his tongue can go. Again, like our bodies are on the same wavelength, Riggs maneuvers me so that my back is against the railing. With the resistance behind us, he's free to lean into me, to press farther into my mouth. Maybe it's because we're in the woods like animals, but this kiss feels rawer and hungrier than anything we've done before. With the toe of his ski boot, he nudges my feet apart, and then he presses one of his legs between mine.

Holy. Freaking. Hell.

Did I just . . . moan? I didn't know that was a thing people did outside of books. Brenton Riggs Jr. must be awakening something inside me.

A gust of wind comes out of nowhere, and from the corner of my eye, I spot our skis moving of their own accord. They're about to slide off the bridge. Panicked, I pull out of the kiss. "Riggs!" I yelp. "Skis!"

In a matter of milliseconds, he dives on top of them just in time to stop them from plummeting into the water below. "Good eye." He laughs. "That was close."

I missed it while we were making out, but the snow has picked up, too. Now it's less peaceful holiday card, more inside of a vigorously shaken snow globe. "This must be the storm Jasper mentioned," I shout over the rising wind. "How far do you think we are from basecamp?"

He pulls down his mitten to check his watch. "Based on how long we've been out here . . . maybe another hour?"

"Crap. We need to move!"

We scarf down what's left of our sandwiches, shoulder our packs, and clip into our skis as quickly as possible. In a matter of minutes, the snow has gotten even heavier, and the wind howls through the trees. Mr. Wheaton would be delighted at the "character-building" potential of it all.

Riggs volunteers to take the lead. "Not because you're a girl," he adds quickly, a callback to the night we met. "Just because I like you and if we hit an ice patch that plunges off a cliff, I'd rather I be the one to die."

"Riggs!" I smack him with my ski pole. "Don't even *say* that!"

"It's the truth!"

We ski off the other side of the bridge and follow the yellow markers onward. The storm is relentless. With Riggs directly in front of me, I know he must be taking the brunt of the wind, snow, and tiny ice pellets, but he doesn't complain once. I'm grateful for his stoicism, because otherwise I might be panicking more than I already am. I don't know how much worse this is going to get, and I'm scared we might get stranded.

About thirty minutes in, we reach a point where the path splits in two. I squint back and forth as I search for the next yellow circle, but it's hard to spot through the snow. If our classmates left any ski tracks, they've since been blanketed over. "Which way do you think we should go?"

"I can't tell!" He points his pole to the left, arbitrarily. "Let's try this one, and if we see a different color, we'll turn back."

Riggs pushes off down the left-hand trail, so I follow him. This path is even hillier than the one we were on before, and pretty soon, we're teetering on the edge of a steep descent that looks like something I'd ski at Whiteface.

"Could this be right?" I scan the area for signs of yellow. "This seems intense!"

"If I can get partway down, I'll be able to see if there's a marker at the base of the hill." And without further ado, Riggs starts to sidestep down, using his poles for support.

"Wait! Riggs, this is so dangerous!"

"I got this!"

"Are you sure? Why don't you at least take your skis off?"

"I'm sure!"

But the wind is blowing from all the wrong directions, and Riggs is nowhere near as good on cross-country skis as he is on a lacrosse field. The fall happens about fifteen feet down the hill;

his bottom ski starts to slide, and as he struggles to gain purchase, his top ski starts sliding, too. We both holler out a string of curse words as Riggs ends up slipping backward down the hill. For the first time, I see how fear looks on my boyfriend's face.

I throw down my poles and bag, rip off my skis, and take the hill like it's a toboggan run, minus the toboggan. Up ahead, Riggs bails to the ground like I did yesterday, but he does something funny to his pole and it snaps in half—then his skis pop off. Forget the equipment—I just need him to be okay. I'm terrified. I feel tears streaking my cheeks.

Finally, he skids to a stop. He isn't moving, and it looks like his eyes are closed. As soon as I reach him, I crawl over him on all fours. "Riggs? RIGGS!"

His eyelids flutter, thank the Lord, and I'm happy my face is the first thing he sees when he opens his eyes. I can tell he's happy, too, because despite the fact that he definitely almost died, not to mention that we're lost in the forest in the middle of a blizzard, he grins up at me. "Hey. You saved me."

"This flat ground saved you!" My voice is still frantic as my brain works to process the shock.

A tear slides off my chin and splashes onto his lips. He licks it. "Are you crying?"

"Yes!" I let out a laugh-sob and prod him in the shoulder. "You can't do that again! You scared the hell out of me!"

He shrugs his arms out of his backpack. As the snow swirls around us, he reaches for the back of my neck and pulls me in for a kiss. The rest of my body follows so that I'm fully lying on top of him and relishing how it feels to have him warm and alive beneath me.

If we were still in our movie, we'd probably end up out of our clothes somehow, frostbite and hypothermia be damned.

Unfortunately, we're in real life. This snowstorm is only getting worse, our equipment is scattered at various points along this hill of despair, and we still have no clue which way we're supposed to be going. I pull out of the kiss and peer over my shoulder. There, nailed to the trunk of a spruce tree, is a circular trail marker. And it's orange.

I push myself up to my knees, straddling him. "We officially went the wrong way."

He pats my thighs. "I think we were going in the right direction."

I smile down at him. I have to say, this view is hot as hell. Who *wouldn't* be thinking about sex in a configuration like this? "I'm a fan of this direction, too."

"But maybe not in a blizzard?"

"Maybe not in a blizzard."

We help each other up and gather his equipment from where it's strewn about in the snow. Then, step by step in our ski boots, we start to hike our way back up the hill.

SUNDAY, APRIL 30

ISABELLE PARK: Welcome back to Channel 5 News.
I'm Isabelle Park. It's been almost a week since
eighteen-year-old lacrosse captain Brenton Riggs
Jr. was reported missing by his coach two days
after prom night. As the search for the young man
continues, we're going live to Sullivan-Stewart
Prep School, where a candlelight prayer vigil is
taking place. Doug Higginbotham is there at the
scene. Doug, tell us what's happening over there.
This must be such a difficult night.

DOUG HIGGINBOTHAM: I'm here at Sullivan-Stewart
Prep School, and as you can imagine, the atmosphere
tonight is very somber. Gathered behind me,
students and faculty are holding candles, singing
songs, and of course, praying for the safe

return of Brenton Riggs Jr. People are hurting, but they're also hopeful. And that goes for Brenton's close friends, Cameron and Alyson, who are here with me now. Can you tell me about your relationships with him?

CAMERON WRIGHT: Riggs and I have been best friends since fifth grade. He's the best dude ever.

DOUG: And you, Alyson?

ALYSON BENOWITZ: I-I'm his girlfriend.

CAMERON: You should see these two together. They give the rest of us hope.

DOUG: That's really beautiful. So, Alyson, is it safe to assume you and Riggs were at prom together that night?

ALYSON: Yes.

DOUG: And no idea where he might be?

ALYSON: I went home early because I had a migraine and I'll . . . I'll never be able to forgive myself.

CAMERON: We should maybe . . .

DOUG: I'm so sorry. We can change the topic. Do you want to tell me what brought you both out here tonight?

CAMERON: Al, do you wanna-

ALYSON: I can't-

DOUG: That's all right, Alyson. I can't imagine how hard this is. Please, grab a tissue. Cameron, do you want to-

CAMERON: Um, we're here tonight because we miss Riggs like hell, and we want to show everyone that we're not gonna give up looking for him, because we know he's out there somewhere-right, Al? Yeah. We know he's out there. And we're staying strong. We've both talked to the police and given them all the information we have, and a bunch of our friends have, too. We're doing everything we can.

DOUG: Speaking of your friends, does it help to be surrounded by community right now?

CAMERON: Yeah, for sure. When you're alone, your mind starts to think about the worst-case scenario. I'm happy they did this tonight.

DOUG: If you could say anything to Brenton right now, what would it be?

CAMERON: We miss you, buddy, and we hope you're okay. Anything else, Al? No? Okay. Sorry, we should probably go sit down. . . .

DOUG: Thank you both for taking the time. I think I speak for all our viewers when I say we're keeping Brenton and his friends and family in our prayers. Back to you, Isabelle.

CHAPTER 7

December, Four Months Earlier

"Hear ye, hear ye, my beautiful babes." Jess taps her mug of ginger tea three times on the coffee table. "The inaugural meeting of the Queen's Cup is now in session."

A rebellious flame crackles in my chest as I peer at the nine other faces spread across the cozy round-arm sofas and overstuffed armchairs. Besides me and Jess, there's the crew from our camping trip—Erica, Zoë, Becca, and Kavita—as well as Marina, Tasha, Tori, and Raquelle. It's an odd collection of people, and if anyone from Sullivan-Stewart saw us, they'd for sure be suspicious about why we're all hanging out together. That's why, on this snowy Sunday afternoon, we've taken over the back room of Cobble Hill Roasters, a coffee shop in a log cabin on Route 86—just a few minutes from school, but far enough from downtown Lake Placid that we're unlikely to encounter anyone we know.

"As you know"—Jess looks at the camping group—"or as you have been made aware"—she looks at our other friends—

"we have reason to believe that the men—nay, *cavemen*—of Sullivan-Stewart Preparatory School are participating in a grossly objectifying competition known as the King's Cup to see who on campus has the most sexual prowess."

A few of us boo; others snicker, because they know what's about to come.

Jess's impassioned hand gestures get even more dramatic. "We will not stand by while they collect our bodies like coins in a goddamn video game—am I right, folks?" We all nod and snap our fingers. "And that is why we, iconic feminist visionaries that we are, are launching a rival competition to see who can reject the boys in the most humiliating way possible—except the twist is, we all fucking win."

She raises her mug, and the rest of us follow suit.

"To the Queen's Cup."

"To the Queen's Cup," we repeat.

"Extra cheers to Alyson, who gets the credit for coming up with this," Jess adds, nudging me affectionately. "Thank you for your service."

"It's an honor and a privilege."

We both turn back to the group. "So," Jess asks, "who has ideas?"

Raquelle raises her hand. "I just had a question, actually? Um, I fully support the Queen's Cup! But I was wondering: If we want to take down the boys, why don't we just go to Mr. Wheaton and tell him about the King's Cup instead?"

Jess and I considered that as we sent out the texts arranging this meeting. "A few reasons," I reply. "First, we read through the whole student handbook, *twice,* and the King's Cup isn't technically breaking any school rules, even if what they're doing is morally reprehensible. Second, if we were to tell him what we know, it might come out that people have been sneaking out of their dorms at night."

Becca gestures at herself and Zoë. "We'd be in Strike City."

"It's also more fun this way," Kavita chimes in with a self-satisfied smirk.

"However, it's not *just* for fun," Jess replies. "Don't get me wrong, watching these boys nurse their poor, fragile egos will literally be the most entertaining thing I've ever witnessed in my life. But we also have to warn girls that this shit's going on behind their backs."

Zoë tucks her knees up to her chest. "We don't want anyone getting pressured into doing stuff they're not ready to do."

"We'll do it all through word of mouth," Jess explains. "Any kind of paper trail or digital footprint makes it easier for the guys to find out what we're up to. Kavita and Becca, will you get the word out to the seniors?"

They nod.

"Tash and Marina, you both know lots of ninth and tenth graders from drama club. Maybe you can start there? And the rest of us can handle our year."

"How do we make sure no one tells the boys?" Tori asks.

"I think we can trust the Stewart people to keep it a secret. I mean, we're all in this together."

"And if the boys find out, they find out." Jess shrugs. "It's good if they start to fear our collective power."

I shift in my seat, imagining how Riggs would react if he found out about the Queen's Cup. He's a good guy; maybe he'd even support it. But I'm scared of what he would think if he traced it back to me: I can't have him doubting my loyalty.

Becca shimmies to the edge of her seat and leans into the center of the room. "Now, on to the next item on the agenda." A mischievous smile plays on her lips. "Alyson, I think I'm gonna need your brilliance here."

"Oh yeah?"

"Tell me how I should take down Riley Prentiss."

And so we begin. Getting sweet, sweet revenge on Riley will take some careful planning; we don't want Riley to suspect anything, but at the same time, it's not like Becca can *keep on hooking up with him* like everything's normal—ew. So on Monday, she tragically informs Riley that she needs to finish her college applications before she can sneak out in the middle of the night to see him.

"I made it seem like I couldn't wait to hook up with him again," she reports to me and Jess in the library that afternoon, as though we're spies in the same resistance network. "Like our next rendezvous would be this special treat for me."

"I mean, it *will* be a special treat for you," I point out.

"Just not in the way Riley's expecting," Jess adds.

Becca can't stay for long; she's on the events committee, and they're busy getting ready for the winter semiformal. Already, glittery silver posters have appeared on all the bulletin boards and the tables in the dining hall, promising a "night to remember" and reminding students to buy their tickets online. There's a tenth grader sitting with her back to us at a desk by the window, and on her laptop screen, I can clearly see her clicking back and forth between her homework and a slideshow of cute holiday party dresses under a hundred dollars on *Seventeen*. (I know the article because I perused it with Marina and Tasha at lunch.)

Jess and I turn back to our work. She's doing some

accounting-related torture that involves a lot of decimals and percent signs, while I put the finishing touches on an AP English Lit essay before diving back into my latest book: a story about friends who pretend to be a couple to get a discount on a vacation package . . . only to realize they might actually like each other when they're forced to share a hotel bed. I mean, is it even a romance novel if it doesn't have a forced bed-sharing scene?

A backpack lands in the center of our table, and Jess and I jump at the sudden commotion. I'm about to call someone out for bad library etiquette—until I look up and discover the "someone" is Riggs. The startled lurch in my chest transforms into something fluttery.

"Hey! What are you doing here? Don't you have practice?"

"Had to stop in real quick to print out a permission slip." He plants a kiss on the top of my head. "Can you watch my bag for a sec?"

"Of course! I won't let any robbers near it."

"That's my girl."

Okay, there's officially a butterfly *convention* in my chest.

"Hey, Jess," Riggs adds.

Jess gives him a tight smile in return and makes a show of jerking the corner of her textbook out from under Riggs's bag. "Hey."

"How's it going?"

"Fine, thanks."

He waits for a follow-up question that never comes. "Cool. Well, I'm gonna go print that thing now. Be right back."

I wait for Riggs to disappear around the corner before I turn to Jess. "Are you okay?"

"Totally," she replies, but she's still doing that tight smile.

"Jess."

She sighs and drops the smile. "I mean, it's weird seeing you go from that conversation with Becca to"—she gestures at the backpack and the lacrosse stick leaning against the table—*"this."*

I wish I could just ask her why she refuses to trust my boyfriend, but I don't want to hear about the stupid "head start" thing again, or any other flimsy "evidence" she might have accumulated since. "It kinda hurts my feelings that you think my boyfriend's using me to win some competition," I mumble. "That he couldn't possibly just like me for me."

She puts a hand on top of mine. "Al, I never said that."

"You implied it."

"All I said was—"

"Can we not have the same conversation over again?" I don't want to feel the way I did that night in the tent.

We fall into tense silence.

"Sorry," Jess says eventually. "I'll try to keep my mouth shut."

"He's a good guy, Jess."

Riggs jogs back around the corner, nearly colliding with a librarian, who hisses at him to slow down. Suppressing a laugh, he speed-walks the rest of the way to our table. "Fight off any robbers?" he asks as he shoulders his pack and picks up his lacrosse stick.

"About six," I reply.

"You should have seen Al wielding the lacrosse stick," Jess chimes in. I squeeze her leg twice under the table to secretly say thank you. She squeezes mine back. "As long as you're happy," she says when Riggs disappears again, "I promise I'll make an effort."

It isn't long before the first successful Queen's Cup operation takes place. Exams are coming up, so Jess, Marina, and I are sitting on the floor of my dorm room making flash cards for French. I'm scrawling out my DR. & MRS. VANDERTRAMP verbs when there's a knock on the open door, and I look up to find Erica standing on my threshold for the first time. Between her heavy breathing and the dirty-blond hair coming loose from her ponytail, it looks like she just ran here.

"You're not"—she pauses to catch her breath—"gonna believe this."

"What is it?" I ask.

She steps into the room and shuts the door behind her. She taps her phone screen a couple of times, then flips it around so we can watch the video playing on loop. Before I can even register what it's about, I spot the likes rolling in like coins in a slot machine that just hit the jackpot.

"Read the caption first," she says, so I scan the words accompanying the video as quickly as I can:

> *There's a guy on my team who hits on me every day. I've been politely turning him down, but he won't stop, and now I dread going to practice. Today I decided not to be so polite.*

"Who is this guy?"

"Trip Amherst."

"Ugh, is that the guy who wears the hat everywhere?" Marina scoffs.

"Well, it's funny you should mention the hat . . ."

The video was shot in the varsity gym, where student athletes do their strength training. Erica must have turned her selfie camera on and then left the phone propped up on a weight bench. We see a sliver of her back, but mostly we see a blond kid in a blue baseball cap who ambles over with a kettlebell in hand.

"Hey. Saw you doing deadlifts earlier."

"Yup," Erica replies curtly.

"You should try shooting your hips back a little less."

"Coach told me to shoot them out farther, so I'm gonna stick with her advice, thanks."

Trip smirks as he leans against the weight rack behind him. He pulls the towel off his shoulder and twirls it around. "You wanna know why I was studying your deadlift form?"

"Not really."

"It's because I couldn't keep my eyes off your ass."

Erica lets out an aggravated sigh, and I can tell she's winding up to strike. "Here's the thing, *Trip*. You interrupt my workouts every day with your bullshit comments, and it makes me uncomfortable. I'm not interested in you, I never will be, and the more you do this, the more I think you're a creep. So for the last time, I'd like you and your Vineyard Vines whale hat to stop hitting on me and let me lift in peace."

Jess, Marina, and I absolutely lose it when the video cuts off with a stunned Trip dropping his towel on the floor: instant meme material.

Chills run up and down my body. If there's one trope I never want to see again in a romance novel, rom-com, or reality TV

113

dating show, it's the guy who vows to "fight for a relationship"—to "win a girl over" by repeatedly ignoring her refusals to go on a date with him. There's nothing romantic about being persistent with someone who isn't into you; it's uncomfortable—like Erica said—at best, and downright terrifying at worst. "Erica, this is the best thing I've ever seen in my whole life."

Erica beams, takes off her coat, and plops down on the floor. "And it already has over ten thousand views."

The three of us freak out all over again.

Erica pretends to dust off her shoulders. "So how does the Queen's Cup scoring work? Are we gonna keep track of all the rejections?"

"Hmmm." Jess strokes her chin. "I'm worried about the paper trail."

"I have an idea!" Marina plucks a black Sharpie from our pile of flash card supplies. "Erica, give me your wrist."

"What?" She looks apprehensive.

"Trust me." Marina takes off the cap and shoves it between her teeth. "It'll be a secret sign that you're part of the resistance."

Erica cautiously extends her hand and Marina flips it over, exposing the pale underside of her forearm. There, on her wrist, she draws a crown.

On a cold, blustery day later that week, Jess and I make plans to get lunch with Becca, Kavita, Erica, and Zoë under the guise of a November Wilderness Excursion reunion. What nobody knows as they walk past our table in the dining hall is that we're actually about to plot the Prentiss Offensive.

The Sullivan-Stewart dining hall is in full holiday mode. In addition to all the posters advertising the winter semiformal, silver tinsel and string lights spiral around the wooden beams, pots of poinsettias perch on every flat surface, and the deer head mounted on the wall is wearing a Santa hat, which is unsettling. During today's lunch period, the Stewart Singers, the all-girls a cappella group from our old school, is serenading diners with a harmony-filled rendition of "Winter Wonderland." Tasha's in the front row, singing in a pair of reindeer ears.

Speaking of my friends, one of them is missing from our table; there are only five of us here. "Has anyone seen Jess?"

No sooner do the words leave my mouth than the heavy wooden doors swing open to reveal Ms. Quigley herself, a smug smile spread across her face. She scans the room, spots us, and struts to our table like she's walking a runway. She even takes off her jacket halfway here and holds it over her shoulder.

"Aren't you gonna get food?" I ask when she arrives.

"Yes, I'm starving, but first . . ." Jess rolls up the sleeve of her uniform shirt and proudly reveals a black crown drawn in marker on the inside of her left wrist. "Like my new ink?"

"We're twinning!" Erica cheers, while I give the other girls the backstory on how the crown came about. Speaking of the first crown "tattoo," I spot Trip Amherst slouched at a table in the corner of the room, picking at his fries with a stony expression on his face. A bunch of people openly stare at him—Sullivan-Stewart's newest viral sensation—as they pass him on their way to the conveyor belt for dirty dishes. A pair of senior girls literally wrinkle their noses at him, which, *good.* Let him know what it's like to feel as uncomfortable as he made Erica feel in the gym every day.

Who knows? Maybe he'll learn from this. Maybe someday

he'll be as good a guy as Riggs, who brought flowers to the door of my dorm the other day so he could ask me to the semiformal. He didn't even have to do it—we were obviously gonna go together—but the gesture showed me just how much of a gentleman he is.

And, okay: it also made me want to climb on top of him the same way I did in the middle of that blizzard.

"I just let Sam have it," Jess explains. "In econ yesterday, he slid a note into my backpack asking me to the semiformal. Well, I just slid a note into *his,* saying 'No thanks, nice try.'"

Kavita does a chef's kiss. "Short and sweet."

Most of Jess and Sam's relationship has consisted of texting each other scholarly articles and FaceTiming about them later, so it's hard for me to say how likely I think it is that he's in the King's Cup, and whether Jess's note was warranted. But there's no way *all* the guys are as bad as Trip and Riley . . . right? There must be some exceptions.

Shortly after Jess leaves to grab food, cheering and applause erupt behind me. I spin around to see Raquelle and her boyfriend, Antoine, locked in a passionate kiss. One of his hands is cupping her jaw, while the other holds a sprig of mistletoe over their heads.

Tori bounds over to my chair, excitement written all over her face. "Oh my God, did you see that?"

"I missed what happened before the kiss."

"Antoine asked her to the semiformal, and she said yes! She's gonna be so happy."

Tori has no idea how happy *I* am to hear this news. Relief floods my chest to know that Raquelle didn't feel the need to reject Antoine, too.

While we wait for Jess to come back, the rest of us bat around ideas for the Prentiss Offensive. Should we have him try to sneak into the dorm and make sure he gets caught? Maybe, but we run the risk of Becca being implicated, too. And besides, after the way he humiliated her, after the way he imitated her to his friends . . .

"I think he deserves something more public," Becca insists.

That's when Jess returns to the table, the cuff of her left sleeve still unbuttoned, and my eyes catch on the black crown. I tap out of the conversation and study it for a moment, remembering the story of how it got there. Then my attention shifts to the Stewart Singers, who are midway through Mariah Carey's "All I Want for Christmas Is You." Sometimes, when I have writer's block, the secret is stepping away from my laptop and doing something different, like taking a shower or going for a walk. That's what happens now; the plan for the Prentiss Offensive just comes to me.

"Wait," I interject. "Becca, is Riley planning on asking you to the winter semiformal?"

The pieces slide into place quicker than I could have imagined, the story coming to me as though I'm sitting in front of a blank Google Doc. My writing always flows faster when I'm emotionally invested in the topic, and, well, I guess you could say I'm pretty emotionally invested in this plan for getting back at Riley. The tension . . . the climax . . . the twists . . . it's all there. Now we just have to put the idea into action.

Because Kavita is Becca's best friend and the only other person in the same year as Riley, she agrees to make the crucial phone call tonight.

"You'll have to tell him Becca wants something big," I stress to her, emphasis on the "big." "After all, she's been working on college apps for *so long* and she deserves something *really special.* Something here in the dining hall, in front of a crowd, so Becca knows how committed he is."

Kavita smiles. "Consider it done."

As for the second part of the plan, I pull out my phone and type a message to Tasha:

> Any chance the Stewart Singers take requests?

I finish it off with a crown emoji.

The winter semiformal is on Thursday, the week before December exams and the day before Riggs is slated to hear back from Duke. I'd be jittery enough as it is, but when Monday rolls around and our plan is ready to go, I'm even more so.

My hands feel numb and shaky as Jess and I walk through the dining hall doors and collect our food like we normally do, because this is *so* not going to be a normal lunch period. This is how it must feel to be a theater director on opening night of a play: you've given everyone their role, you've planned out the staging, and now all you can do is sit back and hope it doesn't turn into a fiasco.

Actually, this is probably scarier than that, because at least the people in a play get to rehearse. We're completely winging this.

I scan the room as we carry our trays to an empty table. There are the Stewart Singers, innocently harmonizing in the corner—well, innocently for now. Tasha catches my eye and gives me a subtle thumbs-up. *Check.*

There's Riley sitting with Devon and a group of their fellow bros . . . and what looks like a stack of blue poster boards under the table! *Check and check.*

"Is it just me, or is this actually going to work?" I mutter.

"You're a creative mastermind and it is a damn *pleasure* doing business with you," Jess whispers back.

Jess and I grab seats with a clear view of the table where Becca and Kavita are chilling with friends and doing a convincing job of acting like they don't know what's about to go down. We eat our sandwiches in quiet alertness, like we're tuning in for the dramatic finale of a TV series. First, Riley has to launch into whatever shtick Kavita fed him on the phone the other night. That'll be the singers' cue to move into position. . . .

About fifteen agonizing minutes go by before Riley and his buddies exchange nods.

Jess grabs my wrist. "Oh my God, it's time!"

Riley hands a poster board to each friend and keeps one for himself. People start to pause their conversations and stare curiously as the six boys stand up in unison, grab their chairs, and drag them in the direction of Becca's table. Once they get close, they arrange the chairs in a line and climb up on top of them, Riley on the one farthest to the right.

By now, everyone in the dining hall has their eyes on Riley and his friends. Some are even holding up their phones to take videos. Over at the teachers' table, Mr. MacMillan pushes himself to his feet. With a slight air of amusement, he calls out, "Boys, what are you doing?"

"I only need a minute!" Riley shouts back. Then he addresses the rest of the crowd with a wave of his arm: "I'd like everyone's attention! There's something important I need to ask Becca Falco."

Wow, he's really going for it. Well done, Kavita.

Becca delivers an A-plus performance of "girl flattered by boy's romantic grand gesture," with one hand pressed to her chest and the other fanning her face.

"Okay, boys," Riley says. "Three, two, one."

They all flip around their poster boards, revealing a word in silver paint on each one. Together, the six words make a sentence—or rather, a question:

BECCA, COME TO SEMIFORMAL WITH ME?

Riley holds the sign that says ME? It would actually be a super-cute way to ask someone to a dance, if the person doing the asking hadn't joined the King's Cup and imitated his partner's sex noises to his friends.

"Bec," Riley begins with a confident smile, "I think you're amazing, and smart, and intelligent, and nice, and . . . yeah, you're just amazing, like I said."

"He really has a way with words," Jess says sarcastically.

While Riley rambles on, the Stewart Singers slink toward Becca and Kavita's table. If people see them moving, they probably just assume they're coming closer for a better view. Little do they know . . .

"Bec, whaddaya think?" Riley asks. "Wanna be my date?"

Becca presses a finger to her lips. "Hmmm. Let me think about that. . . ."

My blood's pumping so hard, I think I might explode.

"Okay, I have my answer!" she chirps.

"Tell me," Riley replies. I can sense from his easy grin that he actually thinks Becca's flirting with him right now.

"Ah, to have the confidence of a mediocre man," Jess muses.

Becca looks over her shoulder to make sure the Stewart Singers are in position. She gives them a nod.

Tasha nods back, blows on her pitch pipe, and counts the group in. First, the other girls come in with their background music. Then Tasha begins her solo.

From then on, I don't take my eyes off Riley. A few seconds go by where he's clearly confused: like, how did Becca get these girls to sing on command—and why? Another few seconds pass where he seems to be wondering if this is a good thing—like, maybe Becca planned something romantic for him, too. A tentative smile plays on his lips.

But it fizzles into dust when, finally, he and his friends register the song they're hearing. When I texted Tasha and explained what kind of song we needed, she gleefully responded that Miley Cyrus's "FU" happened to be in their repertoire. I couldn't believe our luck. The lyrics—which Tasha is currently belting with reckless abandon—are about a woman finding incriminating messages on her boyfriend's phone, so now she's telling him what he can go do to himself. Swap the unfaithful texts for the King's Cup, and the song perfectly applies to the present situation.

Becca and Kavita give Riley double middle fingers as they sway serenely to the music. On regular days, the echo in the dining hall is kind of annoying, but not today—not when the air is filled with earsplitting cackles directed at Riley Prentiss.

Grimacing, the other guys climb down and place their signs on the floor. Riley, still standing on his chair and his face as red as a tomato, viciously tears his sign in half. Above the cacophony of laughter, jeers, and the ongoing a cappella performance, I can just make out his strangled scream in a pathetic attempt to save face: "I DIDN'T WANT TO GO WITH YOU, ANYWAY!"

He stomps down off the chair and whips the pieces of poster board at Becca, but they go about a foot before they flop to the floor. This must make things even more embarrassing for Riley, who flips Becca off and opens his mouth to call her a name.

Whatever it is, nobody hears it; the laughter is too loud. Riley kicks a chair out of his way as he storms toward the door, his face down and shoulders hunched. Becca smiles as she watches him go, leaning back in her seat like a queen on her throne.

CHAPTER 8

The day of the winter semiformal is as dreary as it gets. Heavy clouds hang in the sky, and a bitter wind makes rag dolls out of the leafless trees dotting the mountains.

I hate asking Riggs to spend our lunch hour studying instead of in the back seat of his car, but with exams coming up, I have no other choice; I have to keep my grades up for Overbrooke. When he reluctantly agrees, I end up feeling even worse, like the stereotype of a nagging girlfriend. As I drag him across campus toward the library, I wonder, terror rising in my belly, if Riggs is yearning to break free of me.

The anxiety makes it hard to focus as I pull the AP English Lit readings from my backpack and fan them out on the coffee table in front of us.

"Alyson," he says, "please explain to me how this is what you'd rather be doing right now."

Riggs drags a finger down my spine, as if to remind me what we *should be* doing instead. A warm, tingly feeling follows in the wake of his touch, like he's using magic on me. He peers around to make sure there's nobody else near us, then slides his hand underneath my skirt and up my thigh. Even though it's freezing out, I've been wearing knee socks instead of tights on days when I know I'm going to see Riggs. It makes it easier for moments like this, when his fingers brush against the fabric of my underwear.

The way he's maneuvering his hand underneath my kilt makes the prospect of studying *extra* unappealing. My blood rushes to where he touches me, and all I want to do is make for the stacks and live out my wildest dream of someone pressing me against a bookshelf and kissing me senseless.

But I have to study, and I'm already behind where I wanted to be by now, thanks to all the time Riggs and I spend in his car by day and texting each other by night. And with the semiformal tonight, it's not like I'll have time to review this stuff later.

I hate, hate, hate to turn him down. It's like being offered an opportunity to have dinner with your idol, but telling them you have to stay home and scrub the bathroom instead. "In a perfect world, I wouldn't be doing this, either," I promise him. "You *know* what I'd rather be doing right now. But we have this AP English Lit exam on Monday, and I basically have to get a perfect score."

I resist the urge to cry out when he retracts his hand from my skirt. His finger works its way back up to my neck, then my jaw. "You sure?" He tucks a lock of hair behind my ear and leans closer. "Or are you secretly trying to pull a Becca Falco on me?"

The warm, tingly feeling is replaced by my heart jumping into my throat. "Wh-what do you mean?"

"You're not playing some secret long game to dump me and embarrass the shit out of me?" He puts a little chuckle at the end of the question, but I can tell by the hardness in his eyes and the crease running across his forehead that he didn't really mean it as a joke.

By now, everyone at Sullivan-Stewart and their mothers know about what happened to Riley when he asked Becca to the semiformal. If people weren't in the dining hall on Monday to witness the takedown for themselves, then they surely came across one of the countless videos that showed up on social media that afternoon. Riley has officially joined Trip Amherst in the Society of Humiliated Dickwads—and he isn't the only one. In AP English Lit this morning, Hudson Gale tried to sit next to Maggie Finlay, but the moment his butt touched the chair, she got up and moved to another desk. He looked dumbfounded, and even *more* so when he passed her a note, and she proceeded to get up, drop it in the garbage, and "accidentally" knock his books off his desk on the way back. At the sound of the crash, a red-faced Mr. MacMillan whirled around from the chalkboard and shouted at Hudson to "pull it together."

Every time I spot a crown peeking through the cuff of someone's uniform shirt, my soul lights up with the same fire I felt in the back room of Cobble Hill Roasters that day. But then, when I'm around Riggs, that fire turns to fingernails clawing at the inside of my chest. I don't like keeping the Queen's Cup a secret from him, and as the movement has started to gain traction, I've been worried about exactly this scenario: that my boyfriend might look around at his fallen comrades and wonder, in the back of his mind, if he could be next.

I stop arranging papers and calculate how to react to his question. My answer is obviously that I would never, *ever* pull a Queen's Cup stunt on him.

That's assuming he isn't part of the King's Cup.

"I was kinda hoping you'd be quicker to say no," Riggs adds, without the chuckle this time.

If I'm too defensive—or not defensive enough—Riggs might not believe me. I sit up, face him, and lay my hands on his thigh. "Riggs, oh my God, *no.* Please don't even think that for one second." I lean in and kiss him on the lips—a lingering sort of kiss that hopefully tells him there will be more where that came from tonight, at the semiformal. "It's just that I usually use all my free time for studying the week before exams, and this exam is extra important."

"I know, I know. I'm sorry, I shouldn't have even asked." He kisses me back. "I'm just stressing about Duke and it's making me worry about other shit, too."

"Well, we can only hope for the best with Duke"—I squeeze his leg—"but I can promise you, with every fiber of my existence, that you don't have to worry about the other stuff." Yikes. I hope "fiber of my existence" didn't sound a little much. "Er, should we look at some of these poems now?"

We both lean over the coffee table, but it's impossible to focus with the lingering tension between us. It takes me ten minutes to get through one Shakespearean sonnet because I keep reading the same lines over again. Riggs chews the end of his pen. Then he plays with taking the cap on and off. Then he taps it on the table. It's incredibly distracting.

"Riggs, would you mind—"

He throws down the pen and cuts me off. "Do you know what the deal is with these rejections, though?"

The question catches me so off guard that I stammer a bunch of incoherent syllables and I search for the right thing to say.

"You *do* know something, don't you?"

I quit with the random noises, and my eyes find a vague spot behind Riggs's head. I can't lie to him. Relationships are supposed to be rooted in trust.

If he's the good guy I know he is, he won't freak out if I tell him about the Queen's Cup—not that I started it, obviously; that would be way too risky. Just, you know, that it exists. Speaking of trust, maybe I could ask him about the King's Cup while I'm at it.

"So, um, yeah." *Wow, Alyson, this is off to a rousing start.* I force myself to lock eyes with Riggs, who's looking at me like he wants me to spit it out already. "I heard through the grapevine that some of the girls are trying to get revenge on the guys by rejecting them in super embarrassing ways. I don't have anything to do with it, though." I once read this quote that said over-explanation is a sign of insecurity, so I stop there.

Riggs furrows his brow. "They're getting revenge? For what?"

"Well, apparently the girls are mad because the guys are playing some weird secret game"—here goes nothing—"called the King's Cup. Do you know anything about it?"

His entire body freezes, like we're on a choppy Zoom call. As much as I'd like to turn inside out, I force myself to watch for his next reaction. If Riggs claims he's never even heard of the King's Cup, I'll know he's lying to me; after all, he was there the night Becca overheard Riley talking about it. And if he's lying to me . . . Well, I won't let my brain go there right now. Finally, he squeezes his eyes shut and mutters, "Goddammit."

"Goddammit what?" My pulse is a freakin' jackhammer.

"I was hoping you wouldn't find out about that bullshit."

A knot inside of me loosens. Not only did he just admit to knowing about the King's Cup, but he also disapproves of it. "Why didn't you want me to know? What is it?"

"Will you promise not to tell? It's totally stupid and you're not gonna like it, but I'm not over here trying to rat anyone out, you know?"

"I promise." Everyone knows already, anyway.

"It's this dumb game they played at Sullivan back in the eighties or something. Basically, you get points for hitting each of the bases with a girl, and whoever has the most points at the end of the year is the 'king.' " He makes air quotes with his fingers.

The knot in my chest loosens even more. This *has* to mean he isn't part of it . . . right? "So the competition came back this year? Why?"

Riggs shrugs. "I guess some guys knew about the old tradition and decided to revive it when they announced the Stewart merger. You know: more girls on campus, more opportunities . . . But don't worry: it's mostly losers who could never get girls in the first place who are into it." Suddenly, his eyes are wide—vulnerable. "Not me."

The knot unravels the rest of the way. "For the record, I never thought you were."

"Why would I care about some dumbass points when I already have a hot girlfriend?"

I beam at him.

"For what it's worth, that doesn't mean I support the girls' little rejection game," he adds. "They're sending kind of an extreme message. Not *all* guys are meatheads. Not *all* guys are in the King's Cup."

Oy. Did Riggs just "not all men" me? Whatever—this is a hard conversation, and all things considered, we're navigating it pretty well. I need to focus on the life-changing news that Riggs isn't in the King's Cup. So I nod in response to what he just said. "Right."

"I guess this proves we're both innocent, huh? It's just you and me, rising above the bullshit." He nods at the coffee table. "And trying not to bomb AP English Lit."

We both laugh at that, the tension rushing away like sand through a hole in a bucket. "I can't wait for the semiformal," I murmur. "I just wanna dance with you."

"I can't wait either," Riggs says. He inches closer and grabs my hands. "By the way, I have a surprise for you tonight."

"A surprise?"

"Yup."

"What is it?"

"You know every vocab word in existence. I know you know what 'surprise' means."

"Can I have a clue?"

Riggs smirks. He suddenly pretends to be enthralled by the papers splayed out before us. "You know, I really think we should take a look at these poems now."

Later that evening, I meet up with Riggs at the fountain again. We walk to the gym arm in arm, an electric current buzzing between us. At the coat check, I take off my jacket and reveal the outfit I bought off that *Seventeen* list: an emerald-green velvet slip dress with spaghetti straps, a plunging back, and a cowl neckline that shows more than a little boob action. It seemed sexier than any of my other dresses, which were mostly baby-doll things with tight tops and flouncy skirts. I'd never owned anything *slinky* before. It cost me all of my birthday money from Dad and Harry, but it was definitely worth it for the look on Riggs's face right now, his eyes as wide as dinner plates and his mouth hanging open.

"You look un-freakin'-believable," he says.

"Thank you." I take in his fitted charcoal slacks and crisp, white dress shirt. "You clean up nicely, too."

He jerks his head toward the double doors to the gym and the thumping music coming from inside. "You wanna go in?"

Riggs doesn't know how long I've waited to have a date to something like this—how many times I rode back to Stewart from a Sullivan School dance feeling like a giant failure in the flirting department. I smile up at him and bounce on the balls of my feet, which I strapped into chunky silver heels for the occasion. They feel like medieval torture devices, but Riggs once said I'd look hot in heels, so I'm sticking it out. "Yes, please."

The events committee knocked it out of the park with the winter wonderland theme. Walking through the gym doors is like stepping into Elsa's castle from *Frozen*. Under the blue and purple lighting, icicles and snowflakes dangle from the ceiling, shimmery white curtains drape the walls, and clumps of silver branches wrapped in string lights surround the dance floor. There's a DJ wearing reindeer antlers, a photo booth with goofy cardboard props, and a long table serving up a feast of holiday-themed treats. It feels like there's magic in the air. These dances used to be exercises in imagining what it would be like to experience them with a partner; during slow songs, I would hover on the sidelines surveying the couples like an anthropologist. I reach over and take Riggs's hand, amazed he's real— that *we're* real. And I'm dying to know what his surprise is going to be.

The dance floor is mostly clumps of friends at this point. My crew is already here, jumping up and down in the middle of the room and singing along to a catchy chorus. There's a ring of more apprehensive dancers around the perimeter, sipping cans of soda and screaming in their friends' ears. A few guys punch and push each other, almost like they're daring each other to make a move.

"Should we dance?" I ask him. I know we're going to hook up at some point tonight, but I also want to live out my fantasy of *not* having to do my usual sad routine of half dancing, half peering around to see if anyone cute is looking in my direction. Not only that, but I also want to know how it feels to dance with someone I like. Someone I might even *love*. I've been picturing a spotlight shining down on us as we drift in a circle to a love song, lost in each other's arms like we're the only two people on Earth.

"We should, but we should also grab a drink first." Riggs pats his pocket. "I brought us a little something."

Does he mean alcohol? I feel both sophisticated and paranoid that a teacher's going to see us and kick us out, or give us strikes, or both. But Riggs seems to know what he's doing. Pulling me along behind him, he strides to the snack table and grabs two cans of Diet Sprite with one hand; then he leads me over to the bleachers, where a bunch of people sit and chat and it's easy for us to blend in. He cracks open the cans, takes a swig from each, sets them at our feet, and—without missing a beat—pulls out two minibar-sized bottles of vodka and empties one into each can. Mrs. Cole, who's on dance patrol duty and who I can only assume is taking her job seriously, doesn't even glance in our direction. It's kind of mind-blowing the way guys can get away with things just by doing them with confidence.

"Is this the surprise?" I ask, hoping it isn't.

"Nah, that's still coming." He stuffs the empty bottles back in his pocket and hands me a drink. "Cheers."

"Cheers." Grinning, I clink my can against his.

"Whoa, whoa, we can't make eye contact!"

"Why not?"

"It's bad luck. It means you'll have bad sex for seven years."

"It does *not*."

"It does." He squeezes my knee. "I just saved us."

A warmth spreads through my body that has nothing to do with the vodka and everything to do with the mentions of "sex" and "us" in the same short conversation. I haven't even ventured below Riggs's belt yet, but I get a rush of adrenaline knowing we're both at least thinking about going all the way with each other. I wonder, not for the first time, if Riggs has had sex before. He certainly seems experienced enough. Maybe he did it with Chrissy, and it was super special, and that's why she's still not over him.

That theory would explain a supremely awkward encounter I had with her a few nights ago. I was in the library and in need of a toilet where I'd have some privacy, if ya know what I mean—

shout-out to irritable bowels—so I went downstairs to the cob-webby basement bathroom tucked behind the archives and the storage closets. I've used it a bunch of times before and never encountered another soul, so I jumped when I walked in and saw a figure with black hair pulled up in a lopsided bun standing at the sinks.

When I realized it was Chrissy, I took a step backward so I could flee before she registered my presence. But I stopped when I noticed she was crying. Her eyes were wet and puffy, and her black mascara had stained the warm beige skin of her cheeks. She was trying to wipe the eye makeup off with the crappy single-ply toilet paper from the stalls.

"Hey . . . are you all right?" Stupid question, but "What's wrong?" felt too personal for whatever Chrissy and I were, which was far closer to enemies than friends.

She looked at me in the mirror and froze, the toilet paper still held to her face. She didn't say anything for five seconds . . . ten seconds . . . It felt like a full minute that we just stood there staring at each other. If Chrissy didn't want to talk to me, why not just lie and say she was fine? Or tell me to leave her alone? She certainly had no problem snapping at me before.

A threatening cramp sliced through my stomach, and I knew I couldn't afford to wait there any longer. I'd have to rush to a different bathroom, because no *way* was I going to take care of my situation with Chrissy as my audience. So I stammered, "Um, y-you know what? I'll just, um, give you some space. How's that?" I was out the door too quickly to see if she tried to reply.

From our spot in the bleachers, I scan the dance floor for any sign of Riggs's ex-girlfriend. There's Cassandra and the rest of the friend group Chrissy was with at the Fall Festival . . . but no Chrissy. Maybe she'd been crying because of something that had happened back home, and she'd since left campus to be with her family. I obviously hope the Lins are okay, but I won't pretend it's not a relief to know she isn't going to stomp over and try to break us up again.

Riggs knocks back his drink and crushes the can into a disk.

I'm ready to go dance, so I chug mine, too.

I steer Riggs down the bleachers, toward the spot where Jess, Marina, and Tasha are doing some kind of interpretive dance to the song that's playing. I'm hoping we can dance as a group for a little while: me and all my favorite people at Sullivan-Stewart. I especially want Jess to have fun with Riggs—to see how great he is, and how great he and I are together. While we got ready for the dance, I told her that Riggs swore he wasn't in the King's Cup. All she said was, "Good," her voice (and face) empty of any expression. I know Jess promised she'd be nice to Riggs as long as I was happy, but I feel like if she got to know him more, she'd legitimately want to be friends with him.

At the edge of the dance floor, Riggs pauses. When I look back at him over my shoulder to tug him along, I notice how the room takes an extra millisecond to keep up with the speed of my head. We drank that vodka pretty quickly, and I barely drink to begin with. "Are you okay?"

He pulls me close and puts his lips against my ear. "I'll join you in a minute. I have to go check on something first."

"What do you mean?"

He winks. "The surprise."

My heart skips a beat. I might be willing to give up my dance floor dreams for whatever Riggs has planned for us. "Okay. Come back soon."

He gives me a quick kiss. "I will. Don't let some other guy steal you away in the meantime. They all suck, trust me."

Oh, I trust him, all right. "I won't."

While Riggs is gone, I have a blast dancing with my friends—or, as close to dancing as these death-trap heels will allow. When my boyfriend reappears at the edge of the dance floor, I wave him over to join us, but he shakes his head and waves *me* over to *him*. Then he points at his watch, like it's urgent. I scurry over and let him take me by the hand and lead me back out to the lobby.

"Just go with it," he whispers. The words take me back to when he rescued me at Tasha's party, to the magical night when it all began—only this time, I'm a little bit sad to be whisked away. We haven't even danced yet. Still, I follow him like a loyal puppy as we hang a hard right, away from the coat check, and slip through the door to the stairwell. He takes me down one flight and through a door I never use because it leads to the special varsity facilities, including the athletes' locker rooms and the training area where Erica pulled a Queen's Cup on Trip Amherst.

The varsity floor is a lot like the dining hall, in that it doesn't seem to have been updated since the thirties. Between the paneled walls and the plaques nailed to them, it's all dark wood and gleaming gold. We're in a *literal* man cave, and it smells a bit like bleach.

"Where are we going?" I whisper. "What did you have to check on?"

Riggs stops in front of a wooden door with the words VARSITY MEN'S LOCKER ROOM painted in golden cursive. "Whether this"—he turns the metal knob and pushes open the door—"was unlocked."

He grins at me over his shoulder before leading me inside.

The lights are off, but I smell rubber and sweat and feel carpeting under my feet. I brace for fluorescent brightness when Riggs flicks a switch on the wall, but it never comes. Instead, he turns on the bulbs in each of the wooden stalls lining the walls; they give the room a mystical vibe, like we're standing in a dimly lit shrine to some god of lacrosse.

"Surprise—I've always wanted to come down here with you," he says.

I can still hear the pounding of music from upstairs. Even though it's sexy and forbidden to be down here with Riggs, a piece of my heart aches at the thought of the moments we're missing out on. "Why's that?" I ask him.

"Because this is the place where I'm happiest, and you're the person I'm happiest *with*." Riggs sits down on a brown leather sofa and pats the cushion beside him. "Come sit?"

I love how excited he is to bring me here, but I didn't expect we'd be hooking up before we even enjoyed the semiformal, and certainly not in a smelly locker room. I thought maybe we'd brave the cold and make out under the moon and stars, our cheeks flushed from dancing. I bite my lip and glance at the clock on the wall to make sure there's still plenty of time in the evening for the other things I want to do.

"Wait." Riggs frowns. "What's wrong?"

Shoot. Do I seem wishy-washy? After our heart-to-heart in

the library earlier today, I don't want Riggs to think I don't trust him again. I need to show him I'm into this—and I *am* into this. Case in point: the new lacey thong that's digging into my butt with the force of a thousand suns. I teeter over to the couch, snuggle up next to him, and kiss him on the cheek. "Nothing's wrong."

Riggs leans away from me. "Really?"

"Yes, really."

He cocks an eyebrow. "You're sure?"

"I could not be surer." To show him, I grab hold of his tie and yank him in for a kiss. Our mouths sort of smash together, but in a hot way—like I need to make out with him *now*. Without letting go of the fabric, I forge a trail of kisses up his jaw and down his neck. When I reach his collarbone, I reverse course and work my way back to his lips.

A little while later, he puts his hands around my ribs and pulls me like he wants me to climb onto his lap.

"I think my dress is too tight for that."

He runs his palms over the velvet hugging my hips. "You know I wouldn't complain if you wanted to take it off."

I peek at the clock. We've been down here for forty-five minutes, and the dance is only three hours long. Time is slipping away.

"You're doing it again," he says. This time, his voice has an edge to it I've never heard before, and it makes a paper cut on my heart.

"D-doing what?"

"Freaking me out. Are you playing me or not?"

His voice cuts even deeper this time. What the hell is wrong with me? If I don't let go of this stupid idea I had of the dance, I'm going to lose something way more valuable. "Riggs," I plead, "I told you earlier: I would never trick you like that."

"But you're stressing me out. You're making me fuckin' paranoid."

I stand up, my balance extra-wobbly thanks to the vodka, and hike up my dress so my legs and butt are exposed. I smile coyly at him. "How's that?"

He returns the smirk. "Much better."

I straddle his lap and we kiss again. I'm relieved he isn't mad—or at least, doesn't seem to be. Not with the way his hands explore my body and pull me to him.

"You're so hot," he breathes in my ear.

I keep going. I loosen his tie and unbutton his shirt and put my hands on his chest and shoulders. I want to kiss him so hard he forgets he ever doubted us.

"You can keep unbuttoning if you want to," Riggs says.

My hands pause for a fraction of a second. This is not how I pictured this night playing out, nor my first ever IRL penis interaction, for that matter. But if this is what it takes to prove I'm not tricking him . . .

The next thing I know, my knees are on the carpet and it's scratchy. I help him pull down his pants and the gingham boxers underneath. They pool around his ankles like he's sitting on the toilet.

I want to ignore the mental image and press on, but I can't. Nothing about this feels right. We're missing the semiformal, my knees sting with rug burn, and this room smells like a sweaty gym sock. I hear the opening bars of a slow song seeping through the ceiling. A feeling like homesickness blooms in my belly as I picture what could have been. It spreads up to my chest, then my throat, then the space behind my eyes, and suddenly, I'm on the verge of tears. I thought I could do this, but I can't. It doesn't feel right in my soul. I push back onto my heels and stumble to my feet.

Riggs looks dumbfounded. "What the . . ."

"I'm sorry." I yank my dress back down. "I want to do this, but not here. Not like this."

"Why?"

"Because . . ." *Because I wanted to dance with you.* The truth sounds so pathetic, childish, *desperate.* I stare at the ground, at my stupid high heels, searching for how to explain myself. "You know me. I wanted this night to be romantic, and . . ." As I ramble on, Riggs pulls up his pants and buttons his shirt. His jaw is clenched, and even in the dim light, I can tell his cheeks are beet red. ". . . I didn't want to come downstairs and immediately get naked in your locker room," I confess, "but I went along with it because I was scared you didn't trust me, and . . ."

There's fury carved into Riggs's face as he snaps, "I *don't* trust you, Alyson."

The words slice my heart like a dagger. "Riggs. Please, listen to me."

He lets out a cold cackle that sounds nothing like the boyfriend I know, and it scares me. "I'm not stupid," he fires back. "I should have known you were bullshitting me in the library today. You purposely led me on so you could reject me with my fucking pants down. Good one. Let me guess"—he scans the room in an exaggerated way—"you're secretly filming this so you can post your little takedown online?"

The first tears finally spill down my cheeks. "Riggs, how could I have set up a camera? *You* brought me down here!"

He counters in a low voice, quiet and deadly, like poison. "Yeah, well I shouldn't have. Clearly. I thought we had a good fuckin' relationship going here, but apparently, I'm as big of an asshole as Prentiss and Amherst."

"You're *not,* Riggs!"

"It must really *suck* having to date a guy like me, who gives you cards and flowers . . . who tells you how smart and beautiful you are all the time . . ."

I'm making things worse the longer I stand here and plead with him. My only option is to turn on my heel and race out the door.

This is all my fault.

I'm the reason Riggs doesn't trust me—the reason my perfect love story just got blown to bits. Sure, my friends with the crowns on their wrists made their own decisions, but at the end of the day, I'm the one who invented the Queen's Cup. The evil, useless, stupid, dream-crushing Queen's Cup. I wish I never spoke it into existence.

Crying, I drag myself back up the stairs and into the lobby, where Jess is talking frantically to the coat-check kid. When she sees me, she relaxes her flailing arms. "There you are! I didn't know where you went." She takes in my tearstained face and panics all over again. "Al, what the hell happened? Was it Riggs? What did he do?"

I just want to go home and bury my body in blankets, the same way I did after blowing things up with Aiden. "Nothing," I sob. "As usual, I ruined everything."

Jess opens her mouth to reply, but I stomp past her—past the coat-check kid to snatch my coat off the hanger, then through the lobby to get the hell away from here. Jess shouts my name, but I don't turn around. I elbow my way through the door and into the gathering night.

By the time I reach the fountain, I've given up hope of hearing Riggs's footsteps pounding behind me, his voice calling out for me to wait. A last sliver of hope compels me to check my phone, but when I tap the screen, I see no missed calls or new messages.

Riggs is done with me.

I throw my head back as a keening wail erupts from deep inside me. The sky is as dark as my mood right now, the wind so cold it makes my eyes sting. Every part of my body and soul hurts.

And I deserve it.

MONDAY, MAY 1

CBS

<u>THE JANELLE SHOW VOICE-OVER:</u> It's the missing persons case that's captivated the nation. A varsity lacrosse captain and rising Duke freshman, Brenton Riggs Jr. was at the top of his game. Then, on prom night, the eighteen-year-old vanished in Upstate New York without a trace.

    [INTRO MUSIC AND SLIDESHOW
    OF BRENTON RIGGS JR.]

<u>JANELLE HIGHTOWER:</u> Brenton, Suzanne, thank you so much for being here during this incredibly scary time. Before the commercial break, we talked about the weekend of your son's disappearance, and, Brenton, something you said jumped out at me, which

is that you firmly believe foul play was involved. Can you tell me why you think tha—

BRENTON RIGGS SR.: I don't think it, Janelle. I know it.

JANELLE: How do you know it?

BRENTON: A few reasons. First, a lot of people are saying, well, 'Maybe he got drunk and wandered off and got lost in the blizzard.' With all due respect, my son is a hell of a lot smarter than that—and even if he *was* out there in the snow, he's not some little weakling.

JANELLE: The blizzard killed two people and injured—

BRENTON: Sorry, I'm not buying it. The second reason is that a lot of people have it out for my son.

JANELLE: A lot of people have it out for him? Why?

BRENTON: He's successful. He's captain of the lacrosse team. He's going on to play for Duke next year, like I did. I'll tell you what, Janelle: it's not always easy being a successful young man.

JANELLE: Really? What's so hard about it?

BRENTON: People are jealous and they want to tear you down! Listen, it wouldn't be the first time someone came for Riggs for no good reason whatsoever.

SUZANNE RIGGS: Shhhh . . .

JANELLE: If I may, Brenton, when else did someone come for Riggs unfairly?

BRENTON: I'm angry and I have every right to be. They came for my son with some bullshit accusation at the start of the school year-some girl saying he did something or other. She turned out to be making it all up, and the school dismissed the case, but it goes to show you how dangerous it is to be in his position.

JANELLE: What was your son accused of?

SUZANNE: It was-

BRENTON: Nothing. Some asinine claim, obviously, because the investigation went nowhere. It came out of the blue during the summer varsity training program and it was dismissed before the semester even started. Goes to show you how much of a target he is.

JANELLE: Was the accusation related to sexual misconduct?

BRENTON: What does that have to do with anything?

JANELLE: I'm trying to get the full picture here. Was the accusation related to sexual misconduct?

BRENTON: I already told you, it was an asinine claim.

SUZANNE: The school keeps these things confidential, anyhow.

JANELLE: I see. Well, we're going to take another short break, but we'll have more on Brenton and Suzanne's theories into their son's whereabouts when we return.

CHAPTER 9

January, Three Months Earlier

The Sorceress frowns at me over her steepled fingers. Besides muttering a curt hello, she didn't say anything when I shuffled into her gloomy lair a few seconds ago—just nodded at the chair across from her and waited for me to obey. I hold my breath and dig my nails into my legs, bracing for impact. Mrs. Cole may always be kind of antagonistic, but today she seems straight-up murderous.

And she has every right to be. After she helped me craft the perfect class schedule to impress Overbrooke, my dream college, I repaid her by getting the lowest score of my life on an English exam. I didn't just get a few questions wrong; I left an entire essay question blank because I didn't see it on the back of one of the pages until it was too late. I let twenty-five points go spiraling down the drain, just like that.

With a sigh, Mrs. Cole tilts her monitor so I can see my report card right there on the screen. "I have to say, I was disheartened when I saw this, Alyson."

She doesn't have to specify what she means by "this," because we both know. The bolded B-minus reaches out and punches me in the gut, just like it did when I saw it for the first time over winter break. I drag my eyes away from the screen and fix them to the edge of the Sorceress's desk so I don't have to look at her face and see my own disappointment reflected back at me. The last time we met, I thought I could have it all: an amazing love life and straight As. But as it turned out, both items are now on the list of Things Alyson Benowitz Has Spectacularly Failed At.

"What happened?" she asks.

There's no way I can tell her the real story. She'd probably find a way to become my family member just so she could disown me.

Riggs didn't reach out to me after the locker room fiasco—which, understandable. I found out through social media that he'd gotten into Duke the next day and Riley hadn't. Like the desperate person I am, I texted him "congrats on Duke!" with a GIF of a dancing corgi. Cue me spending my last available study weekend staring at my phone and waiting for his reply instead of reviewing the AP English Lit material, not to mention the stuff I needed to do for my four other classes.

By Monday, he still hadn't responded. The exam itself was held in the gym, which, needless to say, didn't put me in the greatest headspace to begin with. It's hard to focus on the mechanics of iambic pentameter when you can't stop picturing the last time you were in that place, sobbing, the shards of a broken love story at your feet. The dance had only been a few days prior to the exam.

In the sea of desks, I happened to get seated two columns over and one row behind Riggs, meaning I had a nearly unobstructed view of the side of his face. I wondered if he would wave to me, or even glance at me—just acknowledge my existence, *please*— and I didn't want to miss it if it happened. So I stared at Riggs almost as much as I stared at my exam, telling myself it was *English,* and therefore I obviously didn't need all of the allotted time anyway. I checked over my work with two minutes to go, and that's when I saw the essay question I'd missed on the back side of a page. When I begged Mr. MacMillan for a chance to complete it after the time was up, he replied with an unsympathetic chuckle and told me I couldn't have special treatment.

I'll give Mrs. Cole a more palatable sliver of the truth. "I completely blanked and missed this huge essay question."

"You . . . blanked?"

"Yup."

"That doesn't sound like you."

"I think I was stressed out from studying so much, and it got to me."

"I see," she says with the exasperation of someone who doesn't see at all. "How do we stop that from happening again this semester?"

"I don't know." I don't know *anything* anymore, including whether I deserve to be a romance writer someday. How can I create other people's love stories if I can't even manage my own? I'd be a con artist.

"Isn't it still your dream to go to Overbrooke?" she asks.

My throat gets all thick, like I'm about to cry. "I don't know," I manage to squeeze out, but my voice trembles on the last word. It goes against conventional Stewart Academy wisdom to show vulnerability in front of the Sorceress, but I may not have a choice.

"Alyson . . ." To my surprise, Mrs. Cole's voice has lost its edge; it's gentler than I've ever heard before. When she leans across the desk on her elbows and I look up, I notice her face is softer, too. "Is something the matter? Something other than your report card?"

I look back down at my lap. Not to be melodramatic about it, but I'm a wreck. Instead of spending winter break the way I usually do—sitting in bed, eating snacks, and plowing through a new romance novel every day—I mostly moped around Dad and Harry's brownstone like the ghost of a Victorian bride who was abandoned on her wedding day. I couldn't so much as crack the spine of a love story without remembering how badly I'd screwed up my own. Mrs. Cole's last question makes my eyes well up. "I'm totally fine."

"You don't seem like you're totally fine," she says. "Do you want to talk?"

I shake my head. I'm about to collapse like a house of cards and I'd rather not be here when it happens, so I don't have to answer any more questions about what a loser I am.

"All right, then. If you're sure . . ." She sighs and leans back in her chair. "Do what you can to get these grades up, and in the meantime, I hope you feel better."

I mumble some form of goodbye, snatch my bag off the floor, and hightail it out of her office. The moment the door shuts behind me, the tears start to fall.

It's the end of the first day back, and when I leave the student services center, it looks like everyone is headed toward the parking lot, where big yellow school buses wait to drive them down to Main Street. Village Night is a welcome-back treat for the Sullivan-Stewart high schoolers; the school sets the student body loose in town for a few hours, and a bunch of local businesses offer special discounts on a weeknight that otherwise would have been slow. The plan is for Jess to drive me, Marina, Erica, and Zoë into town in her car, but I'm so not in the mood to go. Not only is my face a Jackson Pollock canvas of mucus and runny mascara, but also I know that if I go, there's a good chance I'll see Riggs, and I'm trying to delay our awkward reunion for as long I can—that is, until AP English Lit tomorrow.

I'd prefer no one see me in this state, and the path to the dorms is probably packed with people on their way to Village Night. Instead, I hang a right and slouch toward the library with my arms crossed and my head down. I think I'll spend my Monday evening doing French homework and wallowing in my *très miserable* existence. Maybe I'll drag myself through the fiction section and force myself to commit to another genre—something other than romance—for the rest of my life.

The prospect makes me cry even more as I trudge past the athletics building, and I'm too lost in my sadness to look up when the front doors burst open and footsteps come jogging down the path. I really should have paid more attention. With my head down, I end up colliding head-on with a six-foot-something somebody in a royal blue parka, Sullivan-Stewart track pants, and Nikes with a gold swoosh.

"Oof!"

"Sorry!" I yelp.

I'm about to dart around them and scurry the rest of the way to the library when it dawns on me that I've seen those metallic swooshes before. My stomach does a swoosh of its own as I realize I just slammed into the very person I was trying my best to avoid.

"Shit," Riggs says. My thoughts exactly.

Might as well get this over with. I sniff and look up, the wintry air making my tearstained cheeks even colder. "Hey."

He looks as handsome as ever, his skin golden-brown from the surprise trip to the Bahamas his parents planned to celebrate his acceptance to Duke. (I had a lot of time to stalk Riggs on social media with all the reading I wasn't doing over break.) His blonder-than-usual curls poke out from underneath his white beanie, and even though his hair hangs down in his eyes, I can still read his expression loud and clear, and it isn't "happy to see you." It's more like: "I think I just stepped in dog poop." He adjusts his lacrosse stick so he's holding it diagonally across his body, like a shield.

I hate that I did this to us. I want more than anything to melt into Riggs's arms, but I can't when he holds his lacrosse stick up like a shield and takes a step back from me, like I'm dangerous. The thought of what I'm missing out on—of everything we've lost—unleashes another flood of tears. I put my face in my hands to cover up the mess, but I'm not quick enough.

"Wait—are you crying?" he asks.

"No." I sniff.

"You are." He lowers his stick and takes a small step closer, like I'm an animal that could lash out at any moment. "What's wrong?"

"What do you *think* is wrong?" I blurt out.

"I don't know. You tell me. I'm meeting Cameron to drive down to Village Night in a few minutes, so . . ."

What if I never get a chance to tell him this again?

". . . it's gotta be now."

"I MISS YOU, RIGGS!"

Just like that, a whole winter break's worth of pent-up loneliness and despair comes bursting out of my mouth, and it doesn't want to stop.

"I miss everything about you. I miss talking and texting and hanging out in your car and coming to your lacrosse games and just knowing that you're my boyfriend. I feel terrible about everything that happened last month. I'm so sorry . . . I wasn't trying to hurt you . . . I was just excited about the semiformal because I'd never had a date to a dance before, and it never occurred to me that you were equally excited to show me your locker room. I've gone back to that night a million times in the past three weeks, and every time, I wish I could do it over again. I would tell you how much I like you. Jesus, Riggs, I'm pretty sure I love you!"

Oh.

My.

God.

I just dropped the L-bomb in a delirious stream of word-vomit, and now Riggs is standing there, gaping at me like a goldfish. If I had any hope of winning him back, this awkward silence is solid evidence that I blew it.

"I . . . I'm sorry," I stammer, wiping my eyes. "I'm making this so awkward for you. I should probably just—"

"Don't go." He stops gaping in time to catch me by the wrist. "And . . . and stop saying you're sorry."

The skin-on-skin contact ignites every cell in my body. I look into his eyes, and I see something different than before: a door swinging open instead of locking me out.

"Listen," he says, "I have to go meet Cam, but are you going to be at Village Night?"

"I was planning on going to the lib . . ." Wait. I think he's asking if we can meet up later. "To the library first, to return a book," I respond. "But then I'm coming."

"Perfect," he says. "We should obviously talk more, but maybe we could do it over ice cream?"

Now I'm the one who's stunned. Apparently, my L-bomb wasn't a bomb at all. It got me a date.

"That would be great," I reply, smiling for what feels like the first time in a hundred and fifty years. As Riggs saunters away, I text Jess and tell her I'll be there in five.

CHAPTER 10

There are five of us crammed into Jess's trusty old Kia: she and Marina in front, and me, Zoë, and Erica in back. Marina DJs as we cruise around the lake toward Main Street, and I'm suddenly so full of life that I join the two skiers in lip-syncing and dramatic arm-dancing around our seat belts. The evening is limitless—so full of possibility—and after three weeks of dead ends, I finally feel free.

Jess peers at us in the rearview mirror, shakes her head, and laughs. "Did the three of you take something before you got in here?"

I guess I should probably get the Riggs announcement over with, but Zoë, who's normally on the quieter side, jumps in first. "I have an announcement to make," she declares. "I finally dumped Zeke last night."

The whole car screams, myself included. Over break, we got closer to Zoë when she turned to us—the other original Queen's Cup girls—for help dealing with her boyfriend, who still wouldn't stop pressuring her about sex stuff. She sent us screenshots of their text message history, which was mostly Zeke asking "what r u wearing?" and begging her to send him "cute photos." She always came up with a reason to turn him down, or a way to steer the conversation in a different direction, but it was taking up so much of her mental bandwidth that she started to dread seeing his name pop up on her phone—each ping, another fire she'd have to put out. Her anxiety got so bad that she had a panic attack during Christmas Eve mass and had to extricate herself from the pew to go puke in the bathroom. Reading Zoë's texts, I started to warm to the Queen's Cup again for the first time since the semiformal. Shitty guys were still out there messing with my friends, and we needed to deal with them.

Zeke had to be the next to go down.

"Congrats, babe!" Jess exclaims. She gives the horn a celebratory honk. "How'd you do it?"

Zoë bites her lip and giggles. "You're gonna be so proud," she says. "So last night, he asks me to send him a pic from my dorm room. I don't know how it happened—I guess I was back on campus and thinking about the Queen's Cup and stuff—but I got this idea. I told him I was finally down to do it. Here, I'll read you what I said." Zoë pulls out her phone. She clears her throat and puts on a sultry voice. " 'Get ready, because I'm about to send you the hottest nudes you've ever seen in your life.' I started warming him up with photos of random clothes lying around my room, like I'd just taken them off. He was totally buying it. Lots of gross panting emojis. So then, for the grand finale . . . I sent him a photo of a note on my desk that said, 'Go screw yourself. It's over.' "

The Kia erupts in cheers. Jess honks the horn for so long that three different dog-walkers look up in alarm.

A pang of guilt hits me square in the chest, and I'm the first to quiet down. Don't get me wrong, it was about damn time that Zoë broke up with Zeke—and in as humiliating a way possible— but it just occurred to me how quickly I'd lose Riggs's trust again if he knew I were part of this conversation.

"So how'd he take it?" Marina asks.

"Like a fragile man-baby," Erica declares.

Zoë's triumphant smile fades. "That part wasn't so great. He kind of went off. He called me the . . . B-word."

"Luckily I was there to remind her it was toxic bullshit," Erica insists. "I distracted her by drawing her crown."

"And it totally worked," Zoë adds. "I know it sounds cheesy, but I'm really grateful we started this thing. Ski season's gonna be *extremely* awkward, but I had to break up with him. And I don't know if I ever would have done it on my own."

I don't want to feel guilty about being in the Queen's Cup; I'm proud of what we're doing. Look at Zoë, finally finding her confidence after being pressured by Zeke for so long.

"The Queen's Cup, doing the Lord's work," Jess preaches. "We won't stop until every last boy in the King's Cup has atoned for his sins."

We cruise past the Mirror Lake Inn on the hill overlooking the water, and roll into downtown Lake Placid. Jess happens to snag a parking space directly in front of the ice cream parlor.

"Guess we know our first stop," she announces. "Al, if you get maple and I get black raspberry, can we share?"

"Uh, I'm actually going to wait on the ice cream." I still haven't told them why *I* was so lively on the ride down here. "I told . . . Riggs . . . I'd meet him here later."

I watch her cock an eyebrow in the rearview mirror. I can't

say I thought she'd be over the moon about my news. Jess hasn't trusted Riggs from the night she learned about the King's Cup; she just forced herself to be nice to him so I wouldn't get mad. When she saw me storm out of the dance last month, that was it—the charade was over. She decided he was evil and that I deserved better, and I couldn't change her mind, no matter how many times I recounted what happened, *clearly* explaining why Riggs had every right to be skeptical of my weird behavior.

"I was all depressed from my Sorceress meeting, and I literally bumped into him on my way to the library." I'm breaking my own rule about overexplanation, but, well, whatever. "One thing led to another, and I kind of ended up telling him I love him."

Marina gasps.

"You told him you love him?" Jess asks. "After the shit that went down in the locker room?"

"Didn't he ignore you for three weeks?" Marina adds gently.

I slump against the seatback. This is so much more frustrating than talking to Jess about Bookstore Aiden. I was never *in love* with Bookstore Aiden—never called him my boyfriend, or kissed him, or any of that stuff. "How am I ever going to convince you that Riggs is a good guy?"

Jess glares. "Alyson."

"*Jessica.*"

"You did not just 'Jessica' me."

"I 'Jessica' you when I'm frustrated! He *told me* he's not in the King's Cup!"

"Hey!" Marina waves her hands between us. "Everyone, breathe. Tonight's supposed to be fun."

Jess's eyes light up. "Al—babe—hear me out. What if we all chilled in the car for a few more minutes and figured out a way for you to take down Riggs tonight? It would be epic. He thinks you're in love with him."

"But I *am* in love with him!" I protest. I search my other friends' faces for support. None of them have sided with Jess, but none of them are making eye contact with me either. There's an awkward silence. I hate awkward silences. I always want to fill them immediately. "Listen, it's not like I have to decide right this second if I want to reject him," I say to the car at large. "I'm just going to talk to him tonight, and see what he wants, and yeah, if he ends up being a jerk . . ."

"We're already past that point," Jess argues.

". . . then I'll *maybe* consider doing a Queen's Cup." Just saying it makes me feel guilty of betrayal. I'm never going to Queen's Cup *Riggs*.

"Fine," Jess concedes.

Marina, Zoë, and Erica clamber out of the Kia with barely concealed relief. Jess wriggles around in the driver's seat to face me.

"Hey."

"Hey." My voice feels all thick.

"You know I love you, right?"

"I know," I mumble. "I love you, too." Jess and I hardly ever argue. After it happens, I'm never angry at her—I'm more . . . sad for us. Like, I don't care about "beating her" in an argument— I want us to solve problems together. But when it comes to Riggs and the King's and Queen's Cups, I don't know what that solution looks like, short of one of us having a personality transplant.

"And I'm just looking out for you."

I nod and get out of the car.

As I wait on a bench for my friends to get their ice cream, my phone buzzes with two incoming text messages. They're from Riggs.

Hey you

Meet at the ice cream place at 7:30? Excited ☺

I sniff, and a tear trickles down my cheek. I can't even blame it on the cold, because it's freakishly warm out for January—I'm just bummed about the tension in the car. Before anyone comes out and asks me who I'm texting, I wipe my eyes and send him back three thumbs-up emojis in a row.

When my friends finish their ice cream, we all go to the town's indie bookstore, where, for the first time in a while, I'm able to glance at a romance novel without weeping. I can imagine myself writing them again, too. I'm asking Jess's opinion on which of two books I should buy—"they both seem way too happy for me," she scoffs—when two girls approach us from behind and tap us on the shoulders.

They're a few years younger than us; I think they're in the ninth grade. One is pale with a blond ponytail; the other has bronze skin and dark-brown curls.

"Hi," the first girl mumbles. She's like a mouse who might scamper away at any moment.

I exchange a quick glance with Jess before smiling at the girl. "Um, hi! What's up?"

The girl nods at Jess's wrist, which is visible because she took off her hot-pink parka. The girl's eyes dart to the floor as she clears her throat. "We were wondering if you could tell us what the crown means."

"We heard a rumor and decided to ask the first person we saw with one," the curly-haired girl chimes in. "If the ... Queen's thing ... is still going on, we want to join. If we're allowed."

Jess scans the bookstore to make sure there aren't any boys around. We're good. "The Queen's Cup is still very much going on, and you're very much allowed to join." She looks at me to back her up.

"The more people we can get on board, the better." I avoid meeting Jess's gaze so she can't be all *You should get on board, too, lady.* Instead, I launch into telling the girls how the Queen's Cup works, and how it came to be.

The girls listen, their jaws dropping lower and eyes growing wider the longer I go on. When they hear about the King's Cup, realization dawns on their faces.

"That makes so much sense," the blond girl groans. "The boys in our year play this game to try and ... touch us."

Now *my* jaw drops. "What do you mean?"

She winces and lowers her voice. "They're just always finding ways to bump into us and make it look like an accident, but it's obviously not, because their friends are always watching and laughing." She looks at her boots. "Someone did it to me in the dining hall the other day, and his hand actually went up my skirt. He ran away so fast, I didn't even see who it was."

"Oh my God ... I'm so sorry that happened to you."

Jess nods. "How are you doing now?"

"I'm all right." Her lower lip trembles. "Guys keep making this stupid gesture at me when I walk by." She mimes what looks like an underhand softball pitch.

Flames of rage spring up inside me, like when Becca told us she heard Riley imitating her. I swear under my breath. Jess swears out loud. An older shopper gives us the side-eye, so we shuffle away from new fiction into a quiet corner near the art supplies.

"Has anyone told a teacher?" I ask.

The curly-haired girl rolls her eyes. "I tried telling Mr. MacMillan when it happened to me in English. He said it was probably an accident, and we should all try to be more forgiving of one another."

Jess cracks her knuckles like she's preparing for a fistfight.

"What do you think we should do?" asks the blond girl.

I wave our other friends over from the gel pen display, the creative cogs in my brain already turning. Add this to the list of conversations Riggs can never know about. I look each ninth grader in the eye. "We're going to figure something out."

Once we start brainstorming ways to get back at the gropers, it's easy to lose track of time. It isn't until Erica moves her arm and her fitness tracker lights up that I realize I only have five minutes to meet Riggs. I race to the cash register to pay for the romance novels I've been holding this whole time.

Jess follows me and pokes me in the shoulder as I wait for the cashier to hand my debit card back. "Make good decisions, babe."

"I will," I promise. I stuff the debit card and my new books into my bag and look anywhere else but at her.

As I approach the ice cream parlor, I spot Riggs standing outside, twirling his lacrosse stick and talking closely with a group of his athlete friends. When Cameron looks over and notices me, he smacks Riggs on the back and points in my direction. Riggs must have told the other guys I was meeting him. What did he say? I wonder.

He smiles and waves while his buddies take turns slapping his shoulders to say goodbye. I'm too far away to catch what Cam says before he leaves, but whatever it is, it makes Riggs laugh and punch him on the shoulder.

God, I miss laughing with Riggs.

By the time I get close, Riggs is by himself. He opens his arms—oh my God, he wants to hug me. I rush to close the space between us, slide my arms around his middle, and melt into his chest. It feels like coming home, to hold and be held by him.

We exchange sheepish hellos and head into the ice cream parlor. It's like we're dating again, even though we never did real "date" stuff like this last semester. Riggs holds the door for me, rests his hand on the small of my back in line, and whips out his wallet to pay for my maple cream soft serve and his chocolate milkshake. My pulse thuds harder with each romantic gesture. Does this mean Riggs sees us as a couple again? Because it sure seems like it.

The ice cream parlor is barely big enough for us to stand in, so we take our treats outside. Thankfully, on a scale from one to instant hypothermia, it's like a two point five on this January evening. We turn and start to wander back down Main Street.

"Let's find somewhere to talk down by the water," he says. "It's pretty down there."

He wants to talk where it's "pretty." That has to mean he's going for romance, right?

I follow him to a bench near the rickety wooden toboggan chute on the south side of Mirror Lake. Every winter, when the lake freezes over, people rocket down the ramp on ancient sleds and whiz out onto the ice at the bottom.

He nods to the death trap. "Ever done it? It's super fun."

I shake my head. "I don't trust that thing. It seems like the kind of ride they casually built in the sixties without realizing it could probably kill someone."

Riggs chuckles. "You know, I missed your dorky jokes."

My heart does a backflip. "I missed you laughing at them."

We both go silent for a moment, the ghost of our fallout hovering between us. Riggs, who apparently inhaled his milkshake, takes a final sip and tosses it seamlessly through the opening of the nearest trash can. He reaches over and rests his palm on my thigh, igniting every cell in my body.

Riggs clears his throat. "So, uh, I'm happy we ran into each other."

"Literally."

He thinks about it for a second, then laughs. "Oh yeah. Guess we were meant to be, right?"

When he squeezes my leg, the heat that spreads through my body is enough to melt what's left of my soft serve.

"Listen," Riggs continues, "everything you said back on campus—you made me realize that I totally fucked up and I owe you an apology."

The sexy heat turns to embarrassed heat in a matter of milliseconds. "Wait, you know I wasn't trying to make you feel bad, right?" I cut in. "I wasn't trying to force you to apologize or anything."

"No, no, I know. I just feel like I should, after hearing your side of things." He takes a deep breath and lets it all out. "I was a jerk that night, too. I don't know why I had it in my head that you were trying to play me—probably 'cause I was a mess waiting to hear back from Duke. I was thinking about Prentiss getting in over me . . . and then me having to tell my dad . . . I mean,

163

I was straight-up paranoid, you know? It obviously carried over to what happened in the locker room, and I'm sorry. I shoulda known you'd never fuck with me like that."

"Riggs. *Never.*" I may have invented the Queen's Cup, but the last thing I want to do is turn it against the one good guy this school has to offer. All I want is for us to pick up our love story right where we left off. "All through winter break, it literally *killed* me knowing you thought that."

"It killed you? That sounds bad."

We're being jokey again! "Yes. I'm dead now. I'm like Patrick Swayze in *Ghost.*"

"Is that one of your romance movies?"

"Excuse me? *Ghost* is a classic. Everyone knows the pottery scene."

"Not me. Maybe you could show me sometime."

"I could find out where it's streaming."

Riggs kisses the tip of my nose, an almost unbearably cute gesture. "Sorry it took me so long to stop being an idiot."

"Better late than never."

"Better late than never," he repeats, squeezing my leg again. "So . . . I'm sorry there wasn't time to make you another card, but . . . any chance you want to be my girlfriend again?"

I lean toward Riggs and kiss him on the lips. His mouth tastes sugary sweet.

After a minute or so, he pulls back and rests his forehead against mine. "That means yes, right?"

"Oops." I giggle. "Yes, that means yes."

"Thank God." He kisses me again. "That would've been a really harsh rejection."

Please, no jokes about rejection right now—or ever. I want

to keep Riggs and the Queen's Cup as far away from each other as humanly possible. I force a casual laugh. "Can you imagine?"

"Please don't make me," he responds with a smile. "Which reminds me, um, about the other thing you said back on campus..."

"Which thing?"

Riggs scratches the back of his neck. "Um, the part where you, ah, said you... where you said the... ah—"

My cheeks erupt in flames. "The L-word. I'm sorry. That was a lot."

"Don't be sorry," he says quickly, and tucks a strand of hair behind my ear. "I mean, yes, it caught me off guard, but I want you to know that I could see myself potentially . . . um"—he swallows—"potentially going in that direction."

The people screaming as they shoot down the toboggan run sound like angels singing. *Dear God, thank you for not condemning me to a lifetime of misery after I dropped out of Hebrew school, and blessing me with this gift. Amen.* "Really?"

"Really. Let's do this thing. We can make it work this time."

"I believe in us."

Riggs's gaze shifts to something behind my head. "Speaking of believing in us, I think I have an idea."

I follow his eyes and put two and two together. "Oh no. Absolutely not. No way."

"*Yes* way."

"Listen, I've had enough of you plummeting down icy hills."

"C'mon, let's go." He leaps off the bench and holds out his hand. I roll my eyes—not in an irritated way, but in a keep-showing-me-how-much-you-want-to-do-this-romantic-activity-with-me way—and place my hand in his. I let him lead me down to the kiosk, where he pays for our tickets and hoists a wooden toboggan of dubious structural integrity under his arm.

In every romance novel I've ever read, there's a point where the lovers hit rock bottom. Then, just when it seems like all hope is lost for their happily-ever-after, something changes that sets the relationship right back on track. Next comes the rising action that culminates in the climax, where, despite all the bumps in the road, the lovers realize there's no one else on Earth they'd rather be with than each other. As Riggs leads the way up the thirty-foot ramp, I know this is our rising action.

We take our place in line behind two guys who seem to be talking about the strangely warm weather and the current state of climate change policy in the U.S. It sounds like the kind of thing Jess would try to lecture me on.

The taller of the two boys is wearing a distinctive olive-green beanie. When he turns his head, I see his dark hair and glasses, and that's when I realize it's Sam Young, the guy Jess was totally in love with before she made him her first Queen's Cup victim. She'd been so convinced he was faking his political leanings in order to get into her pants and win points in the King's Cup, but here he is waxing poetic on the virtues of the Paris Agreement— Jess nowhere in earshot.

"I don't know how certain politicians can keep convincing themselves these weather patterns are 'normal fluctuations' or whatnot," Sam insists.

"The wildfires in California are freaking me out, man," his friend says. It's Sahil Jain, a friendly guy who's in a few of my classes.

As I eavesdrop, Sam starts to tell Sahil about the demonstration he attended over the break. I keep coming back to the note

Jess slipped in his bag as a Queen's Cup stunt; something about Sam's earnestness tells me he might have been legitimately crushed when she rejected his semiformal invitation.

"Are you friends with Sam Young?" I ask Riggs after Sam and his friend step up to the top of the ramp.

Riggs snorts.

"What?" I smile, wanting to be in on the joke.

"Oh, were you serious?" he asks. "Sorry—Sam and Sahil are really fuckin' weird."

My smile falters. "How so?"

"I dunno, they watch the news in the common room all the time, and they try to initiate conversations about it, and it's like, bro, I don't care what's happening in some other country. You know?"

Watching the news doesn't seem any weirder than devouring romance novels, but I guess I can see Riggs being exhausted when he comes in from practice and not having the energy to analyze current events. "Mmm, yeah," I mumble.

"Why'd you ask?"

"Just curious."

Sam and Sahil go plummeting down the chute with their hands in the air. Hopefully they're screaming so loud because it's fun, and not because they're terrified for their lives.

When we get to the top, an employee in jeans and a gray sweatshirt takes our toboggan and sets it in one of two narrow tracks. With a deep, steadying breath, I turn around and stare down the slope—and my stomach turns over. It's a lot steeper than I expected. Way down at the bottom, I can make out Sam and Sahil dragging their sled off the ice. They look tiny enough to hold in the palm of my hand.

"Um, I don't know if I can do this," I say. "Are we sure this is safe?"

The man in the sweatshirt pats the front of the sled. "Been doing this for years and never had an issue. Hop in. You're going in front."

Gulp. "I am?"

Riggs gives my shoulders a quick rub. "Don't worry. I'll be right there with you the whole time."

I'd probably say yes to bungee-jumping over a lava pit if Riggs offered to protect me. I sit down and jam my feet into the front of the toboggan as instructed. Then Riggs gets on behind me and engulfs me in a bear hug, his boots literally resting in my lap.

"Don't you feel safe now?" he whispers in my ear.

I stare down the ramp and grimace. My predominant feeling isn't so much "safe" as it is "queasy and terrified," even with all four of his limbs wrapped around me. Maybe I need to rethink the whole lava-pit-bungee-jump thing. "I don't know," I admit.

"You two lovebirds ready?" the worker asks.

"Yup!" calls Riggs.

"Hold on to your hats! Here comes the push. Three . . . two . . ."

There's a split second where we teeter on the point of no return. Then, gravity takes over, and Riggs and I hurtle into the unknown.

MONDAY, MAY 1

Suzanne Riggs is 😖 feeling heartbroken

May 1 at 9:00 PM

Earlier today, my husband and I appeared in a live
TV interview that did not go as planned. We had the
purest of intentions in sitting down with Ms. Hightower:
to raise awareness of the fact that our beloved son,
Brenton, still has not been found. We believed Ms.
Hightower shared that goal, but the direction she forced
the interview in suggested otherwise. Now, as a mother,
I am terribly distressed that what aired on today's show
will eclipse the urgent need to find my son. The truth
is what my husband said: that the incident in question
was a non-event. Let's not dredge up the past. Let's
remain united in our search. Please, if you care about
finding my sweet Brenton, do not watch, like, or share
that clip that's everywhere on the internet right now.
Thank you from the bottom of my heart. —Suzanne

CHAPTER 11

February, Two Months Earlier

We're at the inevitable point in every Adirondack winter when it's impossible to recall what the world looks like without snow, and you start to wonder whether a world without snow even exists, or if you've merely fabricated any memories you have of grass and flowers and leaves. Foot after foot of snow accumulates on the slanted roofs of buildings, so that every once in a while, you'll be sitting in class and hear what sounds like a catastrophic avalanche as it all goes sliding onto the ground. In the oldest buildings on campus, the walls tremble and the windows rattle in their frames whenever it happens.

But tonight, the blanket of snow makes everything peaceful. Riggs and I spent the evening on our couch in the library, and the whole time, snowflakes danced in the windows, lit up by the golden glow of the streetlamps outside. Now, as we stroll hand in hand back to the dorms, the fresh powder swaddles the campus like a soft, white blanket.

"Wow," I murmur. "It's the perfect night."

Riggs twirls his lacrosse stick in his other hand. He still carries it around wherever he goes, even though he's playing basketball this semester. "It's nice," he says, pausing for a few seconds, "but I don't know if I'd ever call a night in the library 'perfect.'"

"Really?" I thought it had been romantic, the two of us curled up together, surrounded by books. I'd even supplied chocolate-chip cookies that I'd wrapped up in paper napkins and smuggled out of the dining hall for us to share.

"C'mon, now." He pats my butt with his lacrosse stick and gives me this look that says, *You know me better than that.*

Riggs would rather have spent our rare free evening hooking up somewhere instead of watching me research our latest assignment for Mr. MacMillan. I've been spending more time on homework this semester in an effort to bring up my AP English Lit grade, and the result is less time spent in the back seat of Riggs's Ford Explorer or some secluded nook in a school building. So I get why he's feeling deprived, but at the same time, he knows how important my grades are.

"Okay, fine, but do you have to make me feel so guilty about it?" I swat his butt with my hand in return. I don't like calling him out on things because it still seems like a miracle that he took me back last month, so when I do, I try to make it seem cute and jokey. (I *know* healthy relationships require honest communication and all that, but you know what? High school is hard.)

"I promise I'm not trying to make you feel guilty," he says. "I just . . ." My insides go melty as he abruptly changes course. He pulls me over to a supply shed and guides me up against the wall. Letting go of his lacrosse stick, he kisses me deeply, the way he did on that bridge when we were cross-country skiing.

He even slides his quad between my legs again, and oh my God it feels out of this world. Riggs trails kisses up my jaw until his lips are at my ear. "... really, really want you," he finishes.

Well. Yes. Okay. Now that he puts it that way, I suppose I can see why our library date left something to be desired. I grab his face and guide his mouth back to mine.

"You know what *I* think we should do?" Riggs asks. There's a devilish edge to his voice that makes me ache between my legs, at the spot where his thigh is pressing.

"What?"

He brushes the pad of his thumb against my swollen bottom lip. "I think you should sneak into my dorm tonight."

I raise my eyebrows. "Sneak into your dorm?"

"Yes."

"Tonight?"

"Yes."

"Doesn't it seem kind of ... risky?"

Last week, I helped Kavita plan a Queen's Cup takedown of Greg Wyatt, the guy who was still sliding into her DMs with reckless abandon. This dude really thought the eleventh time would be the charm when it came to a threesome! Anyway, Kavita told Greg to skip class Monday morning, sneak into our dorm, and meet her in the basement laundry room. She wrote that she was "dying to try this sex move"—we couldn't stop laughing as we typed out the message—"where you sit on the dryer and get off from the vibrations." Before Kavita left for class that morning, she propped the basement window open so Greg could shimmy through. As we learned from a campus-wide disciplinary email sent out later that day, poor Greg carried out Kavita's instructions, only to discover that nine o'clock on Mondays is when our dorm supervisor, Ms. Skidmore, does her laundry. It was nothing short of epic, but now the school is on high alert for dorm intruders, and if I were to get caught, the punishment would be epic, too, and not in a good way.

"Exactly," Riggs replies, "which is why now is the best time to do it."

"What do you mean?"

"They're not expecting anyone to be stupid enough to try it after Wyatt."

"So you're admitting it's a stupid idea!" I poke him in the chest, but I'm worried about this plan. I picture an Overbrooke admissions officer taking one look at my disciplinary record, balling up my whole application, and shooting it into the trash can like a basketball. "Riggs, I can't get suspended."

He kisses me until I'm dizzy again and I can't recall how I ever formed coherent sentences. "I know you want to be good and follow the rules," he whispers, "but what if I want you all to myself for a whole night?"

I don't know if I'm closer to yelling at him or pouncing on him for teasing me like this. I want to keep my disciplinary record intact, but I also want more of Riggs. I'm frustrated because there's clearly a world where I can have both: I just stay in my dorm room tonight and hook up with Riggs somewhere else tomorrow. But it's so hard to say no when I can feel how badly he wants it.

"You are so evil." I say it in the jokey way.

A conspiratorial grin spreads across his face. I reflect it back at him, but my cheeks feel like cold, stiff wax. I *want* this; the blood rushing every which way around my body tells me so. But the real driving force behind agreeing to go through with this plan is that I don't want to let Riggs down. I already feel like I've done it enough, and sooner or later, he might regret that he ever took me back. I can't lose him again.

"If we hypothetically did it," I ask him, "how would we pull it off?"

I've never intentionally broken a school rule in my life, unless you count exceeding the limit on how many library books you're allowed to take out at one time. It seems very on-brand that the first time I'm doing it for real, I'm doing it for love.

Back at the dorm, I cycle through the usual check-in routine of signing the clipboard on the wall outside Ms. Skidmore's room. I go the extra mile of poking my head around her open door and saying hello, so the dorm supervisor can see with her own eyes that Alyson Benowitz is back at home base. It isn't ideal that Ms. Skidmore's room is right off the foyer like this; it adds an extra layer of complexity and danger to tonight's mission. Like a secret agent, I hide the stress from my face as I make small talk with Ms. Skidmore about the scarves she's knitting for her granddaughters. Then I say good night and make my way upstairs to my room, where I proceed to sit on the edge of my bed and stare at the wall with my heart pounding.

When Riggs and I worked out the plan, we realized I only had a very small window to execute my great escape. At ten-thirty, Ms. Skidmore conducts her nightly rounds to make sure our lights are out, starting with the third floor and working her way down. I need to slip out while she's on the move, because once she's back in her room, she'll be able to hear me if I go out the front door, not to mention see me through her picture window.

At ten-thirty, I creep out into the hall wearing leggings and a sweatshirt. I couldn't wear my parka, which would raise too much suspicion if anyone saw me; this way, if I'm questioned, I can say I was going to the bathroom or grabbing a drink of water. When I return to the dorm in the morning, I can totally make it look like I'm coming in from a workout before class. Not that I've ever worked out by choice before, but no one needs to know that.

I creep into an alcove off the stairwell and press my back against the wall just in time to hear Ms. Skidmore's footsteps on the stairs below. They get louder as she approaches the second floor, until she's so close that I can hear her sniffle. I hope she can't hear my shallow breathing. Apparently not, because she continues her path up to the third floor, and I seize my opportunity to make a break for it.

The main paths are too risky, so I turn left and enter the woods, wincing as my sneakers sink into the freshly fallen snow and my calves get soaked. I didn't wear boots for the same reason I didn't wear my parka, and I'm paying for it now. Not only am I cold, but I'm also kind of scared out here in the dark; with my senses on high alert, every little forest noise sounds murder-y. Plus, I'm using my flashlight key chain to navigate, and it's freaky when all you can see is whatever's in the tiny beam of light. Like, what if I moved it and suddenly saw a face?

Relief washes over my body when instead of a face, the side of Riggs's dorm appears in my beam. I click off my flashlight and creep around the building, past the darkened windows, until I spot the one with the lit-up phone screen pressed against the glass.

Riggs's room. Thank God he's on the ground floor.

Shivering in my sweatshirt and snow-covered leggings, I scurry out from the cover of the trees as he wrenches open the window and sticks his whole torso out. I grab hold of the windowsill while he lifts under my arms, and together, we manage to haul my body into his room without making too much noise. Someone give us an Olympic gold medal in horny stealth.

Once I get over the shock of making it here, and as Riggs shuts the window again, it dawns on me that I'm *standing in Riggs's room.* It feels like seeing someone naked: so intimate, I'm almost ashamed for intruding. It smells like his musky boy deodorant, with faint undertones of the gym-sock stench I recall from the varsity locker room. It's a good thing they say your nose gets used to new smells in under a minute . . . especially because scent is so closely linked to memory, and I don't want to think about the semiformal again. Whenever I do, it sets off alarm bells that I'm not holding on to Riggs tight enough.

I reach for his hand. It's dark in here with the lights out, but on the wall, I can make out a cluster of pennant flags—some maroon for Sullivan-Stewart, some blue for Duke—and a poster that says *Weapons of Mass Destruction* with two crisscrossing lacrosse sticks in the middle.

"You like it?" He must have caught me staring.

"It's, um . . ." *Intense?* "Cool."

"Right? Gift from my dad," he says. "Oh! I meant to tell you: My parents are coming up next weekend."

He says it like an answer to a question I never asked, and my heart skips a beat. "Oh yeah?"

"Yeah. I told them I wanna introduce you."

Happiness fizzes like champagne inside me. If Riggs told his mom and dad about me, he must want to hold on to me just as tight. I squeeze his hand. He squeezes back.

I turn to the bed—*oh my God, that is a bed and we're presum-*

ably going to lie in it—and find a blue comforter with an image of a man with pointy little horns on his head. I've spent enough time around Riggs to recognize Duke's mascot, the Blue Devil.

I'm not sure what to do next. I'm still shivering, partly because I'm freezing and partly because I'm nervous. We've hooked up a gazillion times before, but the stakes feel higher because, again, *it's a bed,* and plus, we're not supposed to be doing this. We'll get in so much trouble if anyone finds out I'm here.

"We should probably stop talking so Crothers doesn't hear us," Riggs whispers.

That leaves one remaining available activity. Riggs comes up behind me, kisses the side of my neck, and runs his hands down my sides. When he gently tugs up on the hem of my sweatshirt, I raise my arms and he pulls it off me. I spin around and help him do the same with his T-shirt.

His forty-eight-pack abs and those V-shaped lines at his hips—*penis lines,* I've always called them, because that's where they point to—do wonders for my anxiety. I always think it's hot in books when the characters have to hook up in secret; it's like, "We're so freakin' into each other, we're gonna do whatever it takes to bone, despite the risk of us getting caught." Now I'm one of those characters, and I can confirm: it's as hot as I thought it would be.

One thing leads to another, and I'm lying on my back, in my underwear, on top of the Blue Devil. Riggs, who's down to his boxers, is hovering over me with his elbows on either side of my face. I'm in a cocoon of sculpted upper-body muscles, which, I have to say, is an excellent kind of cocoon to be in. He kisses me at a rhythm: soft and hard, soft and hard. Whenever he presses his tongue deeper into my mouth, he grinds against me down there, and I have to fight not to make a noise that'll travel all the way to the dorm supervisor's room.

"Shhh," Riggs murmurs.

"But I've barely made any noise."

"I mean for what's next."

"What—"

Then I notice his kisses are moving lower. They go from my lips, to my jaw, to my neck, to my collarbone, to— Oh, okay, his whole upper body is moving down, too. He kisses me lower and lower. I bite my lip. Now I see why he gave me the extra warning.

"This okay?" he whispers.

The last time we got anywhere near oral, on the night of the semiformal, everything was all wrong. This time feels different—better. It feels sexy and forbidden and magical. I whisper back, "Yes, please."

I want to drift off to sleep next to him, but I can't. I have to pee.

"Riggs," I whisper.

There's no response. He must be wiped from the time we both spent rounding third base tonight. He's been out like a light for thirty minutes now, during which time I've stared at the ceiling and cursed myself for not thinking through this part of the plan. So far, I've come up with the following options:

1. Pee somewhere in the room.
2. Pee out the window.
3. Do not pee; experience ruptured bladder and/ or kidney failure.
4. Slither to the bathroom and back again.

Every option is bad in its own way, but one and three are especially unappealing. As for two, pee out the window, it seems like a big, embarrassing production that would require Riggs's help. Nothing says "sexy" like your pants-less girlfriend squatting out your window to use the bathroom, and without any toilet paper, for that matter. I climb out of bed, yank on my sweatshirt and my cold, damp leggings—ugh—and creep to the door. If the bathroom is close, maybe this will be easy.

I open the door the teensiest of slivers and peer out into the corridor. There's a hardwood floor—the kind that definitely creaks when you walk on it—and no sign of a bathroom, just more numbered doors that look exactly like Riggs's.

My bladder is fully screaming at me. If I don't do something about this quick, I'm going to end up doing one of my even-less-desirable options. My wish not to burst any of my internal organs outweighs my terror of being caught. I venture a step out into the hall, testing the squeakiness of the floorboards. They're squeaky all right, but this is an emergency.

I tiptoe to the end of the corridor, hating how bright it is out here. I feel so exposed, like a rabbit in a field with a hawk circling overhead. I turn left and have to stifle a gasp when I come face to face with a door labeled:

MR. CROTHERS

DORM SUPERVISOR

Darting in the opposite direction, I finally come across a door with a restroom sign. If there's another student in here, so be it; they wouldn't tell on Riggs's girlfriend. I'm most concerned about avoiding Mr. Crothers, whom Riggs has described more than once as a "vampire in a housecoat."

I enter the bathroom, which ends up being empty, and hurry to the nearest stall. Once I'm done unleashing Niagara Falls, I go to the sink to wash my hands. I glance at myself in the mirror, cheeks flushed pink, ponytail loose and lopsided from rolling around on Riggs's bed. I have to admit, being on the receiving end of oral sex was nothing like the scenes I've read in books, and not in a good way. In all the novels I've devoured, every vulva owner has gone from zero to orgasm like it's no big deal—like it would be harder *not* to orgasm, because that's just how good it feels. That was *not* the case for me, even though everything Riggs did with his tongue felt amazing. While he was down there, I searched for the usual cues that my body was getting close, like a lioness stalking her prey; only, every time I sensed one, and I bucked my hips to let Riggs know, it ended up fizzling out. I think I wanted to have my zero-to-orgasm moment so badly that I ended up psyching myself out. It would have been helpful to read about *that* at some point, instead of person after person "unraveling at the seams" or "shattering into a billion pieces." Where are all the anxious people who spend their hookups telepathically screaming at their own vaginas? Well, hopefully it gets easier over time, and luckily, Riggs assured me he's down to do it as many times as I want.

I go back to the bathroom door and open it a sliver, the same way I did in Riggs's room. The hallway outside is quiet and still. I made it here in thirty seconds or so; now that I know where I'm going, I'm sure I can sprint back in ten. I can't wait to snuggle up to Riggs again and close my eyes, knowing there's nowhere else on Earth I have to be until the sun rises.

Here goes nothing: three, two, one . . . I open the door and slip out into the empty corridor.

I dart left, back toward Riggs's hall. He's going to be so impressed when he wakes up and I tell him about my super-speedy late-night excursion. Here comes the home stretch; one more turn and I'll be able to see his door, which I thankfully remembered to leave unlocked.

When I hang the next left, I collide with something, hard. It knocks the wind out of me, and as I stumble back, gasping, I panic that I misjudged the space, slammed into a wall, and most likely woke Mr. Crothers with the noise.

But the next second, once I've gathered my breath and awareness, I realize the truth is worse—like, worst-case-scenario-level worse. My blood turns to lead and hardens. Each limb is a thousand pounds.

"Care to explain yourself?" asks the dorm supervisor as he jerks his housecoat back into place.

I don't have a choice. Mr. Crothers orders me to lead him back to Riggs's room. When he opens the door and flicks on the light, Riggs blinks awake from his deep sleep. Then he sees me standing in the shadow of his dorm supervisor, and his confusion turns to shock.

"Don't look so surprised," Mr. Crothers says in his stone-cold voice. "You should have known I'd be monitoring the halls more frequently after last week's incident with Mr. Wyatt. I'm stunned you'd both try something so stupid."

This is my first time getting in trouble—not "Alyson, stop reading your book and pay attention in algebra" trouble, but *real* trouble. The kind that could get me suspended and affect my chances of getting into Overbrooke. Somehow, that's not even the worst part of this. I stare at the hideous gray carpet because it's better than looking at Riggs and seeing the disappointment in his eyes that I blew our big night. Can I just shrivel up into a speck and disappear into the dust on the floor?

"Mr. C," Riggs tries in a congenial voice, "Alyson was having a rough night and she needed someone to t—"

Mr. Crothers shuts him down. "If she was having a rough night, she should have talked to her dorm supervisor. Now, you'll both wait here while I go call Ms. Skidmore, who's going to be very disappointed." The words pierce me like an arrow. "I'll be back in a minute. Do *not* move."

Only when we're alone, and Riggs groans my name, do I force myself to meet his eyes. "What the fuck happened?" he asks.

God, I am such a failure. My hot senior boyfriend invites me to his dorm room and goes down on me, and I say "Thanks for the oral!" by doing this. My voice small and shaky, I tell him about the bathroom emergency and how I slammed face-first into Mr. Crothers.

"Are you kidding me?" he hisses. "Why didn't you just"—he looks around the room—"go out the window or something?"

"I don't know!" My logic about not peeing out the window made sense in the moment, but it seems so stupid now.

"This fucking sucks. If I have to miss basketball . . ." Riggs rakes a hand through his bed head. "I think they gave Wyatt two weeks' deten . . ." He trails off, and his expression shifts to something that looks an awful lot like suspicion.

Oh no.

Is he wondering if I tried to screw him over on purpose?

Like what Kavita did to Greg Wyatt? And after he told me he wanted me to meet his parents?

This can't be happening. I must look like a monster. And if I lose him for a second time because of the Queen's Cup, there's no way I'll get another chance.

Before I can attempt to clear the air, Mr. Crothers sweeps back into the room. "Ms. Skidmore is waiting for you back in your dormitory, Ms. Benowitz. I'll be informing Headmaster Wheaton that the two of you—"

"Mr. Crothers, wait." I know what I have to do. I'm already doomed no matter what, so I might as well use my dying breath to prove my loyalty to Riggs. "I just want you to know that Riggs had no idea I was going to show up here tonight." I steal a glance at Riggs, whose face softens as he seems to realize what I'm doing. "This is totally my fault. You're right, I should have just gone to Ms. Skidmore when I was feeling stressed about, um, homework. I'm the one who should be in trouble, not Riggs."

"Thank you, Ms. Benowitz." Before I can say anything else to win back Riggs's trust, Mr. Crothers ushers me from the room.

CHAPTER 12

Because I've never so much as nudged the toe of my black loafer out of line, Headmaster Wheaton lets me off with one strike and a week of detention. Every day after fifth period, I have to report to the student services center, leave my phone and laptop in Wheaton's office, and spend two hours in this depressing conference room as the sun goes down outside the window. It's pretty good, as far as punishments go. I end up getting ahead on all of my homework and finishing both of the romance novels I bought on Village Night.

But the best part of this whole detention situation, aside from the fact that Overbrooke won't see a suspension on my record, is that Riggs doesn't think I set him up. (As for his fate, between my insistence that he's innocent and the basketball coach begging the headmaster not to put his star player in detention, he got off scot-free.) He still wants me to meet his parents tomorrow morning when they come to campus for some fancy alumni athletics brunch, and even though Riggs keeps assuring me they'll love me, I'm still stressed about making a good impression. Like, what if they ask what sports I play? And then I have to be all, "None, but I did just read this novel where rival fencing champions got it on in the Olympic Village. Does that count?"

I've been so in my head about the big meeting that I've barely had a chance to process that next week is Valentine's Day. I've waited forever to celebrate it earnestly, and with an actual valentine. Last year, Jess went on a half-hour rant about Hallmark holidays, Mom mailed me a novelty box of chocolates that said F*%$ LOVE on the lid, and I burned with envy at the girls like Marina and Tasha who walked around campus clutching cards and roses.

Jess will probably be the same old cynic this year. I tried telling her what I witnessed of Sam when I was in line for the toboggan chute, but she shook her head and said she still didn't want to take the risk.

As for me, this could finally be the year things turn around—the year *I* become a girl who floats around campus with a gift from her partner. The events committee did a fundraiser where you could pay to have Valentine's Day treats deposited in people's mailboxes. (I paid five dollars to leave a bag of cinnamon hearts in Riggs's.) While I was in here doing my final stint in detention, I'm certain I heard Becca and her friends fulfilling orders in the mail center across the hall.

At five-thirty on the dot, I launch myself out of the conference room and race to Wheaton's office.

"I don't want to see you in detention again," the headmaster says as he hands back my things.

"You won't, sir. I promise."

He shakes his head. "No more distracting the boys."

I'd like to point out that Riggs *wanted* me to come distract him, thank you very much, but that would contradict the story I told Mr. Crothers. I swallow the casual sexism and say goodbye with a quick nod.

Back at the mail center, I squat in front of box number 417 and stick my tiny silver key in the lock. *Please, please, please let there be a surprise in here.* Holding my breath, I open the door.

I see pink.

The plastic goodie bag is filled with foil-wrapped chocolate hearts and tied with a curly ribbon. Grinning, I flip over the heart-shaped label.

TO: ALYSON
LOVE: JESS

She drew a crown around our names.

My smile fades. I should be happy to get a Valentine's Day gift at all, but I wanted it to be from Riggs. Maybe he didn't know they were selling these things. Boys are bad at paying attention to stuff like that, and in any case, I'm sure he got me *something*. I squat lower and slide my hand as deep as it'll go inside my mailbox, just in case there's a second goodie bag.

Instead, my fingers graze an envelope.

I pull it out and furrow my brow. It has a stamp, and my name and address are scrawled in sloppy handwriting I don't recognize. The top left corner is blank. What the heck? I drop the bag of chocolates and tear into the envelope. Inside, there's a single sheet of printer paper folded into thirds. I open it up and gasp at the handwritten message.

STOP WHAT YOU'RE DOING.

YOU'VE BEEN WARNED.

All the blood drains from my face. I flip the page over; nothing there. I look inside the envelope; nothing there, either. Just this freaky message and no further context.

Could it be from Chrissy? The threatening tone of the message reminds me of her grabbing my wrist at the Fall Festival. "Watch out," she'd said. But why would Chrissy go to the trouble of mailing a letter when she clearly has no qualms about accosting me face to face?

Stop what you're doing. What *am* I doing that's out of the ordinary? I'm dating Riggs. Maybe he has a secret admirer hell-bent on getting me out of the picture. Or maybe it's Jess, escalating her mission to turn me against Riggs. Maybe the chocolates were a decoy. I pull out my phone and FaceTime her.

She picks up after the first ring, lounging against her headboard in her bedroom in Saranac Lake. "Well, I'll be darned. Are you finally free from detention? Wait, why do you look so freaked out right now?"

"Because I'm in the mail center—"

"Oh! Did you get my surprise?"

"Was it this?" I hold the threatening note in front of the camera.

"What the . . . ? No, it was the chocolates!"

The sheer confusion on Jess's face convinces me she's telling the truth, but it doesn't help my overall rising panic. "Okay, well, somebody mailed me an anonymous letter, and this is all it says. 'Stop what you're doing. You've been warned.'"

"You thought *I* sent you that?"

Now that we're talking, I can see what a ridiculous idea it was.

"When there's something you should stop doing, I'll tell you to your face. Like right now: thinking I'd write that weird-ass letter."

"I'm sorry, Jess. I'm just freaked out and not thinking straight." I get up from my Gollum-like pose on the floor, cross the hall, and shut myself in the detention room, where I can speak more freely. "Thank you for the chocolates, by the way. I feel like a huge jerk now."

"Yeah, you kinda were, but in the spirit of Valentine's Day, I still love you."

"I love you, too."

"So who do you think wrote the letter? Can I see it again?"

I smooth it out on the table. As I hold the camera above it, giving Jess a good, long look, I explain why I don't think it's from Chrissy.

Jess agrees. "And that handwriting is messy. It looks like a boy did it. Which makes me wonder . . ."

". . . if they're talking about the Queen's Cup?"

"Yeah."

My stomach drops like a stone. That was the possibility I was trying not to entertain. If it's true, it means someone who's not on our side knows I'm directly involved with trying to humiliate guys at school. I swear a bunch of times in a row.

"What is it?" Jess asks.

I'm somewhere between crying and dropping dead of a heart attack. "How long do you think it'll take for this to get back to Riggs?"

"I don't know." Jess frowns. "I take it you're not going to tell him about this?"

I let out a sigh. In a perfect world, I'd have Riggs kiss away the fear coursing through my veins, then track down the offender and intimidate them into submission with all six foot three inches of his stature. "I can't say anything," I reply. "How could I? He's smart. He'd probably reach the same conclusion we just did and assume I'm part of the Queen's Cup."

"You *are* part of the Queen's Cup."

"Yeah, but not, like, to use on *him*." Jess opens her mouth, but I cut her off. "Don't even start, Quigley. I'm stressed enough as it is."

"Aren't you getting brunch with his parents tomorrow, too?"

Good Lord. The alumni athletics brunch. I have way too many things to freak out about tonight.

"You look like you're going to pass out," she says. "Listen, babe, it's badass that you're getting threats for starting a resistance movement. When bad people hate you, it means you're doing the right thing."

"I don't regret starting the Queen's Cup," I promise, thinking of all the girls walking around campus with crowns on their arms.

"Good," she says.

The part I keep to myself is how badly I wish I could do the right thing without losing my boyfriend in the process.

The next morning, when I meet Riggs at the fountain, he hugs me and pulls down my hood so he can kiss the top of my head. "You look amazing, as always."

"I do? I was worried." I'm not fishing for compliments. I feel like a pile of garbage, and I'm pretty sure I look like one, too. I lay awake until five a.m. worrying about the letter, wondering who figured out my connection to the Queen's Cup and whether they're planning to pass that information along to Riggs. When I got up after four hours of spotty sleep, my eyes were bloodshot and my skin was practically translucent. I took a long, hot shower and blow-dried my hair, but I'm not sure how much it helped.

"Uh, have you seen yourself? Of course you do. Here, put this back up—it's cold." He fixes my hood and zips my jacket up to my chin. "You ready to meet the parents?"

"Can't wait."

Truth be told, I'm apprehensive about meeting Brenton Riggs Sr. after everything I've heard about him. I know he's Riggs's hero, but I also know how much pressure he puts on his son. Riggs is my sweet little golden retriever puppy. I don't take well to people mistreating him.

I try to push the stupid letter from my mind as we walk hand in hand to the gym. "Hey, what are you doing later tonight?" Riggs asks.

Oh, just resuming my panic attack about the anonymous person—most likely a guy—who may or may not want to kill me. "Probably hitting up the library," I tell him, which is also true. After I begged him incessantly for even more opportunities to bring up my grade, Mr. MacMillan finally caved and said I could write an essay on what my favorite literary genre is and why. I'm pretty sure he made it up on the spot to get me out of his office. The due date is "whenever," but I'll take it.

"I have a Valentine's Day gift for you, and I want to do it

today since Tuesday we'll be in class and then I have an away game," Riggs says.

"Riggs!" I suddenly feel a lump in my throat. It just dawned on me that I need to enjoy these romantic moments while I still can. "Screw the library."

He nudges me with his elbow. "I wish you said that more often."

We find Mr. and Mrs. Riggs holding court at one of the twenty or so round tables in the gym. Brenton Riggs Sr. has the same chiseled cheekbones and cleft chin, but his curls have gone silver and he wears them slicked back with hair gel, the grooves from his comb visible. Mrs. Riggs looks to be about a decade younger than her husband, with elbow-length blond hair and Riggs's ice-blue eyes. They both look impossibly clean, like the people you see in first class on the airplane while you make your way back to economy. My parents make enough money to send me to boarding school—Lord knows Mom's billable hours are through the roof—but I've put it together that Riggs comes from a different level of wealth. He's trust-fund rich. Parents-who-donate-big-chunks-of-money-to-the-school rich.

As Riggs guides me by the hand up to the table, his dad is busy telling a story to three other middle-aged couples. ". . . and I said, 'Suzanne, it helps when you're playing golf to have your club hit the ball!' " He waves his arms through the air, mimicking a golf swing, while the table erupts with laughter.

Mrs. Riggs watches her husband with a placid smile. It sounds like she was the butt of his joke, which doesn't do wonders for my opinion of him.

Riggs clears his throat. "Hey, you guys."

Our arrival restores life to Mrs. Riggs's face, and she gets up and rushes to us with her arms wide. She pulls Riggs into a hug first. "My baby boy," she says. "Your father's trying to make me look bad, as usual."

"Aw, I'm sure he's just joking, Mom."

Why won't Riggs stand up for his mom? Then again, it's probably easier to defend your mom when the enemy is her shitty ex-boyfriend, not the father you've looked up to your entire life.

When Mrs. Riggs lets go of her son, Riggs gestures to me. "Mom, this is Alyson."

I do a little wave. "It's so nice to meet you, Mrs. Riggs."

Whenever my friends call my dad and mom Mr. Benowitz and Ms. Becker, my parents always quick to insist on Jeff and Tamar. Mrs. Riggs doesn't correct me, but she does give me a hug. She smells like one of the expensive perfumes Jess and I have spritzed on each other at Sephora. "It's wonderful to meet you, sweetie. I know you two had a little hiccup over the break—"

"Mom—"

"—but it's wonderful to see you back together." I feel simultaneously mortified and touched that Riggs told his parents so much about us. It's like I'm part of the family. "I always tell Brenton," Mrs. Riggs continues, "relationships are hard work."

"What's hard work? Being married to me?" Mr. Riggs walks around the table to greet us.

"Yes, exactly," I hear Mrs. Riggs mutter, but she's drowned out by her husband's booming voice.

"There she is!" My face goes warm when I realize he's talking about me. Mr. Riggs clasps my hand between his palms and pumps it up and down. "A firm handshake!" He looks at Riggs. "Brenton, I like this girl already."

Riggs smiles. "I told you."

My cheeks get even hotter. "It's great to finally meet you, Mr. Riggs."

"Alyson, please! We're honored to meet you. From what Brenton tells us, you're the next . . . You know what? I was going to name a famous author, but I can't think of one. Publish a book so I can name at least one."

"I'll try," I say, laughing. His self-deprecating humor reminds me of Riggs. So does the way he makes me feel important just by giving me his undivided attention. Riggs may be gentler and more loving than his dad, but there's no denying they share the same magnetism.

Riggs and his dad do one of those bro hugs where they grasp each other's hands and slap each other on the back. "Come, come, let's all sit down," Mr. Riggs says, ushering us to the open seats between the other couples. He introduces the men as his lacrosse teammates from back in the day. "And their much better halves," he adds, gesturing to the wives.

Brunch with Brenton Riggs Sr. turns out to be a solid anxiety antidote. Between asking me questions—the first ten minutes or so—and relaying stories about his time at Sullivan—the remaining hour and a half—he keeps the conversation at a rolling boil.

At one point, Headmaster Wheaton comes over to say hello. "Philip!" Mr. Riggs booms. Another bro hug ensues, and I'm legitimately concerned about it shattering the elderly principal's frail bones.

"Brenton!" he replies after a small coughing fit. "It's a pleasure to see you, as always. Thank you for coming all this way."

"Are you kidding me? I'd never pass up a chance to come back here. These were the glory days!"

"They were, weren't they?" It's no great shock that Wheaton preferred Sullivan-Stewart without the Stewart. The headmaster pushes his glasses up his nose and turns to the rest of the table. "Now, who do we have here with you?"

I can pinpoint the exact moment when he registers my presence; he flinches ever so slightly.

"We're getting to know the lovely Alyson Benowitz," Mr. Riggs supplies. "I'm sure you're well aware of what a talent she is."

Wheaton casts the world's most pinched smile in my direction. "Oh yes, well aware," the headmaster says stiffly. "How are you, Alyson?"

It's strangely satisfying to watch Philip Wheaton change his behavior in front of his esteemed guests. I could get used to being part of the Riggs family. "Great, thanks, and you?"

"Wonderful, thank you." He adjusts his glasses again and turns back to Mr. Riggs. "Well, I just wanted to come over and say hello, and let you know we're very grateful for your continued support of the school."

One of Mr. Riggs's former classmates, Cal, claps him on the shoulder. "Once a king, always a king."

The word "king" catches my attention, and I nearly choke on a piece of cantaloupe. Shoot, now I can't stop coughing, and the whole table is looking at me.

Riggs forces a cup of water into my hand. "Here, drink this. Are you okay?"

I chug the water and nod, but I wish my trachea hadn't rudely cut off the men's conversation. I didn't put it together before, but Riggs's dad went to Sullivan in the eighties, which means he was probably here during the first iteration of the King's Cup.

Once a king, always a king. Does that mean what I think it does? Could Brenton Riggs Sr. have competed in . . . well, not just competed in, but *won* the King's Cup? Or am I just on edge because I feel like I'm going to be called out at any moment for starting the Queen's Cup? I never find out the answer, because by the time I'm breathing normally again, the men have said goodbye to Headmaster Wheaton and resumed a conversation about some game-winning lacrosse play Mr. Riggs once masterminded.

After brunch, I say goodbye to Riggs and his parents, who are sticking around for an alumni-versus-students three-on-three basketball tournament. Riggs's dad pulls me in for a hug this time. "I hope we see you again soon," he says after holding me at arm's length and squeezing my shoulders. "Let me know when I can preorder your book!"

"I'll definitely let you know, Mr. Riggs." After the weird "king" comment, his attention feels less magical this time around. In fact, I'm a little relieved to get out of the gym and walk back to the dorm on my own.

My phone buzzes with a text from Riggs.

> They loved you!!! Not surprised. Thanks again for coming. Meet in the parking lot after dinner, like 7:30? Already miss you ツ.

Could this boy be any cuter? I smile as I respond, letting him know I'll be there. If Riggs's dad *did* win the King's Cup way back when, I wonder how Riggs feels about that. Has he told his dad what he told me: that he thinks the competition is stupid? It would be pretty cool if Riggs stood up to him like that, but at the same time, I know firsthand how awkward it can be to call your parents out on their questionable romantic choices. I should probably just be happy that this is one key area where my boyfriend has no interest in emulating his dad.

That night, I find the Ford Explorer in its usual spot in the corner of the parking lot. Riggs leans against the passenger-side door, his hands jammed in the pockets of his royal-blue parka. When I get close, he takes them out, and that's when I notice his fingers are enclosed around a velvet jewelry box.

Oh my God.

Obviously, it's not *that* kind of jewelry box, but seeing as I've never gotten *any* kind of jewelry box from a guy, this is a big freakin' deal for me.

Riggs smiles and holds it out to me. "Happy early Valentine's Day. I know they were doing that candy sale last week, but I wanted to get you something better."

I giggle. "*I* got *you* candy, and now I feel like I should have gone bigger."

"Stop it." He gently places the box in my palm and curls my fingers around it. "You're here with me now. That's the best gift you could possibly give me."

My cheeks are on fire as I open the lid. Inside is a silver bracelet with two shiny charms on it. One's a book; the other's a lacrosse stick.

"They're us," he says a little sheepishly.

I touch the charms gently with the pad of my finger: first me, then him. I would never have picked this out for myself, and yet it's the most beautiful thing I've ever seen. The thought of him going to the jewelry store . . . picking out the chain, and charms . . . imagining how they'd look on my arm . . . I swear I could cry right now. It makes it all the more difficult to hold in my tears knowing the letter-writer is out there, probably waiting to take me down. "Riggs, thank you."

"Do you like it?"

I rearrange my face into a smile. "I love it. Thank you so much."

"Let me help you put it on." He takes the bracelet out of the box and fastens it around my wrist. It's so lovely and delicate, the chain as fine as gossamer. I turn my hand over to admire the charms as they rest on the inside of my forearm.

We get in the car and drive toward town. Lake Placid's downtown strip hugs the shore of Mirror Lake, but drive a minute or two and you'll see the much more massive body of water where the village gets its name. When we came up here on vacation before my parents split up, my dad and I took a canoe out on Lake Placid, failed to realize how windy it was, and ended up stranded three miles from where we started; we had to flag down a Quebecois family in a motorboat and beg them in broken French to tow us back.

At the sign for Lake Placid Marina, Riggs turns down the road that leads to the water and stops in front of the same wooden dock where the family brought us to safety that day. I feel a tug of nostalgia. I was so young back then—seven or eight at the oldest—and now here I am, sitting in the front seat of a Ford Explorer with my senior lacrosse-captain boyfriend who just gave me the most amazing Valentine's Day gift. I've never felt more grown-up than I do in this moment, and it makes me want to throw myself into Riggs's arms.

Riggs shuts off the headlights. As my eyes adjust to the night, I can make out the frozen expanse at the end of the dock and the dark shapes of mountains against the starry sky.

"I'm super into this spot," he says.

"Me too," I reply. "Staring out at this big black hole of nothingness makes me feel like I could do anything."

Riggs snorts.

"What?"

"I was gonna be like, 'Because it's pretty.' As usual, you're smart as fuck. *Buuut . . .*" He reaches over and puts his hand on my leg. "I bet you can't guess why I brought you here."

He has another surprise? Now I *really* feel bad for wishing he bought me candy. "I don't know. Tell me."

"Last month, when we ran into each other before Village Night, you obviously caught me kinda off guard with what you said about, you know, your feelings. I felt kinda bad that I wasn't ready to say it back that night."

"You mean . . ."

He nods. He means the L-bomb.

Oh my God.

"But I know for sure that I'm ready to say it now." Riggs twists in his seat to face me. He takes a deep breath. "I love you, Alyson." His face splits into a grin, and he lets the rest of his air out in a shocked sort of laugh. "Whoa. I can't believe I just said that. It felt so good. I love you. I fucking *love* you."

And then I really do throw myself across the center console and into Riggs's arms. There's a frantic unbuckling of seat belts, and I clamber onto his lap, careful not to kick the gearshift and send us rolling into the lake. Our kiss feels like an earthquake that sends shock waves through my body, makes me tremble with a force I didn't know was inside of me. This must be what happens when you're in love and the other person loves you back. I finally made it.

Now I just hope I never have to leave.

WEDNESDAY, MAY 3

Press conference, Lake Placid Police Station

POLICE CHIEF RALPH NOSTRAND: Good morning. I'm
going to ask everybody to please hold your
questions until we've given our briefing, and
please wait until you're called upon. This morning
we're going to give an update on the ongoing
search efforts for Brenton Riggs Jr. In addition
to conducting interviews of family, friends, and
members of the school community, we have been
conducting extensive searches of the Wilmington
area. Over the past week, we've started to see
increased snow melt and that has aided us in our
search by opening up sections of terrain that we
were previously unable to search. We are going to
continue to expand our search and have involved
the state police and the county sheriff's office.

We've established a hotline for tips specific to this case, and we encourage anyone with relevant information to please give it a call. At this time, we're going to take some brief questions, but let me remind everybody that this is an active investigation and there are certain elements that we will not discuss publicly at this time. Go ahead.

CHRIS COLLINGWOOD, THE NEW YORK TIMES: Chief, do you have any information regarding past allegations of sexual misconduct involving Brenton?

CHIEF NOSTRAND: No. To my knowledge, our department has never investigated Mr. Riggs for any crime. Geraldine?

GERALDINE JOHNSON, ADIRONDACK DAILY ENTERPRISE: Is foul play being considered here?

CHIEF NOSTRAND: At this time, we have no evidence that any crime has taken place, so this is being considered a missing persons case.

GERALDINE JOHNSON: And a quick follow-up: what are the search conditions like out there?

CHIEF NOSTRAND: As many of you know from living in the Adirondacks, the terrain is challenging, to say the least. The deep snow we got last weekend made it difficult for our search teams to move, especially when it came to utilizing our canine units. But as I said, with the melting of the snow this week, we're hopeful conditions will improve and we'll be successful.

WEDNESDAY, MAY 3

Riley Prentiss @RPlax6000 · 5m

Come by the mirror lake public beach at 4pm today—the SSPS
lax team is fundraising for the search effort for Brenton Riggs
Jr. Our buddy Riggs was a great guy & we just want to find him.

Cameron Wright @camwright32 · 3m

Replying to @RPlax6000

"Was"? WTF man

Emerson Moreno @emoreno_69 · 3m

Replying to @camwright32 and @RPlax6000

Dude seriously??

Riley Prentiss @RPlax6000 · 1m

Replying to @emoreno_69 and @camwright32

It was a typo, relax

CHAPTER 13

March, One Month Earlier

Jess parks in the driveway and the five of us shimmy out of the Kia, our arms laden with shopping bags and shiny rose-gold Mylar balloons. We crunch through the snow, bright white in the Saturday afternoon sun, to the side of the house, where Marina twists the knob on the rarely used side door and leans into it with her shoulder.

"It feels like we're breaking and entering," Raquelle says.

"We're breaking and entering for *love*," I point out.

"Don't worry, Mrs. Thompson said she would leave it open for us." Marina grunts as the door peels open with a suctioning sound.

We take our boots off in the laundry room and follow Marina into Tasha's kitchen, which looks as Instagram-worthy as ever. "I always feel guilty messing this place up," Tori confesses.

"Whatever, it's gonna be romantic." I plop my bag onto the counter and start to unload the LED tea lights.

While Tasha and her parents run some manufactured errand that Marina worked out with Mrs. Thompson in advance, we get to work decorating. Despite her leather jacket and black choker, Marina's in full sappy mush mode as she explains her vision to have Tasha follow a winding path through the main floor, ending on the back patio.

I outline the sides of the path with the lights, and Jess scatters rose petals in between. Tori stuffs mini Union Jack flags into bud vases, and Raquelle covers every available surface with glossy prints of the girls doing cute couple-y things together. When the stage manager is satisfied with the way we're arranging everything, Marina carries the Mylar balloons out to the back deck. There are five of them in total: four letters and one question mark.

It isn't long before she's racing back inside with her phone in her hand. "Mrs. Thompson just texted—they'll be here at quarter past two!"

That's only ten minutes away. We scurry around, stuffing trash into empty bags, and doing one last inspection to make sure everything looks perfect. Then, everyone except Marina, who's going to wait in the foyer to greet her girlfriend, heads outside to wait on the deck with our confetti cannons.

Are we totally falling prey to the "commodification of love," as Jess insisted on putting it while we waited in line at the party store? I guess so.

But is it also going to be totally freaking romantic? *Yes.*

Three car doors slam nearby. The Thompsons must be home. Bouncing on the toes of my boots, I exchange excited smiles with the other girls.

We hear a telltale Tasha shriek as she presumably opens the door to find her girlfriend standing in her foyer and ushering her down a path of tea lights (you're welcome) and rose petals. I chart their path in my head, estimating where they must be, getting closer and closer. . . .

And then Marina opens the sliding glass door and leads Tasha out by the hand. Tasha is already laugh-crying from the surprise of it all, but when she sees the four of us standing around the metallic balloons that spell out "PROM?" she really starts to sob.

Jess shoots me a panicked grimace, as though she's worried Tasha is going to say no, but I flash her a thumbs-up. I know better. I know *love*. And sure enough, Tasha screams, "Ohmigod, yes!" before launching herself at Marina like a flying squirrel leaping toward a branch. That's our cue. There's a series of pops as we each twist the bottom of our cylindrical contraption, and we shower our friends in silver confetti as they kiss in the early-spring sun.

Since Sullivan-Stewart only has around a hundred kids to a grade, the juniors *and* seniors are invited to prom so we can fill out the banquet hall at the Sentinel Lodge in Wilmington. I've never been there before, but Jess's mom has. When we were hanging out at the Quigleys' last weekend, she told us how gorgeous the views are from way up high in the mountains. "Your photos will be to *die* for," Maura Quigley gushed. "They have all these scenic overlooks. Just don't drop your phones over any railings, because you'll never get them back again." I'm already aching to stand there with my head on Riggs's shoulder and watch the sun set behind the rocky peaks; I hope we take every cheesy prom portrait imaginable, including the classic pose with my back against his chest and his arms wrapped around me.

I'm beginning to think God really *did* forgive me for dropping out of Hebrew school, because despite the anonymous letter-writer's threat, the Queen's Cup is still chugging away on campus, and nothing bad has befallen me. Girls whisper about the latest come-ons and rejections while in line for the shower at night and at the common-room coffee machine in the morning; when they notice a new crown on a classmate's wrist, they ask, in a knowing way, how they got it. "Carson sent me an unsolicited dick pic over break, so I welcomed him back to campus with a bunch of moldy eggplants in his mailbox," I heard a girl explaining the other day.

Contrary to my worst nightmare of Riggs finding out I invented the Queen's Cup, our relationship keeps getting better. One morning while I was home in Albany over spring break, I got the surprise of a lifetime when a bouquet of roses showed up on our doorstep. The note attached was only two words long—"FaceTime me"—and signed Brenton Riggs Jr. I shrieked so loud that a pug being walked down the street started yapping in a panic, and I had to apologize to its human.

"I got these flowers from my boyfriend," I called out by way of explanation.

"Cool," the guy replied, sounding zero-percent interested.

Whatever. He didn't *get* the romance of it all. I grabbed my phone and FaceTimed Riggs, who answered on the first ring.

He grinned. "You look hot in pajamas."

I burst out laughing. "I promise I don't normally wear them outside."

"Does this mean you got a little delivery from me?"

"A *huge* delivery. I'm still unclear on whether it'll fit through the door, but it's gorgeous."

"Good. Well, I sent it because I've been missing you like hell, and I needed something to look forward to, so I wanted to ask you: Alyson, will you go to prom with me?"

"YES!" I screamed it so loud that the pug, who was two blocks away at this point, started yapping again.

So I know firsthand how excited Tasha and Marina must be right now. Since my friends and I have completed our confetti duties, I suggest we leave the girls to celebrate on their own. Jess, Tori, Raquelle, and I hug the couple goodbye and get back in the car.

Jess reverses down the driveway, but she pauses before we hit the road. "Anyone else not feel like going back to homework just yet?"

Yesterday, I finished the first draft of my extra-credit English essay. "I'm down to stay out longer."

Jess looks in the rearview mirror. "Tori? Raquelle? Permission to not go back to school?"

"Permission granted," Tori says.

An idea pops into my head as Jess starts steering us toward town. "Hey, should we stay on theme and go look at prom dresses?"

"I'm down," Jess replies. "Let's go to the mall."

I twist around in my seat. "That okay with you guys?"

For some reason, Tori looks anxious. Biting her bottom lip, she turns to Raquelle. "It's okay with me if it's okay with you."

"I guess it's fine," she says in a small voice.

I didn't notice earlier because we were so wrapped up in our mission, but now that I think about it, Raquelle hasn't been her usual giggly self today. "Raquelle, are you okay?" I ask.

She sighs. "Not really, no."

Tori pats the back of her hand. "She found something gross on Antoine's computer yesterday."

"Aww, Raquelle." I flash her a sympathetic smile. "You know it's totally normal for people to watch—"

"It wasn't porn," she cuts in. "That would've been fine."

"Oh. Okay. So then . . . ?"

Raquelle takes a deep breath, her shoulders shooting up to her ears with the effort. "We're working on our laptops in the library and Antoine gets up to go to the bathroom. Now, while he's gone, my Wi-Fi starts being all weird—you know how it gets like that on the second floor sometimes?—so I grab his computer to see if he got disconnected, too, or if the problem is just me. And when I look at his screen, I see this sticky note on his desktop."

"What did it say?"

"I already have a feeling I'm going to want to punch him," Jess adds.

"It was this list of four dates, and at the top, it said 'pipe.' I was like, 'pipe'? What? Then I realized one of the dates was Valentine's Day, and another was his birthday. I was with him on both of those days, and there weren't any pipes involved. So I got the idea to put 'pipe' into Google Translate, since everything on Antoine's computer is in French."

I think back to all the French vocab tests I've taken over the years. "I don't think I've ever heard that word in class."

Tori shakes her head. "You wouldn't have."

"It means"—Raquelle pauses and closes her eyes—"*blow job.*"

Jess's jaw drops. "No."

Raquelle replies with a solemn nod. When she speaks again,

her voice is thick. "He was tracking the times I went down on him. The other two dates lined up, too. It has to be for the King's Cup. I tried to hide it today so I didn't kill the vibe at Tasha's, but, you guys, I'm so upset and embarrassed." She wipes away a tear before it spills down her cheek. "I thought it was just between us. I thought he was better than that."

"I'm so sorry, Raquelle." I reach back and squeeze her knee, hating how limp her body feels. Raquelle usually bounces around, radiating positivity.

She smiles weakly at me. "Thanks."

"Are you sure you wanna go prom dress shopping, now that . . . ?"

"Now that *what*?" Jess exclaims. "Now that she's going to prom with me—and any other iconic ladies who want to join us? We'll shop for dresses for ourselves, not some dumb boys."

Tori whoops. She's been single by choice since she and that guy Karl broke up shortly after the Fall Festival, before we'd invented the Queen's Cup.

A hard knot forms in my chest. I feel like an outcast for going to prom with the guy I'm in love with. Not that I want to join them—I wish *they* could have partners like Riggs, too. Not jerks like Antoine. "So," I ask Raquelle, "how are we gonna Queen's Cup him?" We bat around ideas the rest of the way to the mall, but nothing stands out as a surefire winner.

We make a beeline for the department store, where every spring, half of one of the floors turns into a prom dress extravaganza. There are sequins, beads, ruffles, and puffy skirts in every color of the rainbow. Over spring break, Mom generously told me I could use her only-for-emergencies credit card to buy anything under two hundred dollars. "The dress," she said, giving Riggs's bouquet the once-over, "is the most exciting part."

We hit the racks like a tornado, grabbing hangers and holding up gowns to see how they'll look on us.

"I want something with drama," Jess declares. "Something that screams *me.*"

"How about this?" Tori holds up a sequined magenta A-line dress.

Jess cocks her head. "Hmm . . ."

"Wait, how about *that*?" I point to a nearby mannequin in a sequined magenta *suit,* with nothing beneath the deep V of the lapels.

Fifteen minutes later, we're hauling as many outfit options as we can physically carry into four neighboring fitting rooms. I'm, like, an inch from dislocating my shoulder in an attempt to tighten my lavender corseted dress when Tori screeches, "Oh my God! You guys, come out here!"

I drop the corset ties and yank open the door, clutching my bodice to my boobs so they don't fall out. We promised each other we'd sound the alarm if we thought we found "the one." Tori's standing across from me in a black velvet halter dress, her phone in her hand.

"You look incredible!" I tell her.

"Thanks!" she says. "Love that color on you. Raquelle, Jess, get out here."

The other two doors open. Raquelle comes out in a pale blue jumpsuit, and Jess emerges in the sparkly magenta ensemble.

"Wait," Tori says, holding up her palm, "you both look unfucking-believable."

Jess puts her hands on her hips and poses in front of the three-way mirror. "Really? You think so?"

She turns to look at her butt, which looks amazing and she knows it. "If you don't get that," I tell her, "I will sue."

"Wait, Tor, is that the one?" Raquelle asks.

"No, no!" Tori replies. She holds up her phone. "I have intel. From *Antoine*. Raquelle, I think he's gonna ask you to prom tomorrow afternoon."

"No."

"Yes. He just texted me saying he's planning a surprise for you, and he wants to know which side of the dorm your window looks out on."

A look of fierce determination appears on Raquelle's face. "I'm going to Queen's Cup his ass."

While Tori and Jess cheer, the cogs in my head start to turn, the same way they did for the Prentiss Offensive and Kavita's takedown of Greg Wyatt. "You know, I bet he's gonna pull a *Say Anything . . . ,*" I point out. The other girls blink at me. I sometimes forget my friends don't share my encyclopedic knowledge of old rom-coms. "Oops, sorry. It's this movie where the guy stands in front of the girl's house with a boom box over his head." I look at Raquelle. "The point is, Antoine's probably gonna do something outside your window. We can work with that."

Raquelle flashes me a conspiratorial grin. "What do you think I should do?"

Lacrosse season is back, and the next morning, Sullivan-Stewart hosts a rare Sunday home game. Unsurprisingly, I have no luck convincing any of my friends to sit on the ice-cold metal bleachers and watch boys running around with sticks, so after breakfast, I make my way to the field behind the athletics center solo, my gloved hand clutching the GO RIGGS GO sign I made on a piece of cardboard.

Watching the game is mostly miserable, thanks to the chilly gusts of wind and the small but vocal group of deranged lacrosse dads screaming obscenities after every call. But my attendance pays off when a rosy-cheeked Riggs jogs over after scoring the game-winning goal. "I thought I was fucked out there," he says, still panting, "Then I looked over and saw your sign again, and I was like, nah, I got this." He kisses me hard on the mouth, and even though his lips are like ice, they set my whole body on fire. "What are you doing now?" he asks.

"Going home to take a hot shower because I can't feel my butt."

He laughs. "What about after that? I want to spend time with you. And your not-frozen butt."

Well, then. That would be a nice reward for sticking it out through an entire game of sports. I check the time on my phone: one o'clock. Antoine's prom-posal is supposed to happen around four, and I need to make sure I'm alone before then so I can help Raquelle with her Queen's Cup operation. Four is still three whole hours away. "Meet in the library in like, forty-five? I have some research to do on eighteenth- and nineteenth-century music history that I was hoping you could help me with." We've used this joke about a million times by now, but it never fails to make me smile.

Riggs kisses me again. "I know a thing or two about that."

Forty-five minutes later, we park our backpacks and lay out our homework at our usual couch, but we don't stay there for long. He takes my hand and guides me between two rarely browsed stacks, then positions me so that my back is against the books and kisses me hard, his tongue pressing between my teeth and deep inside my mouth. He gets like this after a big win: confident, hungry for whatever he can get his hands on. It's caveman-like—or it would be if I didn't enjoy being the aforementioned thing-he-can-get-his-hands-on so much.

His hands find my wrists, and I offer exactly zero resistance as he lifts them up above my head and pins them against the thick spine of a leathery book. I love it when he does this. Still kissing me, he shifts his grip so that he's holding both my wrists in one hand, while his other hand slides between my legs. He's gotten very good at touching me down there with all the experience we've built up, and I smile into his lips at the feel of his fingers against my yoga pants. He works his hand there for a while, the tension and heat and spasms of pleasure building and building, until . . .

"Shit, bro, get a room!"

It's like being doused in ice water. I swear loudly as I yank my arms down and wrap them around my torso for protection. Riley stands in the opening of the stacks, wrinkling his nose at us.

Riggs, a thousand times smoother than me, keeps his upper hand where it was and makes it look like he was just leaning against the bookshelf like that. He takes the hand that was just between my legs and rakes his fingers through his curls. Smiling lazily, he asks, "Jealous, Prentiss?" Shame burns up my neck to my cheeks. I look at my shoes and squeeze myself tighter. "Hey, remind me who you're going to prom with, again?"

I can't bring myself to drag my eyes away from the floor,

but I hear Riley scoff. As far as I know, he's still dateless for the dance. "Fuck off, Riggs. I'm just tryna find a book."

"Well, don't let us stop you."

Even though I love Riggs, I could scream at him right now. *"We can go,"* I mumble at the carpet.

"I think your girlfriend would rather I come back later," Riley says. I hear his footsteps as he walks away.

Riggs laughs. "What a loser." His hand finds my chin and tilts it up, but as he moves in for another kiss, I turn my face to the side.

"Wait."

"What?"

I'm still hot with embarrassment, and the pressure behind my eyes feels like tears are on the way. I can't just go back to making out, as badly as I wish I could. "Riggs"—my voice is small, barely above a whisper—"that was so awkward."

"Yeah, awkward for *Prentiss.*"

"And for me."

"Aww, c'mon, he didn't see anything."

"It's not about what he *saw.*"

"What is it, then?"

"The way you talked to him . . . It made me feel . . ." I swallow hard. I'm used to bringing up issues in a jokey way, but I'm past the point of doing that now.

"Made you feel how?"

"Like I was just some . . . some shiny object that Riley could have . . . could have won for himself, if he'd tried harder."

"Alyson. Oh my God." He wraps me in his arms and I relax into his chest. Then he kisses the top of my head and says, "That's ridiculous."

I flinch. It didn't feel ridiculous to me, but I'm not sure if I should press the issue. I'm the one who suggested we hook up here in the first place.

That's when I remember: There was a time limit on today's tryst. "Hey, what time is it?"

Riggs looks at his watch. "Three-thirty. Why?"

Oh no! We must have been hooking up for way longer than I realized. Time flies when your boyfriend knows what he's doing down there. I meant to be out of here by three at the latest. I shuffle to the side, breaking his hug. "I have to get back to the dorm."

Riggs looks worried. "Are you mad?"

"No, not at all." *That's not exactly true, but it's not the reason I'm leaving.* "I have to, uh, FaceTime with my mom."

"Well, at least let me be a gentleman and walk you home."

"Oh . . . it's okay. I know you have that history thing you still need to start on." In reality, I need him to leave me alone so I can do my Queen's Cup stuff in peace.

"If you think I've ever come to the library to do homework, you don't know me very well."

Argh. I could stay here with Riggs and bail on Raquelle, but I want to be there to support her. I could let Riggs walk me home, but if we get there and Antoine's already setting up, I'm assuming my boyfriend will want to stick around and watch. Who wouldn't?

"Let's go, then." If we leave now, maybe we can still make it back to the dorms before Antoine sets up shop. I hurry back to the couch, shoulder my backpack, and hightail it for the stairs.

"Whoa, whoa, wait up!" Riggs calls.

As we pass the fountain and veer left, a junior on the lacrosse team named Emerson jogs up from behind us and punches Riggs on the shoulder. That's weird—guys usually only come this way if they're walking somebody home.

"What's up, man?" Riggs asks.

"My buddy Ant's about to ask this girl Raquelle to prom. He wants us to hold balloons or some shit."

Oh no. That must mean Antoine's already setting up.

"Raquelle?" Riggs looks at me, oblivious to my mounting anxiety. "You guys are friends, right? Didn't you say she went dress shopping with you yesterday?"

I force a grin that probably looks more like a grimace. "Yeah! This is so exciting."

"You guys should come with me," Emerson says. "The more people holding balloons, the less stupid I look."

Riggs laughs. "We got you, bud."

We are, indeed, too late. When we round the next corner, Antoine comes into view—along with enough helium balloons to lift the house in *Up*. If I'd been walking home alone, I could have easily slipped past him and gone inside, but not anymore. I take out my phone and shoot off a stealthy text to Raquelle, explaining I can't come up to her room, but that I'll be outside and smiling up at her.

"Ant, I brought friends," Emerson announces, motioning to us. Antoine flashes us a grin. I fake one back and accept a balloon from him, dread pooling in my stomach. Riggs knows I hung out with Raquelle yesterday, and I don't want him to think I had anything to do with what we're about to witness.

We take our place in the crowd of thirty-some-odd people gathered outside the dorm. Some are here to hold balloons; others just seem curious about what's going on.

"You think Raquelle has any idea?" Riggs asks.

"I dunno!" I lie.

Riggs cranes his neck to take in the crowd, then turns back to me and lowers his voice. "But she's super into him, right? She's not gonna pull some dumb shit?"

The last two words hit me like stones in the center of my chest. I don't know if I'm still shaken up from what happened in the library, or sad that I can't be up there with my friends right now, but I can't let the comment go. "It isn't dumb shit," I mumble.

Riggs doesn't hear me, which is probably a good thing. At the same time I say it, Antoine screams, "Okay, okay, I'm calling her!" The crowd quiets down at his announcement. Everyone watches with blissfully ignorant expressions as he holds his phone up to his ear. *"Bonjour, mon chou.* Can you come to the front of your bedroom and open the window as far as it will go, *s'il vous plaît?"*

A few seconds later, Raquelle's red curls appear on the other side of the third-floor window. Tasha must have given her an acting lesson beforehand, because her look of joyful surprise as she cranks open the glass would convince me if I didn't already know what was coming.

"Raquelle Dennison!" Antoine yells. "As you know, there is something special I want to ask you!"

She flutters her eyelashes and fans her face. "What is it?"

"Iras-tu au bal avec moi?"

"I can't hear you!" she calls down to him. "Can you come closer?"

We analyzed this part meticulously yesterday afternoon. Because the upper-floor windows don't open all the way, we needed Antoine to be directly below Raquelle's room for the plan to work.

He walks right up to the building wall and cranes his neck. Perfect. "I said, *Iras-tu au bal avec moi?* Will you go to prom with me?"

Raquelle smiles wide. "I have an answer to your question."

"And?"

When we came home from dress shopping, we stopped at the dining hall on the way back to Raquelle's room, and each picked up a few pieces of fruit: a mix of bananas, apples, and oranges. We ate them for a snack as we went over the specifics of the operation, exchanging triumphant smiles every time one of us deposited a peel or a core into the trash bin.

Even though it was my idea, it stuns me to see what happens next: the aforementioned trash bin appearing behind the glass; Raquelle's hands tipping it out the open window; the pile of smelly brown fruit carcasses and other random garbage cascading through the air. There's a truly poetic moment when a slimy banana peel slaps Antoine in the face.

The crowd erupts in noise: the boys booing; the girls laughing. I refuse to boo, and I can't laugh—I don't want Riggs to suspect me of anything—so I grab his arm and pretend I'm still shocked, my eyes wide and my jaw hanging open.

"This is getting ridiculous!" Riggs yells in my ear over the cacophony of reactions. I don't say anything back.

Fuming, Antoine screams something in French at Raquelle—another word I don't remember learning in class and I'm probably okay not knowing. Then he turns on his heel and storms through the crowd, pushing people aside and ripping balloons out of their hands, setting them loose into the sky. He's like a toddler throwing a temper tantrum at a birthday party, and he only gets angrier when he notices the girls with crowns on their wrists holding up their phones to immortalize his embarrassing exit.

When Ms. Skidmore explodes through the door and threatens to give us all strikes if we don't clear the area, I give Riggs a quick kiss and say goodbye—grateful, honestly, not to have to field more of his anger at the Queen's Cup.

I go straight to Raquelle's room, where we celebrate with a crown-drawing ceremony and a dramatic reenactment of the epic rejection. The upside to my failure to make it up here in time is that I can describe, in detail, what it looked like from the ground, including the poetic banana-peel slap. The gathering turns into a dance party, which turns into Ms. Skidmore banging on the door and telling us to turn the music down, at which point we figure it's a good time for dinner anyway. Jess, who drove to campus this afternoon to help with the operation, offers to pick up pizza so Raquelle doesn't have to come face to face with Antoine in the dining hall.

Later that night, when I finally head to my room, I reach into the side pocket of my backpack, and my fingers crunch against paper. That's weird; I only ever use this pocket for my key chain so I never lose my keys.

Alone in the hallway, I pull out the paper, which was folded neatly into quarters before I crushed it with my hand. I open it up, and the high of the past few hours disappears. It's a note, scrawled in the same handwriting as the last one.

I THOUGHT I TOLD YOU TO STOP.
YOU'RE GOING TO REGRET THIS.

CHAPTER 14

"How? How am I going to regret this?"

I sit on the edge of my bed and stare at the stupid paper, wishing I could intimidate it into revealing its secrets. The first time this happened, it plunged me into a world of panic that Riggs would find out the truth and break up with me. But then . . . nothing happened. The Queen's Cup kept going, and so did our relationship.

"Who are you, and what do you *want*?"

Shockingly, the page doesn't answer. Just like the first letter, there's no indication of who the hell wrote this, and when I think back on my day, it could literally be *anyone*. I brought my backpack to the dining hall, to Riggs's lacrosse game, to the library, then to the middle of a freakin' crowd of people. I brought it to Raquelle's room, too, but none of the girls went anywhere near the piles of bags in the corner, and besides, everyone there was *clearly* in favor of the Queen's Cup.

I throw the letter in the general direction of the garbage

and flop onto my side. I hope my performance down there was convincing enough that Riggs isn't suspicious of me, especially given that he knows I hung out with Raquelle yesterday.

When he asked if I thought Raquelle was expecting anything, I feel like he believed me when I said I didn't know. But was it enough? This is so frustrating. All I ever wanted was to live out a love story—not a freaking spy novel where the main character has to hide stuff from her boyfriend and live in fear that he might find out.

Whatever this letter writer has in store for me, it couldn't hurt to remind Riggs how I feel about him. I search my disheveled bed for my phone, and after I find it wedged between the mattress and the wall, I send him three texts.

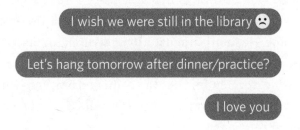

Nothing yet—no ellipsis bubbling in the corner. Where is he? Still walking home? Talking to a friend? Or deciding I'm not trustworthy enough to deserve his love? Maybe he's thinking of how to revoke his prom-posal and ask someone else instead. A nervous cramp takes hold in my stomach. I leap off my bed and sprint for the door, gastrointestinal distress imminent.

When I get back to my room, my skin six shades paler than usual, I have three unread text messages—and they're from Riggs. I hold my breath, open them, and read:

> Love you too

> So fucking much, btw

> Can be in the library by 6:45/7. Movie night on our couch?

Relief washes over me. We're good, at least for now. I type back:

> See u there!!!

Riggs volunteers to pick the movie the next day; he says he has an idea and wants to surprise me. After lacrosse practice and team dinner, he meets me at our couch in the library, where I've already been parked for a few hours, chipping away at my extra-credit English essay.

He plops down beside me and opens his laptop but tilts it away so I can't see what he's pulling up. "Okay . . . are you ready?"

I put a period at the end of a sentence, hit save, and shut my screen. "Ready."

Smiling proudly, like a kid showing off their report card, he flips the laptop around. "Ta-da! I figured this would be high on your list, knowing you."

Right away, I recognize it. It's this sexy-as-hell romance movie about rival private investigators working for a married couple who suspect each other of cheating. The PIs have sex; the married couple has sex with each other *and* with their side-pieces. . . . Basically, everyone with a pulse in this movie has sex. I know this because Jess and I went to see it in theaters one weekend in January. I'm almost certain I told Riggs about it at the time, when he called me from the bus heading back from an away basketball tournament.

Should I be honest and tell him I've already seen it? I don't know. It's adorable how he picked out a movie that he'd probably never watch on his own but that he knows I'll appreciate, and that he's *this* excited about it. He clearly forgot that I told him about the movie, but I don't want him to feel like he failed in any way. After yesterday's letter, I'm not sure I have the currency for that. And besides, my chest has started to flutter at the thought of rewatching some of those steamy scenes; I don't know if I'm nervous to essentially watch soft-core porn with my boyfriend, a little turned on by the prospect, or both.

I bounce on the couch cushion. "Ooh, good choice. I've been wanting to see this."

"Do I know you, or do I know you?"

"You know me."

Riggs looks over each of his shoulders. "So I heard it's good, but pretty, uh, graphic." He stands up and peers toward our usual hiding spot. "I think we should probably research some eighteenth- and nineteenth-century music history. If you know what I mean."

"Oh, *absolutely*," I reply, going along with the joke. "We have that group project on . . . bassoons . . . to finish."

Riggs breaks character and laughs. "Get over here, you weirdo. Let's bring some pillows."

I follow Riggs's lead and grab one of the squishy couch cushions. We carry them, along with the laptop and Riggs's earbuds, to the end of the secluded and rarely visited stacks, where we lean them up against the wall so we can sit on the floor and use them as backrests. The space isn't super wide, so I wriggle into his side and layer my inside leg over his. We each take one of the earbuds. When he presses play and the story begins to unfold—the story I don't need to follow *super* hard this time around—all I can think about is how grateful I am to be here.

He trusts me.

He loves me.

He's stroking the skin on the inside of my leg.

Two characters in the movie rip off each other's clothes and fall into bed in a tangle of limbs. I remember this part. Jess and I jokingly fanned our faces in the theater. Riggs leans in even closer to me and gently takes out my earbud. "I've been wondering . . . Would you ever wanna do that?" He kisses the spot behind my ear, and delicious shivers spread all over my body.

When I regain consciousness, I answer, "I would *love* to do that. . . ."

I've been ready to have sex with Riggs for a while now. I'm already on the pill because of my uncooperative ovaries, and Riggs could just nip to the drugstore for condoms. We're, like, *right there* every time we hook up in private, but I keep pumping the brakes when we get too close. I guess my inner romantic always thought it would be, well . . . *romantic* . . . if my first time felt special.

I know, I know, society makes way too big a deal out of the first time you have P-in-V sex. Plenty of couples don't even *have* that kind of sex in the first place. But the heart wants what the heart wants, and mine wants not only to be in love with the first person I do it with, but also to do it someplace that isn't the back seat of a Ford Explorer, with my neck bent against the door at some horrifyingly unergonomic angle.

Riggs smashes the space bar to pause the movie. "Really?"

"Someone's excited."

"Well, yeah. How could I not be?"

"I'm just wondering when we'll do it. And where."

"What's wrong with the Explorer?"

"Riggs, I love you, but my first time can't be in your car." I rest my head on his shoulder. "And I don't think it's a good idea for me to sneak into your room again."

"Okay, okay, yeah, I get that." He rubs his chin. "There has to be another option."

"Don't you think it'll just be easier if we wait until summer? It's not like I'm going anywhere." We haven't officially discussed what we'll do when Riggs goes to Duke in the fall, but I've been taking that to mean we're on the same page about giving long-distance a go. Why should geography trump love? "I'm sure both of my parents would be cool with you coming to visit, or I could take the train to the city or something."

He nuzzles his cheek against my hair. "Yeah, but the thing is, I'm probably gonna go down to Duke super early for training stuff. And I have my cousin's wedding at some place in the Caribbean, and this family reunion thing at some point."

I lift my head and look at him, concerned. "You mean we're not gonna see each other over the summer?"

"No, no, oh my God, of course we are." He cups my face between his hands and kisses me once on the forehead, once on the nose, and once on the mouth. "We're gonna figure out a time to see each other, I promise. Multiple times, because I wanna meet both your parents."

I grin. "Phew. You scared me for a second."

"Sorry, I totally didn't mean to. I just love you and I really wanna do this with you, and with my schedule so up in the air this summer, I figure it's easier to do it sometime before graduation, you know?"

"Yeah, I get it." I sigh. "But that doesn't fix the problem of where we're gonna find a bed."

An idea dawns on Riggs's face. "Holy shit."

"What?"

"Why didn't I think of this before? We could do it on prom night."

My heart skips a beat. We'd be like the main characters in a classic teen movie. We'd take an already-amazing night and make it perfect. "Whoa, I'm into this idea. Would we get a room at the Sentinel Lodge?"

"Well, we don't wanna miss the after-party at Prentiss's. His family has this sick lake house—but we could do it there. The place has, like, ten bedrooms. We could snag one of those."

"As long as there's no chance of Riley walking in on us . . ."

Riggs laughs. "If I know Prentiss, he's gonna be wasted by the end of the *pre*-prom party. He'll probably be dead by the end of the night. Don't worry." He taps the tip of my nose. "I'm gonna make this perfect for you. You deserve it."

"You deserve it, too."

"Me? I'm just some dumb lax bro who somehow ended up with the best girlfriend in the world."

"You are not a dumb lax bro!" I smack him on the arm

playfully before returning my head to his shoulder. "You're a very smart, sweet, sensitive, sexy lax bro. They really need to make more of you."

"I'll send your feedback to the manufacturers."

"Thank you. You know, I'm excited for the day when we don't need a whole strategizing session to figure out when we're gonna sleep together."

I don't think Riggs heard the last part. His earbud is already back in his ear, and he pushes play.

THURSDAY, MAY 4

10.0k upvotes

**Still Haunted by my Sullivan School experience.
(Trigger warning: sexual assault)**

Made a throwaway account and might delete this later . . .
we shall see. For now, it feels good to get it off my chest.
I've never spoken about this publicly before, but I couldn't
stay silent with all the news going around, especially all the
people shitting on Riggs's accuser and parroting the same
toxic trash his dad said on the *Janelle Show*. Regardless of
what happened between Brenton Riggs Jr. and that girl, and
regardless of the missing persons case, the shit I'm seeing on
social media about women making false reports is incredibly
damaging and needs to stop ASAP.

Let me tell you what happened to me when I reported my sexual assault to Philip Wheaton, then the headmaster of Sullivan School, which was all-boys at the time. In 1987, I was a ninth grader at Stewart Academy, Sullivan's sister school. I was starry-eyed and hopeful as my girlfriends and I boarded the school bus that would drive us to Sullivan for our first coed dance. Later, I would board it again in tears.

Only a few guys actually wanted to dance and have fun with us. Most of them would materialize out of nowhere, grope you in some horrible way, and run away again, laughing their heads off. One of them ripped my friend's dress in the process. She developed the rather convincing theory that it was some kind of game for them, because nothing else could explain their unwavering determination to show off their supposed sexual prowess.

I made the mistake of leaving the gymnasium alone to use the bathroom. I got lost trying to find it. A Sullivan boy I'd danced with earlier in the night—one who'd actually seemed nice—offered to show me the way. Instead, he guided me to the varsity men's locker room and took advantage of me. I won't go into detail but he was a lot bigger than me and I couldn't fight him off.

When I finally made it back upstairs, I decided I was going to tell someone. I was too young and naïve to know how hard it is to get people to believe you. The first teacher I found was Wheaton, who was milling around the lobby, shaking hands with his students and their dates. I asked if I could talk to him, and we went outside. I gave him the gist of what had happened, including the student's full name. I showed him the mark on my wrist. I assumed he'd be horrified and take action—I know, I know, young and naïve. He asked if we'd known each other beforehand, and I said yes, a little, we'd been dancing. He took this long, uncomfortable look at me, and said, "My dear, I'm a busy man, and I don't have time for 'he said, she said.' Might I suggest you be more judicious in what you choose to wear to these events, and how you choose to conduct yourself in front of the young men in there?"

I never set foot on Sullivan's campus again after that, but I heard of similar things happening to so many other girls.

TL; DR: The fact that Brenton Riggs Jr. is missing doesn't take away from the fact that his school has a history of sweeping assault allegations under the rug, and I know because it happened to me.

CHAPTER 15

April, Twelve Days Ago.

I try to take lots of deep breaths as I sit cross-legged on the floor of Tasha's bedroom, using a curling iron plugged into a power strip alongside a half dozen other hair appliances. Tasha's desk has been cleared off and transformed into a makeup table, and the duvet on her queen-size bed is hidden beneath the new "quilt" composed of our colorful, sparkly prom dresses and—in Jess's case—a sparkly magenta suit.

Tasha waggles her eyebrows at me. "I can't believe you're gonna do it tonight. How does it feel?"

I let out a long exhale. "Exciting, but also extremely nerve-racking?"

"Oh my God, I was terrified before my first time, too," Kavita says.

"Did it end up being okay?"

"Nothing bad happened," she responds with a laugh. "But nothing *good* happened either. He pumped away for, like, forty-five seconds, rolled over, and asked if I 'liked that.'" She shrugs.

"I lied and said yes because I was happy to have finally done it, but then the problem was he had no incentive to work on his skills."

"You really have to communicate," Tasha says. "At first, I assumed that Mar and I liked the same stuff, because, ya know, same parts, but . . ."

". . . we are *very* different," Marina finishes. "I had to be like, 'Babe, to the left.'" She mimes giving directions with her hands, and Tasha swats her playfully.

"At least I've always kept my nails short!"

Marina turns to the rest of us, rolling her eyes. "I forget to clip my nails *one time,* and this girl acts like I've never heard of the lesbian manicure."

"Antoine—may he rest in peace—did not know his way around down there, nor did he care to learn," Raquelle confesses. "Both times we had sex, it was just in-and-out thrusting the whole time. It was fine for like, a minute, but once the spit dried out, it did *not* feel good."

Tori cocks an eyebrow. "You know there's lube, right?"

Raquelle blinks at her. "Oh. I never even thought of that."

"I can't speak to P-in-V stuff," Zoë chimes in, "but Zeke was the same with the in-and-out thrusting, with his fingers. Is that really supposed to feel good?"

"I like it, but only if they touch the outside, too," Becca says. Erica nods.

"Well, that makes sense," Jess replies. "I read about this study that found something like eighty percent of cis women either need clit stimulation to orgasm, or say it makes the whole thing better. I saw a study about it."

This is a lot to process right now. My fingers shaking slightly,

I put the finishing touches on my last lock of hair and turn off the curling iron. Then I stand up, weave around my friends, who are busy concocting their own looks, and pluck my purple gown from the pile. Even though everyone else is still in their comfy clothes, I need to get dressed now, because Riggs is going to be here in fifteen minutes to take me to the pre-prom party at Riley's house.

I carry my dress into Tasha's en suite bathroom and shut the door behind me. I strip down to just my underwear and check myself out in the full-length mirror, seeing myself the way Riggs will see me later tonight, after prom, when we get to our room at Riley's. There's the dark-brown birthmark shaped like a three-leaf clover next to my belly button; the thin, white scar above my knee from when I slipped on a rock by the lake as a kid. I want Riggs to know every last detail of me, for every inch of my body to feel like home.

I step into the dress I bought at the mall that day in Plattsburgh. It's the shimmery lavender one with the corset top that's kind of impossible to do up—but at least it gives me decent boob support. I'm going to pair it with silver stilettos that I may or may not be able to walk in.

There's a knock at the door, followed by Jess's voice. "Need help with those ties in back?"

How did she know I was in the process of trying to dislocate my own shoulders again to fasten this corset contraption? I guess that's what best friends are for. "Yes, please!"

Jess comes into the bathroom, her black hair in a thick fishtail braid. She looks me up and down. "Damn, you look hot."

"*You* look hot."

"Just wait 'til you see me out of this flannel." She shuts the door and comes around behind me, taking the strings from my helpless hands.

"I think you can pull it tighter." I'm envisioning myself looking like one of those medieval bar wenches with cleavage up to their chin. "I want my boobs to look . . . you know . . ."

"Like something they'd describe in the olden days as a 'heaving bosom'?"

"Yes. That, please."

"Okay, but I also want you to be able to breathe. And not break any ribs."

"I mean, I could sacrifice a *few*."

She finishes tying the knot and looks up at me in the mirror. "You know you shouldn't have to sacrifice anything, right?"

The look on her face tells me she's not just talking about my heaving bosom, but I swallow and try to keep my expression casual. "Yep, I know." Whatever she wants to lecture me on, it's always worse when I try to resist it.

She rests her hands on my shoulders. "Sometimes I wish I could believe in love the way you do, and not be such a jaded bitch all the time." She laughs weakly, and the laugh turns into a sigh, and she spins me around to look at her for real. "But, Al, sometimes I also worry that you believe in love *so much* that you could end up"—she brushes a stray curl away from my eye—"overlooking things."

A wave of frustration rises inside me. I'm already bummed I have to leave Tasha's early, and I don't want to spend what little time I *am* here having a version of the same argument we've been having all semester. "Do we have to talk about Riggs again?"

"I don't just mean Riggs," she insists.

"What do you mean, then?"

"I mean . . . I don't want you overlooking your own happiness, either." She pokes the top of my chest. "Or your own heart."

The frustration ebbs, replaced by something else: an ache. It feels like longing—like missing a version of myself I've never even met.

"Be careful tonight, okay?"

"Okay."

"I love you, Al."

"Am I allowed to say it back, or is that believing in love too much?"

"Oh, the opposite rule applies to me. You're contractually obligated to love me until the ends of the earth."

We share one of our classic snort-laughs. "Done and done."

She throws open her arms and wraps me in the warmest, softest hug—the one that's always been there waiting for me whenever I've needed it: in the fifth grade, when we'd only just met and my parents called to tell me my Bubbe had died—she saw me crying alone under a tree, and she came over and embraced me, no questions asked; in the ninth grade, after I embarrassed myself by trying to chat it up with that guy who was grinding with me; in the tenth grade, after the Sorceress practically skinned me alive in our first meeting; and I can't even count all the times she's held me up this past year, between dating stuff and school stuff. I turn my head and rest my cheek on her shoulder. Her scent, a blend of peppermint gum and warm vanilla body lotion, feels like home to me.

"By the way, Miss Jaded B-word, you can take this advice or leave it . . ." I step back so I can look her in the eye. "If

Sam's there tonight, I still think you should give him another chance."

Jess leans her butt against the counter and crosses her arms. "You know, it's funny you say that."

"Why?"

"Because we got put on the same team for an econ project the other week, and . . . well . . . we've sorta been talking again." A smile spreads across her face. I don't believe it: after all this time, there's a crack in Jess's rock-hard façade. "I should have listened to you after Village Night."

"Hey, better late than never. What finally swayed you?"

"I mean, part of me believed you were right about him, but I didn't want to go there because I'd already rejected him. So instead, I was like, 'Nah, screw that guy.' I got pretty good at convincing myself he was just some other dude in the King's Cup. But then this econ project came along."

"And . . . ?"

She smirks. "And I saw how much he shared my burning hatred of the other two bros in our group."

"I think we found two of the good ones."

"Yeah." Jess toys with the end of her braid. After a short pause, she chuckles. "Sam actually called the guys out on their bullshit the other day. I was proud of him, because they're both seniors. We sit down at the table in the library to figure out a plan for our presentation, and one of the bros is like, 'Someone should take notes.' And then he looks straight at me. I didn't even have my laptop open at that point, and he did. I was tired and *so* not in the mood to explain why it's sexist to assume women will take on administrative tasks, and was literally about to agree to it, when Sam jumps in and is like, 'You're right, Paxton. Someone should take notes. Why don't you do the honors?' It was such a small thing, but, like, I *felt that.*" She holds her hand to her heart.

"That's so awesome," I tell her, but a part of me burns with jealousy. I think about Riley discovering Riggs and me in the library, how exposed and embarrassed I felt, and how Riggs could have stood up for me, but instead he said, *Jealous, Prentiss?* Why couldn't he have shut Riley down the same way Sam shut down those guys who were messing with Jess?

My phone vibrates on Tasha's marble counter. It's a Face-Time from my dad. Grateful for the distraction, I pick up the call and get an intimate view up Dad's and Harry's nostrils.

"HAPPY PROM!" they scream in unison.

Jess claps her hand over her mouth, holding in a laugh.

"Thanks, you guys. Hey, can you hold the phone out in front of you? I can see your nose hairs."

"Good Lord, Jeff, that isn't cute," Harry says.

Dad moves the phone to a better angle and takes me in through his round tortoiseshell glasses. "I'll tell you what *is* cute, though: my daughter."

Jess pouts and mimes a tear rolling down her cheek.

"Honey, you look beautiful."

"Thanks, Dad."

"Can we see the whole dress?" Harry asks.

I switch to the front-facing camera and turn toward the mirror. Along the way, Jess says a quick hello to my dad and his husband before slipping out the bathroom door to finish getting ready.

Dad and Harry ooh and aah at my gown and make me spin in

a bunch of directions. "When's Riggs coming?" Dad asks. "Are you so excited to see him?"

"Yeah, he'll be here in a few minutes." The uncomfortable feeling from a minute ago burns with new life. Maybe I could use some perspective from people who've been teenage boys before. "Hey, can I ask you guys a question?"

"What's wrong, honey?" Dad already has a crease between his bushy eyebrows. "Is there an issue with Riggs?"

"No, no, no." I don't need him getting any negative ideas about Riggs, since I'm hoping he'll let Riggs come and stay with us in Philly this summer. "It's something really small. I was just wondering why guys have such a hard time calling each other out on problematic stuff sometimes."

"What kind of stuff?"

"You know, like, sexist stuff. Locker-room talk, and all that."

"I thought Riggs wasn't like the other lax bros," Dad says.

"He isn't!" I clarify. "I know deep down that he and I share the same core values and stuff. He just . . . doesn't always . . . express them."

Dad's face softens. "Listen, I know firsthand how hard it can be to go against the grain, so I feel for the guy—"

"But at the same time," Harry cuts in, "if he doesn't speak up, he's technically supporting whatever's going on."

I remember when I asked Riggs about the King's Cup that day in the library. He admitted the competition was stupid, but he also made me promise not to tell anyone about it. He said he wasn't trying to rat anyone out. I've known all along that silence is the same as complicity, but I guess I've been giving Riggs a break because I like him so much. If we're going to be together for the long haul, I want to see him walk the walk a bit more.

"Riggs needs to stand up for what's right," Harry declares. "He's a tough guy. He can handle the blowback."

"You're right," I tell him, nodding. "He can. Oh, shoot—he's here." Riggs just texted me that he's pulling into the driveway.

"Have so much fun tonight, hon," Dad says. "Send me lots of photos."

"I will. And thanks for the advice, you guys." I blow a kiss.

It's sad to say goodbye to the rest of my friends before I meet up with Riggs. Even though I'll see them again soon at the Sentinel Lodge, it would have been fun to stick around and take pictures with them on the back deck. Besides Tasha and Marina, they're all going as one big group: Jess, Raquelle, Tori, Kavita, Becca, Zoë, Erica. All the original Queen's Cup girls, minus me.

I sling my overnight bag over my shoulder and head downstairs to meet Riggs. Before I go, I pop my head into the living room to say goodbye to Mr. and Mrs. Thompson, who are sharing a bottle of wine and watching the local news station. "Welcome back to Channel 5 News," the anchor says. "I'm Isabelle Park. As we mentioned earlier in the program, despite the warmer weather we've been seeing recently, a major nor'easter is on its way, potentially bringing quite a bit of snow with it. We're going to go over to our meteorologist, Shay Kimball, for the latest on that. Shay?"

Shay Kimball starts to wave her arms across a screen with a bunch of wind and snow icons.

"They're projecting *twenty* inches?" Mr. Thompson gasps.

"I can remember a few big April snowstorms, but not like that," Mrs. Thompson says, turning to me. "You're taking proper shoes, right, hon?"

I pat the side of my bag. "Yep. And a jacket."

"Good. I'll make sure Tash and the others do the same." She looks at her husband. "Neil, maybe you should run over to Hannaford to get some pantry stuff for the next few days." She peers into the almost-empty glass in her hand. "Hmm, maybe you'd better hit up the wine store, too."

While Mr. Thompson shakes his head and mutters something about cancelling his bird-watching plans, I thank the couple for hosting me and head toward the door.

CHAPTER 16

Outside, there's a cool breeze that still has a bit of a bite to it. Goose bumps travel up my arms and the hair on the back of my neck stands up. Riggs does an exaggerated double take when I teeter down the front walkway in my silver stilettos. Thankfully, Tasha loaned me a pair of flip-flops to stash in my bag so I don't break both of my ankles on the dance floor later.

"Alyson, you look beautiful."

His words warm me up from the outside in and help to ease my jitters. "Thanks. You look great, too."

He's in a light-gray suit that must have been tailored, because it fits him the way clothes look in magazine ads, the fabric hugging his quads in the same delicious way his uniform pants do. Underneath his jacket, he wears a crisp, white dress shirt, and—because I told him the color of my gown—a light-purple tie with tiny silver dots. He opens the plastic box that was resting on the hood of the car and takes out my corsage: a pretty purple rose with white baby's breath around it. I'm wearing the charm bracelet he got me for Valentine's Day on my right wrist, so I hold out my left hand for him to slide it on. Suddenly, I don't have FOMO about leaving Tasha's early.

With shaking hands, I try not to stab myself as I fasten the matching boutonniere to his lapel. He looks over my shoulder and nods at Tasha' house. "The place where it all began," he muses.

Oh my gosh, he's right. Seven months ago, at this very house, Riggs rescued me from Riley's clutches and asked me to be his date to the Fall Festival. This is the place where we first became an *us,* and now, here we are again, writing a new chapter in our love story. I couldn't have written it better myself.

I look up into his eyes and murmur, "I love you."

His kiss sends shock waves through my body, because tonight, a kiss isn't just a kiss; it's a precursor to something much bigger. I'm nervous, but I think we're making the right choice by going all the way tonight. "I love you so fucking much, Alyson Benowitz," he says.

Scratch that. I *know* we're making the right choice.

Riggs opens the passenger-side door for me and pats my butt as I climb into the car. Once we're buckled up, he pulls out of the driveway and steers the car around Mirror Lake.

As we turn off the tree-lined street, I glance at the sky through the front window. It's a soulless expanse of silver-white, the way the lakes look when they're frozen over. Way off to the north is where things get dicey: there's a clear line where the sky turns dark purple, like a two-day-old bruise.

"Yikes, that doesn't look good." I point out the purple sky to

Riggs. "They were saying on the news that we might be getting, like, record-breaking amounts of snow."

"I'm sure it won't be that bad. The media loves to exaggerate that shit. Riggs slides his hand through the slit in my skirt and rubs my leg. "Whatever happens, I'll keep you warm."

I twist sideways in my seat and take him in. I know he isn't perfect—that there are still a few things I'd love for him to work on—but he's pretty darn close. And we have all the time in the world to learn from each other and grow together; that is, as long as my anonymous letter-writer doesn't go all Hollywood and decide to ruin my life on prom night—a nightmarish idea that I'm trying to keep locked in the deepest, darkest corner of my brain, so as not to be even more anxious than I already am. Great, now I'm thinking about how I'm not thinking about it, which is the same as thinking about it. I need to distract myself.

"Riggs, did I mention I love you?"

He sneaks a glance at me and smirks. "I think you might have, at some point." He turns back to the road just in time to steer us around a traffic jam that's formed at the entrance to the grocery store parking lot. "Whoa, Hannaford is bumping tonight."

"I think people are stocking up before the storm." Shoppers exit through the sliding glass doors pushing carts that are practically overflowing. A guy walks out of the liquor store next door with both arms wrapped around giant paper bags. Mr. Thompson had better hurry up before all the supplies are gone.

"Oh snap, this is our turn." He pulls off the main road onto another tree-lined street, and we carry on toward Riley's.

*   *   *

By the time we're taking photos with the lacrosse team and their dates at the Prentiss's lake house, I don't have it in me to worry too hard about anything: not the storm, not Riggs, not the two threatening letters I've declined to obey. I'm under the spell of prom night, giddy and smiling and laughing at everything. The crystal flute of champagne Riley handed me when we walked in is probably helping.

I lean against the deck rail, finishing my drink, as Riggs and Cameron pose for photos with their arms around each other's shoulders. Suddenly, there's a hand on the small of my back. It doesn't just rest there, but scratches, like a stiff claw. "Can I get you a refill?"

It's Riley, his other hand strangling the neck of a champagne bottle. I'm surprised by how friendly he's acting, given the obvious rivalry he has with my boyfriend. It wasn't long ago that he was staring down his nose at us in the library and ordering us to get a room. I hold out my glass. "Uh, sure."

He flicks his blond hair out of his eyes and tops me up. "There you go. You can always come find me if you need more . . . or if you just wanna hang with me instead of your golden boy over there."

As if I would ever go out of my way to spend one-on-one time with Riley. "So you're flying solo tonight?"

His face darkens. "Fuck prom dates, man. Why take a date when you could save yourself the hundred bucks and spend it on booze?" He's definitely slurring his words. I'm guessing his starring role in one of the original Queen's Cup takedowns made him a less-than-desirable prom date option for the girls of Sullivan-Stewart. Then, to my horror, Riley takes a swig of champagne directly from the bottle.

I glance at the drink in my hands. Thank God I didn't ingest any of his backwash. I set the flute on the railing, abandoning it, before smiling politely at Riley. "Well, I'm glad that's working out for you. I'm pretty happy about going with Riggs, though."

"Of course you are," he mutters. "Who wouldn't love to be Brenton Riggs Jr.'s prom date?"

"Did I hear my name?" Riggs calls as he saunters across the deck. When I turn back to Riley to ask what he meant by his last comment, he's already gone.

Riggs pulls me into a one-arm hug, a drink in his other hand. "What the fuck was Prentiss bugging you about?"

"I think he's pissed he doesn't have a date. He seems jealous of you."

"Everyone's jealous of me," Riggs says matter-of-factly. "Did you kindly remind him you're all mine?"

"I did."

Riggs squeezes me tighter. "Atta girl. C'mon, let's go have a look at our room."

He takes me by the hand and pulls me into the house, up a sweeping curved staircase, and through a door at the end of a hall. Inside, there's a king-size four-poster bed. My heart thumps at the thought of what we'll do there later.

Riggs points at the window. "You should go check out the view."

While he busies himself with something behind me, I cross the room and stare out at the churning lake. The wind is picking up, making whitecaps on the water. The purple is taking up more of the sky since I last looked.

"Okay, enough view-checking-out," Riggs says. "You can turn around now."

When I follow his orders, I clap both my hands over my mouth. Apparently, while I was looking the other way, Riggs scattered rose petals all over the comforter. I would let myself cry if not for the makeup Tori did for me, so instead I settle for saying "oh my God" over and over again.

"I'm glad you're into the whole rose petal thing." Riggs pulls an empty sandwich bag out of his pocket and dangles it between his fingers. "I felt like a freak carrying them around this whole time."

I physically *can't* handle his cuteness. I close the gap between us and wrap my arms around his waist. "All men should walk around with baggies full of rose petals in case of an emergency."

"No way. Then any random clown could impress you."

"Nuh-uh. You're the only random clown I want."

Bam!

Something smacks the other side of the wall hard enough to rattle the framed painting of a hunting dog in the snow. I jump, and the top of my head smacks Riggs in the chin.

"What the hell was that?" I ask.

"Ah, fuck." He pulls his hand away from his mouth, and there's blood on the tips of his fingers.

"Oh my God, did I just do that?" My face burns.

But it's nothing compared to the way I feel when there's a second smack on the wall, and someone screams in a high-pitched voice, "Oh, Riggs! Yes!" It sounds like a boy pretending to be a girl having sex—pretending to be *me* having sex. "Take me from behind, Riggs!" Another boy guffaws.

Just like that, I'm back in the music history section of the library, the flames of embarrassment spreading from my cheeks down to my neck, my shoulders, my chest, my hands. Only that time, Riggs didn't come to my rescue. He let me burn. This time, his bloody mouth contorts into a scowl, rage written all over his face.

I had that whole pep talk with Dad and Harry, but in the end, I don't even have to ask Riggs to stick up for me. He wipes his lips with the back of his hand, blood smearing down his middle finger. He wrenches open the guest room door with so much force that hairline cracks form in the paint near the hinges, then storms out into the hall. There's a crash, followed by a series of yelps from the guys who were guffawing a few seconds ago.

"What the fuck, Riggs? Get off me!" It sounds like Devon.

"Learn to take a joke, bro." *Riley*.

"It wasn't funny," Riggs growls. "Don't you dare fucking disrespect her like that again."

"Why?" Riley drawls. "Because she— *Ow!*" When he talks again, it sounds like he's holding his nose. "That fucking hurt!"

"Good. I'm glad."

When Riggs marches back into our room, I no longer feel bad about accidentally driving his teeth through his bottom lip with the force of my skull. Instead, I feel like I want to skip the prom and dive into these rose petals ASAP. I throw my arms around his shoulders, and when I stare into his ice-blue eyes, I see our future more clearly than ever before.

Except for one unsettling thing that just occurred to me. "Wait, did you tell the other guys about our plans tonight?"

"*No,*" Riggs answers emphatically. "I think they just saw us come upstairs together and decided to be dumbasses. Prentiss is drunk already." He tucks a strand of hair behind my ear and cups my cheek in his palm. When he speaks again, his voice is softer and more serious at the same time. "I've always kept our relationship between us," he promises. "You know I'm not like the other guys, Alyson. You've known it all along. It's why I had such a huge crush on you from the first time we talked at Tasha's. You didn't treat me like I was just another problematic lax bro."

"Because you're *not.*"

"But not everyone would take the time to realize that."

I smile, and so does he. "Jesus, Riggs, there's still blood on your lip."

His grin turns devilish. "Kiss it better, then."

And I do, with every ounce of love I have to give. The weight of his body pushes me backward, and we stumble, kissing each other hungrily, until my back is against the cool glass I was looking out of while Riggs scattered the petals on the bed.

A few seconds later, Cam calls up to let us know the limos are in the driveway. We break apart, the same delirious grins on our faces as before.

Riley must have just gotten downstairs, because we hear someone ask why there's Kleenex shoved up his nostrils. "Don' worry aboudit," Riley grumbles.

Riggs and I burst out laughing.

Prom is going to be amazing; I can feel it. Showing off the sexiest goddamn dimples I've ever seen on planet Earth, Riggs pulls me toward the door—toward the greatest night of our lives—and away from the window with a view of the gathering storm.

CHAPTER 17

Between the setting sun, the incoming weather, and the huge elevation, the air has more than a little bite to it when we climb out of the limo in front of the Sentinel Lodge. My teeth chatter as we wait in line to show our tickets to the Sorceress, who's stationed at the door of the venue in a characteristically foreboding black cape.

When we get to the front of the line, she scrutinizes us with a piercing stare. Why does she volunteer to chaperone every fun social event when she clearly hates joy more than anything else on Earth?

"Good evening, Alyson," she says to me. To Riggs, she merely holds out her palm to accept the tickets.

"Hey, Mrs. Cole. How are you?"

"I'm fine, thank you." Her gaze travels to Riggs, then back to me. "How are *you*?" She puts a little extra emphasis on the "you."

She's acting like there *should* be something wrong with me, although in defense of her strange behavior, the last time we had a one-on-one meeting, I was about 0.4 seconds away from a full emotional breakdown. Since I mostly avoid her at all costs, we haven't had a chance to talk since I hauled myself back from rock bottom. "I'm great!"

She purses her lips. "Really?"

"Yes, really."

"Okay." It's the kind of "okay" that says *I think you're wrong, but I'm also not gonna stop you.* "Well, if you need anything, I'll be around," she says.

What a buzzkill. "All right, thanks!"

She nods and ushers us in with a sweep of her arm, then turns her attention to Riley, who spent the better part of the car ride gargling mouthwash and spritzing himself with cologne to hide the scent of alcohol oozing from every pore. Now he reeks in a different way, and I'm happy to put some distance between us.

We follow the thumping bass up a sweeping flight of stairs and into a big, round ballroom with fancy tables surrounding a dance floor that's lit up with the Sullivan-Stewart logo. Shiny red and gold streamers drape the walls, and string lights snake around the wooden beams that stretch across the vaulted ceiling. There's a buffet table, a photo booth with a bunch of fun props, and a DJ who's already fist-pumping.

The opposite wall is entirely glass, looking out on a sea of trees and rocky cliffs. I point to a set of French doors. "Let's go see what's outside before it gets too dark and cold."

"Whatever your heart desires," Riggs says.

We cross the dance floor, weaving around the brave (or drunk) couples who are already letting loose. We exit through the French doors and find ourselves on a flagstone patio ringed by an iron railing, where people snap photos in front of the scenic overlooks Mrs. Quigley described. We say hi to a few of Riggs's senior friends.

"Would you mind taking a few shots of us?" Riggs asks one of his buddies, already holding out his phone. I'd been hoping for the same thing, but didn't want to interrupt their conversation.

"No prob," the friend says.

Riggs pulls me over to the iron railing. We pose with his arm around my shoulder and my hand and cheek resting on his chest. "Nice," the friend calls out.

I look up at Riggs and kiss him.

"That one was good, too," the guy says.

Maybe I'll get these photos framed and give them to Riggs as a graduation present. He can put them up in his dorm room next year so it's like I'm always with him. If I end up getting into Overbrooke, which is in Washington State, we'll need to work extra hard to stay connected. I, for one, am not above Zoom sex.

Ready to explore the rest of the outdoor area, we descend a steep staircase to the lower terrace. Down here, the patio area ends in grass, and a bunch of different hiking paths split off into the trees. There's a sign that says:

WARNING:
STEEP TERRAIN
PATHS SLIPPERY IN RAIN AND SNOW
DO NOT ENTER IN INCLEMENT WEATHER

I'm about to make a joke about our prom night hiking plans being foiled, when I spot my friends over by a wildflower garden. With a rush of excitement, I grab Riggs's hand and lead him over to Jess.

"Please say hello to my boyfriend, who kicked off the night by punching Riley Prentiss in the face."

At first, Jess blinks in shock at the announcement. "Wait, what?" she asks, looking back and forth between us. "What happened?"

"Riley and Devon were imitating me having sex—it was really disgusting—and Riggs just took off and . . . *bam!* Riley rode in the limo with Kleenex in his nose." I know I'm talking fast, but I want Jess to know Riggs *did it.* He stood up for me the same way Sam stood up for her. Riggs and Sam: feminist icons.

Jess's expression goes from shocked to impressed. "Holy shit!" She turns to Riggs. "Well done, sir."

"It was my absolute pleasure," Riggs replies. "Seriously, though: it's fucked up the way they treat girls. I can't let that shit slide anymore."

"Brenton Riggs Jr., welcome to the resistance."

And then something incredible happens. Jess extends her hand, and Riggs shakes it.

As my boyfriend greets the rest of my friends and compliments their outfits, Jess pulls me close and slings an arm over my shoulder. "Benowitz, I'm about to do something I don't do very often," she says.

"Oh? What's that?"

"Admit that I was wrong. Maybe. Just a teensy bit."

"About . . . ?" But my heart's already soaring.

"Riggs. He's actually . . . kind of charming."

"You know, he carried a plastic bag of rose petals in his suit pocket all afternoon so he could surprise me and scatter them on the bed."

"He did *not*."

"Indeed he did." I bump my hip against hers. "So, have you seen Sam yet?"

She bites her bottom lip. "We ran into each other for a hot sec, and I told him he looked great, and he said I did, too, and that we should talk more at some point soon."

"Yay!"

"I was on my way to take photos, so I was like, 'I'll find you later tonight?' And he looked straight in my eyes in this super-hot way, and he was like, 'That would be great, Jess.'" She sighs dreamily. "You know, Al, maybe we really *did* find two of the good ones."

And they all lived happily ever after. Okay, fine, I'm not a psychic, but those are the vibes I'm getting from this night. Riggs, evidently working overtime to make sure this night goes better than the winter semiformal, makes no objection to joining me on the dance floor, where we jump up and down singing along to the music, sway to a couple of slow songs, and yes—my lifelong goal, unlocked—even have a conversation while he grinds on me from behind. If we were back in the rom-com I envisioned during the November Wilderness Excursion—the one with our falling-in-love montage—this would be the other montage that comes at the end, the one that says *Don't worry, despite all that other shit that went down, everything's gonna be all right.* There might even be a freeze-frame on our smiling faces, and a cheesy text bubble that says, *Alyson and Riggs are going strong despite the distance. They've been flying cross-country to visit each other, but if airfare gets too expensive... there's always a dogsled.*

Riggs slides his arms around me from behind and plants a kiss on my cheek. "It looks like Coach Pierce just got here!" he shouts over the music. "You mind if I go say hi for a bit?"

"Go for it!"

I could use a minute to cool off, anyway. We've been dancing for like an hour straight, and the amount of underboob sweat I'm currently producing could probably fill a swimming pool. While Riggs jogs off to the group of lax bros circled around their coach, I make my way to the bar.

By the time I have my water, a giant ring has formed on the dance floor, with none other than Tasha and her theater friends performing in the middle. Sipping my drink, I drift to the outer edge of the circle and take in the scene so I can bottle it forever. Everyone seems so alive and in love. Marina watches her girlfriend adoringly, while Jess and Sam talk with their faces an inch apart. Jess is twirling the end of her braid around her finger, which probably means they're discussing the prom industrial complex, or something else that's *really* turning her on. As I lift my glass to my lips, my charm bracelet from Riggs twinkles in the glow of the string lights.

A hand lands on the top of my butt. I assume it's Riggs, back from his chat with Coach Pierce. "I missed you!" I call over my shoulder. "Did you know Sahil could break-dance like that?"

The fingers curl into a claw and scratch at the fabric of my dress. Then a wave of cologne slams into me, and I whirl around and find myself face to face with Riley, whose cheeks are flushed *very* pink and who already has a bruise blooming underneath his left eye.

"Heeeyyyy, Alyson." He burps and blows it out the side of his mouth, because time is a flat circle and we might as well be back in Tasha's kitchen. When he shifts his weight, he stumbles, and it takes a second for him to regain his balance.

I really don't want to hang out with him, but I also don't want him collapsing onto the floor and cracking his head open or something. "Hey, are you okay?"

"I'm fine. This whole thing is fiiine." He tries to flick his bangs out of his eyes, but they're plastered to his sweaty forehead and they don't move. "But you know what would make it waaayyy better?" His hand lands on my shoulder like a slab of meat. "You . . . and . . . me."

This conversation is getting *way* too similar to the one we had at Tasha's. I scan my surroundings. This was around the point last time when my knight in shining armor swooped in and rescued me. But I don't see him.

A harsh, cruel laugh explodes from Riley's mouth. He must have continued drinking since he got here, because his breath smells like sour liquor. "Awww, are you looking for Riggs? Your perfect boyfriend who everyone loves *sooo* much?"

I glare at him, my irritation rising. "So what if I am?"

Riley takes a lurching step closer. "He doesn't love you. Never has."

This is the most pathetic ploy imaginable to get me to hook up with him. "Thanks for that." I look around, but Riggs still isn't within eyeshot. I'm going to have to extricate myself this time around, if I can find a way to get his hand off my shoulder. "You know what, Riley? I think I'm gonna go to the bath—"

"I'm serious. He doesn't give a shit about you." He squeezes my shoulder harder. "Sorry to be the bearer of bad news, but that motherfucker's in the King's Cup. You know what that is?"

I stop looking for Riggs and turn my whole focus to Riley, my annoyance molting into white-hot anger. "Wow, Riley, that's low, even for you," I spit. "Go be a jealous idiot somewhere else and leave me and Riggs alone." It feels good to unleash on him, to let go of the instinct to be polite at all times. If he's gonna try to trick me into hating my boyfriend, he can go and fall on his head all he wants.

"You're not listening to me," Riley implores. "I said . . . that . . . mother . . . fucker . . . is . . . in . . . the . . . King's . . . Cup. You don't think he texted the whole team and told us how he was gonna fuck you in that room at my lake house?" He puts on a bro-y caveman voice, apparently imitating Riggs. "'Yooo, check out these rose petals. Girls get wet for the dumbest shit.'"

It feels like tripping and falling into a well. I know I'm still standing at the edge of the dance floor, but I can't hear the music or feel my face and everything's gone dark at the edges. It's one thing for Riley to say Riggs is in the King's Cup, but it's another for him to know a specific detail like the rose petals. Still . . . there has to be an explanation. Riggs could have told his friends about our plans to have sex because he was *excited*. I mean, I told my friends, too. We had a whole conversation about it in Tasha's bedroom. "I still don't believe you," I tell Riley, but my voice isn't as strong as it was when I unleashed on him.

"You want the proof?"

What I want is to erase this conversation from existence and go back to my end-of-movie montage, but it's too late. Riley's scrolling through a group thread on his phone. He hiccups, then reads aloud: "From six-thirteen p.m., today: 'King's Cup-date: Put rose petals on the bed, lmao. I'm getting it tonight, and I'm gonna win. Suck it, pussies.' That was from Riggs, by the way. The competition is *tight* this year. You guys hooked up enough that he's neck-and-neck with a buncha guys who had sex. Including me." He waggles his barely-there eyebrows.

"You're making this all up."

"Oh, am I? Look." He flips the phone around and holds it up to my face, so I have no choice but to read the words my boyfriend typed. He sent it while we were in the limo—while my hand was probably resting on his knee. "You wanna see more?" Riley asks. "I have months of this."

I'm still plummeting down the well. Prom has disappeared; the only thing I see at the end of my tunnel vision is Riley. He means nothing to me—nothing except a vehicle for more information. "Show me." As he starts to scroll, it occurs to me that Riggs could come back at any moment and see what we're doing. I grab Riley's wrist to stop him. "Let's go to the terrace."

I march through the French doors, Riley stumbling along behind me. I hardly feel the cold wind as it whips against my skin. I lead us over to the iron railing, where we won't be lit up by the sconces on the outside of the building. Then I hold out my palm for Riley's phone.

"Read as much as you want," he slurs.

I don't want to, but I know in my heart that I have to. Under the starless sky, I start to work my way backward through Riggs's texts to his teammates. It would take ages to

spot every text about me in a year's worth of conversation—
except for the fact that Riggs started every one of them with
the same words.

From after we watched the movie in the library:

> Riggs: King's Cupdate: Sat through the worst
> movie ever but she agreed to fuck so how bad
> was it ACTUALLY, lmao. You know what? Give
> this movie an Oscar.

From when he asked me to prom:

> Riggs: King's Cupdate: Hey Prentiss, pro tip:
> if you don't wanna get your ass kicked by
> a bunch of girls, ask a chick to prom over
> FaceTime. Btw, she said yes. Y'all know what
> that means. 🍆

From after Valentine's Day:

> Riggs: King's Cupdate: Dropping the L-bomb:
> a small price to pay for continued 🍆. Had
> to deploy it ASAP bc she totally heard some
> douche call my dad "king" at the athletics
> brunch. She straight-up choked on her food.

> Cam: Now she's gonna choke on your 🍆

> Riggs: LMAOOOOOOO

Every text is a dagger that stabs me in the heart. I was right: Riggs's dad must have won the King's Cup way back when . . . but I was wrong to convince myself Riggs was nothing like him. Does Mrs. Riggs realize her angel son is just as bad as his father? God, I should have known from the way he's always idolized him. Why didn't I see it? Or *did* I? Maybe I chose to look away, to see our love story instead.

I use my phone to take pictures of the incriminating texts on Riley's screen. I don't know what I'm going to do with them, but it seems like a good idea. I keep scrolling and hitting my camera button.

From Village Night:

> King's Cupdate: Yooo, huge Cupdate. I'm walking to the car when I run into Alyson. She's crying and shit because of how much she's missed me, and then she says . . . drumroll . . . SHE LOVES ME. I was wrong about this chick. She's not trying to reject anyone. She's safe. I'm going balls deep, lmao.

Another dagger to the heart.

When I told him I loved him, it was the first time I'd said those words romantically to anyone. They . . . they felt like a gift.

A gift that meant nothing to him. Nothing except reassurance that he could keep on using me.

Gritting my teeth through the pain, I force myself to read that last text again so I can piece together the terrible truth: Riggs didn't get back with me in January because he'd missed me; he did it because my word-vomit L-bomb gave him proof that I hadn't been trying to humiliate him at the winter semi-formal. It proved to him that I was "safe"—that he could keep on using me without risk of rejection. And there I was thinking *I* was safe—that I'd locked in the one good lax bro at Sullivan-Stewart, or maybe on planet Earth.

I scroll faster, not caring if I miss some. I already have the truth about Riggs: he's been conning me all along. There's just one burning question I still need to answer.

"You should read the one about the card," Riley blurts out. I almost forgot he was here.

"The card?" But no sooner have I spoken the words than a text from early November jumps out at me.

> Riggs: King's Cupdate: Bow down to the king, assholes. Made a card asking Alyson to be my girlfriend. Kept it in my backpack, ready to deploy when needed. The other day, we're hooking up in the car and she gets all shy about taking off her shirt. So I give her the card. And it fucking worked!!! Today . . . 😈

"Told ya," Riley sneers.

"Shut up, Riley."

I so badly want to hurl his phone off the balcony and into the void. But I keep scrolling, searching for the text that'll tell me the only thing I still need to know: the reason he picked me to begin with. The dagger may be in my chest, but there's still a flicker of life in me, a tiny shred of hope that we may, at one point, have had a genuine connection.

I go all the way back to September, to the first days of the school year. My breathing clipped and shallow, I read some of Riggs's first "Cupdates."

> Riggs: King's Cupdate: According to my dad (who won btw), the best move is to pick one and stick with her all year. Easy access whenever you want it, lmao. Now I just gotta find my target . . .

> Riggs: King's Cupdate: Lots of possibilities but I wanna choose the easiest one. Maybe I go down a grade . . .

> Riggs: King's Cupdate: OMFG I FOUND HER. Junior in my English class. Stares at me all the time. Seems desperate. Hot, though. Asked MacMillan to make her my partner on the first group project lmao. 💣💣💣

Desperate. The word forces the dagger the rest of the way in, all the way up to the hilt. My tears splash onto Riley's phone screen.

"Don't," he says. "That piece of shit doesn't deserve it."

But now that I've started crying, it's impossible to stop. It's not that my love story went off the rails; it's that I never even *had* a love story to begin with. After everything I thought we experienced together, I'm still the same desperate girl who left books in Aiden's mailbox. I haven't learned a fucking *thing.* I should make like my mom and give up on love; she's had the right approach all along. Better to have loved and lost? No. Better to have never loved at all.

"Listen," Riley continues, "I fuckin' hate the guy, too. He thinks he's *sooo* much better than everyone else, right? Don't you just wanna knock him off his high horse?"

I nod because it feels good to hate on Riggs.

"So this brings me back to what I was saying earlier." He comes closer, his hand finding my shoulder again. He uses it to steady himself. "There's a spreadsheet where everyone logs their points for the year. Riggs thinks he's gonna take down the other guys at the top, but we could crush him if we wanted . . . you and me, getting back at him . . ."

The hand that was on my shoulder slips down and grabs my chest.

"What the fuck, Riley?" I jump back, trying to get away from him, slamming into the iron railing and smashing my elbow in the process. His phone clatters to the ground, but instead of reaching for it, he grabs the bars on either side of me, pinning me in place. It's the same way he trapped me at Tasha's party, only that time I had a rescuer. I try to shove him off, but he's too heavy. I start to panic.

Riley smirks. "Don't scream or I'll push you over."

What the hell? Is he joking? I have no idea. He's drunk and acting erratically; for all I know, he could do it. His face comes closer, his lips parted and his sour breath suffocating me. With what little self-command I can muster, I wriggle around so my back is to him.

"Come on." He grinds into me. "I saw you in the library. You're normally a slut."

He pushes me into the railing with all his might, and pain explodes across my ribs. I can barely breathe. My head, neck, and shoulders jut dangerously over the edge, and I'm glad for the dark, for the clouds obscuring the moon and stars, because at least I can't look down and see my death.

And then something happens. I can taste the air again. Riley grunts as he gets knocked to the side, and a hand—small, but strong—closes around my wrist and yanks me away.

"Fuck you, Riley!"

The voice belongs to a girl, but I can't place it. My panicked brain is struggling to process anything beyond putting one foot in front of the other as we escape down the stairs to the lower terrace. I wince in pain with every step, but I focus on following the fast-moving figure in front of me. Finally, we make it onto flat ground.

"He didn't follow us, did he?" the girl asks. When she looks over her shoulder, I finally gaze into the face of my rescuer.

And it's the last person I expected to see.

CHAPTER 18

"Thank God," Chrissy breathes.

But there's fear written on every inch of her face. She squeezes her eyes shut and drags her nails down the sides of her head, like she's trying to fight off bad thoughts.

"Th-thank God you were there." My jackhammering heart makes my voice come out shaky. "Y-you got him off me. H-he was so heavy. I c-couldn't move. Chrissy, *thank you*."

She still has her eyes shut.

"Are you okay?"

She doesn't reply. It's like that time we were in the library's basement bathroom.

"Chrissy?"

Her throat bobs like she's swallowing something down. She opens her eyes, but her fingertips stay pressed into her temples. "Are *you* okay?"

No, not by a million light-years, but my brain's still playing catch-up with everything that's happened since I finished documenting Riggs's text messages: Riley grabbing me and pinning me to the railing; me trying to fight him off, then fighting for air; someone—Chrissy—wrestling him off me and whisking me to safety. I remember the things Riley said to me as he pressed me into the railing, words I can already feel etching themselves into the inside of my skull. The terror and shame slam into me like a tidal wave.

Sobs overtake me, but before I can crumple into a ball on the ground, Chrissy wraps her arms around me. When I return the gesture, I can feel her shaking, too.

We hold each other up.

Jess's voice comes from the top of the steps. "Al? Are you down there? Are you okay? I looked out the window and saw someone pulling you down the stairs."

"I'm here," I call back weakly, my cheek resting over Chrissy's heart. It's still pounding a mile a minute, even as my own panic subsides.

Jess hustles down the steps and hurries over to us. "What hap— Chrissy?"

We break apart, but I don't want to let her go completely, so I keep her trembling hands in mine. I get the sense she isn't ready to talk—not that I am, either, but I owe her one. I owe her everything.

I turn to Jess, my voice still weak. "Chrissy just saved me." I swallow. "From Riley."

She claps a hand over her mouth. "What?"

As little as I want to relive it, I need Jess to know. Jess loves me. Jess can help. I take a deep, shuddering breath. Then, starting with Riley approaching me on the dance floor, I rattle off the details as quickly as possible. If I linger on anything for too long, I'll start to feel, and feeling hurts too much.

By the end of the story, Jess is seething. "I swear to God I could kill Riley Prentiss. And Riggs—"

"I know." I turn back to Chrissy, who's been quiet this whole time, hoping to briefly distract myself from the memories playing on a loop in my head. "What was Riggs like when you were with him?"

Chrissy gives me a pleading look, like there's something she's dying to tell me but can't. Then . . . it's like something inside her snaps. She wrenches her hands from my grip and cups them over her nose and mouth. Tears spring from her eyes, and Jess rushes to her side as she starts to cry in angry, heaving sobs.

"Chrissy," I beg, desperate to know what she's bottling up, "what's going on?"

In between sobs, she finally lets it out. "He was a monster, Alyson!" She wraps her arms around her torso in her black spaghetti-strap dress.

"What did he do?" I whisper, my heart pounding.

Chrissy looks at me with glassy eyes, tears clinging to her lashes. "He raped me."

My body goes numb.

"I've been trying to tell you all year, but he—he and his dad—have made it impossible for me to say *anything* to *anyone*!"

As Jess comforts Chrissy, I stand there, frozen, remembering our first-ever interaction. Chrissy squeezed my wrist, dug her nails into my skin, and told me to watch out. She wanted me to stay away from Riggs, but it wasn't a threat.

"You tried to warn me at the Fall Festival."

As Jess rubs her back, Chrissy nods. I *knew* a threat seemed out of character for the bubbly girl I knew from assembly. Riggs sold me on the whole "crazy ex-girlfriend" trope, and I believed him, just like I believed all his evil lies. Mortified, I rack my brain for what else I might have interpreted the wrong way.

Oh.

Oh my God.

"Did you write me those letters?" I thought they were threats at the time, too, but the warnings were right there in front of my eyes. *STOP WHAT YOU'RE DOING. YOU'VE BEEN WARNED. I THOUGHT I TOLD YOU TO STOP. YOU'RE GOING TO REGRET THIS.*

Chrissy nods again.

"I feel so stupid," I groan.

"I had to make them cryptic," she says, her crying softer now. "I didn't have a choice."

"What do you mean?" Jess asks gently.

Chrissy manages to take a deep breath. "You can't tell anyone, okay?"

I move even closer, cocooning her between me and Jess. There are thousands of feelings and questions swirling around inside of me, but right now, I just want to be there for Chrissy the way she was there for me. "Your secrets are safe with us."

Something cold and wet lands on my nose: a snowflake. Looking up into the glow coming from the Sentinel Lodge, I can see them starting to fall.

"It happened during this varsity training program they did over the summer," Chrissy says, fighting to keep her voice steady. "Riggs and I had been together for a few months at that point, and I actually really liked him. When we first started hanging out on the lacrosse bus, I felt like he genuinely wanted to get to know me, which sounds like the lowest bar in the history of the world, but . . . *ugh.*" She rolls her eyes and sniffs. "I guess that's why I trusted him? God, I bet he was just searching for King's Cup targets early."

"Don't blame yourself," I tell her. "He knows how to turn on the charm."

"We were at this party at Riley's lake house," she continues. "I was wasted. I remember sitting in an Adirondack chair on the dock, and Riggs offering to put me to bed. Apparently, I gave him a double thumbs-up. The next thing I remember, he was on top of me." She swallows and moves along. "I did the thing they tell you to do. I told Coach Pierce, who was running the program, and he called a meeting with Philip Fucking Wheaton."

"What did they say?" Jess asks, her eyes wide.

"That I shouldn't have been drinking underage and that it was complicated because Riggs was my boyfriend."

Jess's jaw drops. "That shit doesn't matter! There wasn't enthusiastic consent."

"Yeah, well, try explaining that to two old white guys who want their golden boy to get into the best lacrosse program in the country."

"And who want his dad's donations to keep coming in," I add.

"Jesus Christ, his dad is a whole other story," Chrissy mutters bitterly. "After Riggs saw me trying to talk to you at the Fall Festival, I get this phone call from Brenton Riggs Sr., essentially threatening me. He's like, 'You're walking on thin ice, Miss Lin. If you keep spreading dangerous lies about my son, I can make your life very difficult. I have friends at every top college you're probably looking at. Don't test me.' " She gets a hopeless look on her face. "I was applying to all the Ivies, and I want to go to law school someday. I didn't know what he could do, but I couldn't risk getting denied. I just can't."

"So you quit lacrosse this year because of Riggs?" I ask.

Chrissy nods. "If I'd stayed on the team, we would have had all these long bus rides and tournaments together. I couldn't be around him like that—my whole body tenses up and I feel like I'm gonna cry when I see him from a *distance*." She sighs. "I was so, so sad to miss my last year of lacrosse."

"Do your parents know any of this?" Jess asks.

She shakes her head. "They think we just had a bad breakup and that I changed my mind about lacrosse, since I never planned to play in college anyway. But my friend Cassandra knows, and so does my therapist."

Another memory rushes back to me. "Now I understand why you just stood there staring at me that time I found you crying in the bathroom."

"Yeah. I didn't know you at all, and I was scared that if I told you anything directly, you might funnel it back to Riggs and his dad."

She sighs.

"Ever since Riley's party, guys have been coming up to me and flashing me the double thumbs-up. Like it's some inside fucking joke we have and not a memory of the worst night of my life. That's why I was crying when you came into the bathroom. I was feeling okay that day. I hadn't had a panic attack, and I was finally starting to believe the stuff my therapist was telling me. And then a group of guys I didn't even *know* walked by me in the library, made the stupid thumbs-up sign, and laughed their asses off."

Jess and I put our arms around Chrissy, holding her tight until a howl of wind makes us realize how bad the weather's getting. The snowflakes are more like snow-chunks now.

Chrissy shivers. "Thank you both for listening."

"You don't have to say thank you," Jess replies. "I'm so sorry you've been through all that."

"I'm so sorry, too, Chrissy."

"There's one silver lining to this shitty year," she says. "Now I know what kind of lawyer I want to be."

"What kind?" I ask.

When she looks into my eyes, I see kindness and fierce determination swirled together. "I want to defend people in situations like mine."

"You'll be amazing at that, Chrissy."

"Thanks." She smiles at me. Then she lets out a long sigh. "Now you know the full story of why I tried to warn you. I couldn't just stand by and watch a shitty guy ruin another girl's life."

"I appreciate you trying." Her words reverberate in my chest because I've said them before: about my mom, about all the girls I've helped through the Queen's Cup. Jess gives me a pointed look, and I know what she's thinking. I've rationalized going into vigilante justice mode for everyone else but me. Maybe it's time I end the double standard. I massage the side of my torso, where my ribs smart from Riley crushing me into the railing. *None* of us deserves to be treated like this.

"What are you going to do about Riggs?" Chrissy asks.

My mind goes blank. I've barely had a chance to absorb all

the disturbing revelations, let alone decide what I'm going to do about them. There's no question Riggs and I are over, but as far as he knows, we're still going back to Riley's together.

"Did I just hear my name?"

The voice that calls down to us is heavy with liquor, but there's no mistaking it. It makes my blood run cold—colder than it already is as I stand out here in the snow without a jacket. I peer through the flurries to the top of the steps, where Riggs's hulking form bears down on us.

I'm the one closest to the bottom of the staircase, and when he sees me, he grins. "There's my girl! I've been looking everywhere for you!" He starts to stumble his way down the steps. He's moving slower than usual, which buys me some time, but shit, I don't know what to do when he gets here. "Why are you out in the snow?" he muses. "Let's go inside, I'll warm you—"

He's midway through his descent when he notices Chrissy and Jess hovering behind me. Like a man who just realized he drank poisoned wine, his smile fades to shock.

"What are you doing with *her*?"

I don't say anything. I can't find the words.

"Al, c'mon. Get away from Chrissy. I told you she's fucking crazy. She makes shit up and I don't want her putting her lies in your head."

Something inside me shifts, and the pathway becomes clear. It's the one I forged with my own hand. It's the one Jess, the partner who's *truly* loved me this whole time, urged me to take from the start, when she warned me about . . .

Oh my God. The conversation Jess overheard about Riggs's "huge head start over the summer." Were the guys outside Jess's econ class implying Riggs got King's Cup points for . . . for raping Chrissy?

I've felt rage before, but never like this. This isn't a flame inside my chest. It's a huge ball of fire engulfing me, and I want it to destroy Brenton Riggs Jr.

Jess and Chrissy step closer, and I can feel the bond linking us together. It's a chain of steel, ten thousand times stronger than this gossamer chain around my wrist. And that's how I know that when I make my next move, whatever happens, I won't be alone.

It's time for me to join the Queen's Cup.

CHAPTER 19

I lift my chin and roll my shoulders back. "We're done, Riggs. I know you're in the King's Cup." *And* I know what he did to Chrissy, but I promised Chrissy I'd keep that between us.

"Al, no. You can't believe anything she tells you." He takes a few more steps down the stairs. "Tell me what she told you and I'll tell you why it's wrong."

"Chrissy didn't tell me anything. R-Riley did." It's hard to get his name out without bile churning in my stomach.

"You're gonna believe *Prentiss*? Al, are you—"

"I didn't have to take anyone's word for it. He showed me your whole group thread—all your 'King's Cupdates.'" I yank my phone out of my dress pocket and wave it in the air. "FYI, I took photos of everything you wrote. Can't wait to let the world know how you coerced a girl into hooking up with you all year so you could win some disgusting competition." I pretend to look scared as Riggs reaches the bottom step. "Oh no, do you think someone from *Duke* might see?" I'm making this up as I go along, trying to hit him where it'll hurt the most. "Can you be *sure* they'll be willing to protect you and keep you on the lacrosse team after they see all this? I mean, you're not a star there like you are here." I let out a harsh laugh in his face. "You almost didn't get in."

The curl of his lip lets me know my strike landed, but I gasp when he retaliates not with his words, but with a swing of his arm. I jump back, and his fingers close around empty air.

"Gimme the phone," Riggs snarls.

"No." I jam the phone into my pocket, adrenaline surging through my veins. "This is what you get for everything you've done."

Riggs bares his teeth like a wolf about to strike. "I said, gimme . . . the fucking . . . *phone.*"

I mimic him in as bro-y a voice as I can muster. "How about you leave us . . . the fuck . . . alone?"

Chrissy screams.

Riggs lunges at me, all six foot three of him, and in the moment before his fingers reach my neck, I know he wants more than just the phone. He wants to hurt me—worse than any lacrosse player he's ever checked to the ground. I hold up my arms to protect myself, but the impact never comes. Jess hurls her full body weight into Riggs's side, knocking him way off balance.

As he trips over his own feet and falls to the ground, he reaches out and grabs a fistful of Chrissy's dress, pulling her down with him.

"Chrissy!" I shout.

Chrissy releases a strangled cry for help as Riggs rolls her over and pins her underneath him, holding her hostage.

No. Jess and I react at the same time, and in the same way: with kicks aimed straight at his ribs. The combined force sends him toppling off Chrissy, and panting, we drag her to her feet.

I don't need to ask if she's all right; her bloodless face says it all. "Stand behind me, okay?"

She replies with a rushed nod.

"What do we do?" Jess whispers to us in a panic.

Riggs is climbing to his feet at the foot of the stairs, and we sure as hell don't want to go anywhere near him. I look around for another way into the lodge, but there isn't one. The lower terrace is built into the side of the mountain.

And then Riggs is standing again. He rounds on us, and the look in his ice-cold eyes leaves no question about how badly he wants to hurt me—to hurt all three of us. I know what we have to do. There isn't any other option.

I answer Jess with one word: "Run."

She leads the way to the only other place there is to go: a trail into the woods with a warning sign telling us not to enter in inclement weather. The wind howls, and the blizzard drives the snow down at a diagonal. It doesn't matter. We can't let him catch us.

It has nothing to do with preserving the text messages. For all I know, he could kill us.

The route would be hard enough to hike in optimal conditions, but running in prom dresses, in the light of our phone flashlights, and with the snow obscuring rocks and tree roots, is almost impossible. Without Jess's outdoor skills, we'd be in a lot more trouble.

"Keep following me," she calls over her shoulder as she leads the way down the steep, narrow trail. "Put your feet exactly where I put mine. And don't look behind you."

I'm the last in line. Over the wailing wind and the creaking of trees as they're bent out of shape, I can hear Riggs crashing along behind us. We hit a fork in the path, and Jess makes an arbitrary decision which way to turn; getting lost is better than getting caught. For a second, I think we might have shaken him, but then I hear the snapping of twigs and a deep grunt of frustration, and I know we have to press deeper into the trees.

I'm in flip-flops, and Jess is in Converse, but Chrissy is wearing strappy sandals with a low heel. None of our shoes were made for this, but hers especially so. She twists her ankle on a divot in the path and falls to the ground.

Riggs's grunts getting louder behind us, I stop to help Chrissy climb back to her feet. When I grab her by the arms, her skin is damp and freezing cold.

My stomach turns over.

How much longer can we go on like this?

"Shit, shit, shit." Jess stops moving and shines her flashlight up ahead. "This is gonna be bad."

Squinting through the heavy snow, I see the trees thin out as the path wraps around the side of a peak. On the right is a wall of rock. On the left is a steep drop that might as well be a black hole.

Jess inches forward. "Keep to the right as much as you can."

With her right hand, she grabs hold of the rock, using it to steady herself as she navigates the tricky terrain. Chrissy goes next, then me. The rock feels like ice; it's cold and slippery, and I know it'll be useless if any of us loses our footing again.

Don't look down. Don't look down. Don't look down. I repeat the words in my head with each step along the perilous path.

Jess swears again. When she calls to us, I can hear tears in her voice. "You guys, I can't even see where I'm going anymore."

She stops moving. Chrissy and I follow suit.

There's a loud crack as a branch snaps—way too close for comfort.

Shaking from fear and near frostbite, I turn to the right, switch the hand that's on the wall, and shine my flashlight back the way we came. There's Riggs, standing at the tree line, a twisted grin plastered across his scratched-up face. He must have careened into more than a few branches as he chased us.

I look into his eyes, searching for the boy who got lost in the woods with me back in November. The one who kissed me as the snow swirled around us, who pulled me onto his lap at the bottom of a hill, who showed me he was alive, who helped me imagine our future together. There's no trace of that boy in the cold eyes glinting before me. He was never there at all.

The real Brenton Riggs Jr. is a boy who sees power as his birthright, who fears no rules because they never apply to him. He's a Sullivan School legacy who's been taught that he's untouchable.

Maybe that explains the decision he makes, as the wind and snow pummel us from all directions, to run at me.

They say your body enters fight-or-flight mode at times like this, but I feel strangely calm. I guess because I can't do either of them. There's only one way this ends, and it's me going over the edge. I steel my body for impact. I have no idea how high it is—if the fall is survivable. For a split second, I fully accept the worst-case scenario.

But when the smooth sole of Riggs's dress shoe lands on a patch of snow, it goes sliding out from under him.

We all gasp—but not Riggs. His face freezes in shock as all two hundred and something pounds of him go airborne. Then, as his grim reality sets in, a terrified cry escapes his lips. "HELP ME!"

But it's too late, and we all know it. Pinned to the wall for our own safety, there's nothing we can do except watch in the beams of our flashlights as his body collides with the earth, slips off the edge, and plummets into the abyss.

CHAPTER 20

"Oh my God. Oh my God. Oh my God." I crouch down, hyper-ventilating. Beside me, Chrissy does the same.

Jess takes a half step away from the rock and shines her flashlight over the edge. "We're safe," she breathes. "I can't see him."

The relief of having the target off my back gives way to a new kind of panic. Mrs. Quigley kept talking about the steep drops around here. And I didn't hear him land.

"Riggs!" I scream. "RIGGS!"

The only reply is the howl of the storm.

Squinting against the wind and snow, I crawl to the edge of the path. I try his name again, screaming so hard my lungs hurt. "RIGGS!"

Still, nothing.

Cold fear works its way through my already-shivering body; I can hear it in my own voice. "W-we have to g-get help."

"Wait," Chrissy objects, her voice wavering, too. "I . . . I don't know. What are they going to think when we tell them what happened?"

"Wh-what do you mean?"

"What if they don't believe us that he slipped? What if they think . . ."

Chrissy's point sinks in my belly like a stone. She's a step ahead of me, and she's right: Riggs's fall won't necessarily look like an accident—not with *us* as the only three witnesses.

Jess lets out a string of curses. "Fucking hell. They're going to think we pushed him."

"Oh my God. Oh my God. Oh my God." I tug at my tangled hair, wet from the snow. "You guys, what the hell are we going to do?"

"You're going to listen to me!"

The words come from a dark figure that just materialized in the spot where Riggs was standing before he fell. A fleeting thought tells me it *is* Riggs, and I hallucinated the last two minutes. Maybe it's hypothermia setting in; isn't delirium one of the symptoms? But no, it can't be Riggs—because I know that voice: deep, gravelly, intense.

There's no avoiding her. From the ground, I look up and force myself to gaze at the dark outline of Mrs. Cole, the Sorceress, her curls and black cape blowing wildly. How did she know we were here? And most importantly, what does she think happened?

The idea that someone might think we pushed him haunts me; it wraps its hand around my throat and squeezes, and before I know it, the truth spills from my lips. I shout the full story:

the King's Cup; the Queen's Cup; the text messages saved on my phone; the life-or-death chase through the forest; and finally, the fall. "Mrs. Cole, please, you have to believe us," I beg.

And then, something remarkable happens. She says, "I do."

Did I hear her right? Chrissy and Jess don't say anything, either. I assume we were all expecting instant crucifixion.

Mrs. Cole isn't finished. "But others won't." She unclips the cape from around her neck and holds it open to us, like a blanket. "First things first, I'm going to ask you to get the hell off Widow's Pass and wrap yourselves in this. The three of you must be freezing."

Now I'm certain this is stage three hypothermia, because only delirium would make me think the Sorceress was on our side.

She beckons me again with a wave of her arm. "Let's go. Now."

We're already so screwed; how much worse could things get? My limbs shaking, I rise from the ground and gently, gently, ease my way back into the cover of the trees. When Jess and Chrissy follow suit, the Sorceress arranges our bodies into a tight clump and drapes the cape around our shoulders. "There you go."

"Mrs. Cole," Jess begins, "did you say we were on . . . Widow's Pass?"

"Yes."

Jess gasps. Clearly she knows something I don't.

"W-what's Widow's Pass?" I ask.

"The single most dangerous route in the Adirondacks," Mrs. Cole answers.

Jess sounds like she's going to be sick. "The drop . . ." Her voice trails off.

". . . is five hundred feet," Mrs. Cole supplies. "No hiker has ever survived that fall."

The blood drains from my head and I feel like I'm going to pass out. I keel over, hands on my knees, gasping for air. When the dizziness only gets worse, I collapse to the ground. I hear his panicked cry for help, I remember his body suspended in the air, and I imagine the whoosh as he fell through the sky—the darkness swallowing him. Riggs is dead.

Riggs.

Is.

Dead.

"It's too late to help him," the Sorceress says matter-of-factly, "but I'm going to do everything in my power to protect you girls. Alyson, stand up, please. You're going to start by deleting the photos of Riggs's texts from your phone."

Jess holds out her hand and helps me to my feet. I don't understand what's going on, or why, but I follow Mrs. Cole's order.

"Now, look at me," she says. If I thought I'd been on the receiving end of piercing Sorceress stares in the past, they were nothing compared to the look she gives each of us now, in turn. It's a look that tethers us together—a silent but powerful spell. "You can never tell a soul that you were out here, or that you saw Riggs fall. Do you understand me?"

The three of us nod.

"I don't mean to scare you, but this is serious. If the school, the authorities—*anyone*—finds out about this, my gut tells me they'll try to put the blame on you." Her eyes are as cold as the storm when she adds, "The world will bend over backward to protect a promising young man like Brenton Riggs Jr."

"Why are you helping us?" a tearful Chrissy asks.

Mrs. Cole's hardened voice fractures. "It's what I've been trying to do all year. It's why I moved over from Stewart in the first place, after the merger." She looks at the ground and sighs. "I know how I can come off, so I know it doesn't always seem this way, but I care about you girls deeply, and I was all too aware of what merging with Sullivan School"—she spits the name out—"could mean for your safety."

"What were you aware of?" Jess asks.

"I was a student at Stewart," Mrs. Cole replies, "which means I had my fair share of experiences with Sullivan boys."

A memory from the beginning of the year sticks out clear as day. "You told me you knew what Sullivan boys were like, and you were worried about the 'distractions.' I . . . I thought you said it because you'd *worked* at Sullivan." I feel terrible for assuming she was just some Puritan.

"No," she says, "I said it because I was assaulted at Sullivan in 1988. It happened at the cast party after the school play. I didn't tell anyone, because I knew of a girl who'd reported something at a dance the year before, and they said it was her fault. I carried my trauma around alone, for years and years."

I picture a young Mrs. Cole, happy and carefree—a theater kid, like Tasha. Dancing on a kitchen island with a drink in her hand. After that cast party, she must have built a shell—anything to protect her in a world that wouldn't do it for her.

The Sorceress.

I'm never going to use that name again.

"I ended up making it my mission to help Stewart girls get ahead," Mrs. Cole says. "To the point where I know I can be a little . . . harsh . . . but I want to see you flourish more than anything." She shakes her head and looks out toward Widow's Pass.

"I knew of Brenton's father when I was in school, and I've always assumed the apple fell close to the tree. Tonight, when it started to snow, I went outside to take a photo to send to my husband. That's when I saw him chase you into the woods, so I followed as fast as I could."

"Thank you," we say in unison.

"And for believing us," Chrissy adds.

When Mrs. Cole speaks again, the fracture is gone. She commands us like a general on a battlefield. "You don't need to thank me. You just need to follow my directions."

CHAPTER 21

It's a blessing to be under Mrs. Cole's command as we make our way back to the Sentinel Lodge. I'm too much of an empty shell to make my own decisions. Jess and Chrissy are in the same boat, I think. The three of us just stood there, nodding rhythmically and answering questions, as Mrs. Cole pieced together our next steps. The night had taken such unfathomable turns that nothing seemed real and anything seemed possible. It was like a dream. *Sure, Mrs. Cole. I can memorize that alibi and tell it to police so I don't get charged with murder.*

As the trees start to thin, we branch off onto another trail that circumvents the back terraces and spits us out at the far end of the parking lot.

"You wait here," Mrs. Cole says to me and Jess. The plan is for the two of us to leave now, and for Mrs. Cole to drive Chrissy home when prom wraps up. We say our rushed goodbyes and take turns squeezing Chrissy's hand. Mrs. Cole and Chrissy head back to the Sentinel Lodge, leaving Jess and me shivering in the driving snow. I want to break down and cry but I'm too cold.

"Y-you're l-lucky you b-bought that b-blazer," I tell her.

No sooner have the words left my lips than Jess's arms are around me, dragging me in to her body and leaving no gaps. I press my face to the soft skin of her neck and think maybe I'll live here forever.

Mrs. Cole returns a few minutes later with our bags from inside. Jess releases me to fumble through the pockets for her keys. She clicks the button, and the trusty old Kia Soul lights up a few rows of cars away.

"Chrissy's in the lounge with Cassandra," Mrs. Cole says. "We said I found her outside having a panic attack, and that we ended up talking for a while." She squints at the sky. "You sure you're okay to drive in this?"

Jess nods. I know we'll be okay. This blizzard might be unusual for this time of year, but it's nothing we haven't seen in an actual Adirondack winter.

"Be safe," Mrs. Cole says. "Remember everything I told you. If you ever want to talk, don't put anything in writing, but you can come by my office anytime." She puts a hand on each of our shoulders and squeezes tight. Then, with a whirl of her cape, she turns to go back to the prom, to chaperone a roomful of blissful kids who have no idea what we just went through, or what nightmare is still to come.

We get into the car, where Jess turns on the ignition and cranks up the heat as high as it'll go. She pulls out of the parking lot, windshield wipers pumping back and forth.

"Do me a favor and text the girls from my phone?" she asks. "It's in my right pocket."

I dig out the phone, and with numb fingers, I type a casual-sounding message to Tasha, Marina, Tori, and Raquelle. Mrs. Cole said we needed an excuse for me to have left the prom early, so that nobody conducting my inevitable questioning will be suspicious when I say I don't know where Riggs has disappeared to. We went with a totally legit medical condition I've had since I was little. I read it back to Jess, who nods, and I hit send:

> Me: Hey babes, Al had a migraine coming on and I needed to get her home ASAP. She gets them really bad during storms, with the air pressure and all that. Lmk if you still need a ride to the afterparty—I can come back and drive you once I get her settled at my place.

> Tasha: Omg no!!! Tell her to feel better! I'll text my parents and see if they can get us. Ty for the heads up!

"Done," I report.

Next, I send the crucial message to Riggs:

> Me: Hi, my love, I'm so sorry to be this girl, but I literally have a horrible migraine and I have to go home and rest. My head can't take the music anymore. I'm not sure where you went off to, but I'll be leaving with Jess in a few minutes if you want to meet me by the doors. No worries if you're having fun with your friends, though!! I'm so sad we can't spend the

The alibi is born. It's daunting to have it out there, to know the wheels are officially in motion, and there's no turning back.

It's hard to say exactly when people will notice Riggs is missing. Probably not tonight, with so much going on, not to mention so much alcohol flowing. It could happen tomorrow, or on Monday, when he doesn't show up for lacrosse practice in the morning. I'll have to claim I thought he was mad at me for leaving prom early, which is why I didn't think it was odd when I didn't hear from him the next day. I'll have to keep up the lie for the rest of my life, but I don't have a choice. Not until real justice exists.

As warmth seeps into my body, my teeth stop chattering and my limbs stop shaking. I can kind of, sort of, think straight again.

And that's when the full weight of Riggs's death slams into me. The sound of his voice screaming for help that won't come. The thoughts that must have flashed through his mind as he plummeted through empty space. The fact that it just as easily could have been me.

I start to cry uncontrollably.

"Oh, babe," Jess says, her own voice wavering, "I want to hug you but I'm scared to take my hands off the wheel. I love you so, so much."

I remember all the times *Riggs* said he loved me. Too many times to count, and each and every one of them a lie. A part of me wishes I could talk to Riggs one last time, to see for myself if our love story was really just a game to him. The whole thing is so sick and twisted, none of it seems true.

But I saw those heinous texts with my own eyes.

Fury works its way into my sobs, and they start coming out part-scream. Riggs will never know how much he hurt me. He'll never have to pay for what he did to Chrissy, either. Meanwhile, she'll be forced to remember that night for the rest of her life. If death is the ultimate punishment, why do I feel like Riggs got off easy?

We pull into the Quigleys' driveway in Saranac Lake and carry our bags to the house. Jess's parents went to see her brother's college theater production in Vermont this weekend, so we thankfully have the place to ourselves. Well, almost. As soon as we walk through the door, a very round, beige furball bounces down the stairs and immediately weaves a figure eight between my legs. It's so innocent, so mundane, that my eyes well up all over again. It's amazing I still have tears left in my body.

I bend down to scratch the cat behind her ears. "Hey, Marcy."

Marcy does a classic cat face-wipe against my hand, and Jess manages a weak laugh. "She loves you, too."

My tears splash into the tuft of fur between Marcy's ears, but she doesn't seem to mind. She trots along behind us as we trudge upstairs, where we take turns showering before crawling into Jess's bed. As ice pellets pelt the window, I roll onto my side, face to face with Jess, and pull the fluffy white duvet cover up to my chin. My eyes sting from crying and windburn and exhaustion. "I've never been more grateful to be safe and warm."

"Same. And we've been in a camping situation where we literally had to eat lard all night to survive."

This makes me smile. "Can we keep on distracting each other for a bit?"

"Obviously."

"How did things go with Sam tonight?" I ask. "I saw you two talking pretty close."

"Oh . . . *that*." She fidgets with the edge of the duvet. "So when I find him later in the night, I go into the conversation all flirty . . . and he ends up telling me he got back together with this girl from the camp he works at." She sighs. "I guess I can't blame him, given that I *did* Queen's Cup him."

"Oh, Jess. I'm sorry."

"Nah, it's all right. I'm happy for him. And we're gonna stay friends. We still really like talking to each other."

"It's probably for the better that you didn't end up dating," I point out. "You wouldn't want feelings getting in the way of your plans to overthrow capitalism together. *Ow!*"

Marcy got into bed with us, but she still hasn't settled down thanks to the storm outside. She's spent the past few minutes walking back and forth across my rib cage, and she just landed a paw on a tender part of my chest.

"She's obsessed with sleeping on that pillow." Jess nods at me. "She probably wants to share with you."

Wiggling forward, I make room for her to lie behind my head so I won't inhale Siberian cat hair all night. Marcy, satisfied at last, settles into a lump on the freed-up side of the pillow, her fur tickling the back of my neck and making me shiver.

"Wanna be little spoon?" Jess asks.

"Yes, please."

I roll over so she can pull me into the soft curve of her body. "Come share my pillow so you don't cough up a hairball in the morning."

Her chest expands as she yawns. It's been the longest night of both of our lives. I try to breathe in tandem with her, matching her deepening inhales and exhales, but exhausted as I am, I can't relax. Without conversation to distract me, my brain goes to the dark places—to heartbreak and trauma and injustice. It goes into panic mode, too—to the lies we'll have to tell, the secrets we'll have to keep, the endless variables that'll determine whether we make it out unscathed. It all plays through my head on a loop. Before long, I'm taking like ten breaths for every one of Jess's and feeling dizzy.

"Jess?" I whisper.

"Hmm?"

My voice is small and trembling. "I can't sleep. I can't even close my eyes."

Jess presses a hand to my chest. "Oh my God, your heart. Breathe, Al. Breathe. *Breeeathe.*"

"I'm going to have to lie to the police. What if they don't believe me?"

"We're all gonna back up your story."

"And what if they talk to Riley? What if he tells them I found out Riggs was in the King's Cup tonight?"

"With what Riley did to you, I doubt he's gonna mention you at all. Especially because Chrissy witnessed it. He'll probably say he was wasted and doesn't remember a thing."

"What if—"

"We'll figure it all out tomorrow, I promise. *Breeeathe.* Your heart's still racing."

"I feel like I'm dying."

"Alyson Benowitz, you are very much alive." She buries her nose in my hair and kisses the spot behind my ear. "And I'm right here with you."

FRIDAY, MAY 5

Press conference, Lake Placid Police Station

POLICE CHIEF RALPH NOSTRAND: Good morning. Today
we're going to provide an update in the case
regarding the disappearance of Brenton Riggs Jr.
Yesterday, at approximately nine a.m., members
of our country search-and-rescue team located
human remains at the base of Widow's Pass in
the Wilmington area. Family members have since
positively identified the remains as those of
Brenton Riggs Jr. At this time, the search phase of
our investigation has closed, and we are beginning
the process of determining cause of death and the
manner in which Mr. Riggs's death occurred.

FRIDAY, MAY 12

Press conference, Lake Placid Police Station

<u>POLICE CHIEF RALPH NOSTRAND:</u> Good morning. Today
we're going to provide an update in the case
regarding the death of Brenton Riggs Jr. An autopsy
was performed on Saturday, May 6, and the cause
of death has been determined as trauma sustained
from a fall. Widow's Pass is widely known among
experienced mountaineers in the area to be a high
cliff with very narrow walkable terrain at its top.
The results of our investigation are as follows:
Mr. Riggs attended the Sullivan-Stewart Preparatory
School prom at the Sentinel Lodge between the hours
of seven and eleven p.m. Witnesses interviewed by
the Lake Placid Police Department report seeing
Mr. Riggs inside the Sentinel Lodge ballroom as
late as nine p.m. This is the last time Mr. Riggs

was accounted for visually on the night of April
twenty-second.

According to National Weather Service data,
the weather on the twenty-second was blizzard
conditions, consisting of heavy snowfall, high
winds, and freezing temperatures. We do not believe
that any person was with Mr. Riggs after this point
and to the point at which his death occurred. We
believe Mr. Riggs walked to the area of Widow's
Pass, where a fall from the cliff occurred,
resulting in injuries that caused his death. At
this time, we don't know why Mr. Riggs decided to
embark on this hike.

As part of the standard toxicology analysis done
during an autopsy, it was determined that Mr. Riggs
had a significantly elevated blood alcohol level.

CHAPTER 22

June, two months after prom night

Jess and I have a tradition on the last weekend of the spring semester: We hike one of the High Peaks. Two, if the summits are close together and the sun's out.

Jess loves the whole experience: waking up before sunrise; stopping at the sandwich shop in town to pack lunch; smoothing out her map on the hood of the car to visualize our route before we hit the trail; leaping over streams, scrambling up rocks, and weaving through forests for hours; reveling in the sweeping views and the sense of accomplishment.

I'll admit that the views from the summits are breathtaking, and it's fun to eat a sandwich on top of a mountain, but mostly, I love that Jess loves it.

This year is a two-summitter: Wright and Algonquin. Jess tossed in the idea of sneaking in Iroquois, too, but she took it back when she saw my I'm-trying-to-be-supportive-but-dear-God-please-no grimace. We just left the top of Wright, where Jess and I ate our turkey sandwiches and shared a bag of dill pickle potato chips. Now we're making the climb up to Algonquin, where Jess promises the view will be even more spectacular. At 5,114 feet, it's the second highest of the 46 Peaks—just behind Marcy, which she says we'll climb for graduation next year.

"What's new with Tamar?" Jess asks, hopping over a mossy tree trunk like it's nothing more than a crack in the sidewalk.

"Actually"—I clamber over the tree trunk a lot less gracefully—"I confessed something big to her yesterday."

Jess stops in her tracks and whirls around. *"What?"* she whispers, her eyes darting around for other hikers.

We have a rule, which is probably obvious: no mentioning Riggs or the truth about prom night when other people are, or could be, around. For the first few weeks, it felt impossible, like I could burst at any second. It wasn't just the lying—to detectives, friends, family—that clawed at me; it was also not being able to express how much pain I was in. The hardest day of all, in that respect, was Riggs's funeral in Manhattan, the week after they found his body. I had to sit there with his family and friends and my parents and Harry and act like a grieving widow as the whole church hero-worshipped him. Riggs, who manipulated me for almost the entire school year. Who would have seen me die sooner than ruin his reputation. The only silver lining was that nobody pressed me when I said I wasn't in the mood to talk.

These days, the wounds aren't healed—they may never be— but they're less fresh. More like scabs that hurt when you press them. Add to that the case being closed, and the memorial services behind me, and I'm starting to feel more like myself again. Like I can finally think clearly.

"I meant vigilante justice mode!" I quickly clarify.

Jess lets out a visible sigh of relief before continuing along the trail. "You gave me a low-key heart attack," she says. "So what did you tell her?"

"Well, I asked her what she got up to the night before, and she said she went on a crappy date with some guy who talked about his ex the whole time. So I finally decided to tell her about Operation Egg Attack."

"How'd she take it? You always said she'd be mad if she found out."

"Well, she *was* kinda mad at first. She said I totally over-reacted, since *she* was the one who messed things up."

"Hmm, where have I heard that before?" Jess asks, looking pointedly over her shoulder.

"I know, I know." I shake my head. There's so much I wish I'd known sooner, including how I demonized myself after the Bookstore Aiden fiasco. "I told Tamar she deserved way, way better. I think she kind of believed me by the end. Or we're getting there."

"The power of the Queen's Cup," Jess muses.

After a steep final ascent that leaves me huffing and puffing, we emerge onto the summit, and—

"Whoa," I gasp.

Even Jess, who hikes way more than I do, turns in a slow circle with her mouth agape. We're standing on a rocky plateau ringed by a fluffy sea of clouds. Off in the distance, other mountaintops poke through like breaching whales. There's a point where the clouds break and the blanket of white disappears to reveal a rolling green landscape thousands of feet below.

"We're on top of the world," I say, still hardly believing my eyes.

Jess takes a few steps toward the closest edge, a spot where there's no cloud cover to block the sprawling view below. She pauses and looks over her shoulder. "Do you want to get closer?"

I nod, even as my pulse picks up. The views are my favorite part of any hike, besides being with Jess. But despite how far I've come in the past two months, it's hard not to think about *that night* when you're standing at the edge of a sheer cliff. Jess, reading my mind, extends a reassuring hand. I take it and let her lead me forward, the view getting better with every step, until at last, we're there. The edge of infinity.

As we stand there looking out, she strokes my thumb and presses her arm to mine. "Wing to wing," like Robert Frost wrote in that poem we read in AP English Lit. The line made me melt the first time I read it. Slowly but surely, my pulse calms down again.

And suddenly, instead of being afraid, I'm struck by how electric it feels to be alive: to feel my heart pound and my lungs expand with each breath; to hear the *whoosh* of the wind and smell the cool, clean air; to squeeze Jess's hand and have her squeeze mine back.

After a few minutes, Jess pulls out her phone to shoot a panoramic video for Instagram, but when she opens the app, her thumb freezes. A post at the top of her feed seems to have caught her eye.

"Oh my god, *cute*." Jess scrolls to the caption and beams. "Oh, this is so nice!"

"What's so nice?"

"Look at what Chrissy just posted." She shoves the phone into my hand.

It's a photo of a dozen preteen girls posing in the sunshine in front of a lacrosse net, smiles wide and arms slung around each other. I instantly recognize the girl front and center—her face caught midlaugh as a friend hugs her waist—as a younger Chrissy. She looks so happy, so carefree.

I read the caption below:

> I spent some of the best months of my life as a camper at Windham Woods. It's where I fell in love with lacrosse, made lifelong friends, and learned to believe in myself. That's why I'm pumped to share that this summer, I'm headed back to my home away from home to work as a lacrosse counselor! Can't wait to share the lax love with my Windham fam!

The words wrap around my heart and squeeze. Nothing can bring back the lacrosse season Chrissy lost this year, but I'm relieved to know that she'll get to play again—and in a place where she's safe and loved. Then, in the fall, she'll get a fresh start at Harvard, and start working her way toward the law career of her dreams.

"Hi—excuse me?"

We turn around at the stranger's voice. A middle-aged woman with an expensive-looking camera hanging from her neck smiles warmly at us.

"I'm a photographer, and I was taking pictures over there by the boulders when the two of you wandered into my shot," she continues. "You were posed so perfectly, I just had to keep going. Do you want to see?" She turns the camera around and shows us a stunning landscape that literally looks like one of those preset desktop backgrounds, but with our two silhouettes standing out against the clouds, holding hands.

"Oh my God!" we gush in unison. I'm already picturing it on the wall of my dorm room next year.

"If you give me your emails, I'll send you the photos. I have a few more."

"That would be amazing," I tell her, and Jess and I type our addresses into her phone.

"Thank you so much," Jess says. "This is the best surprise ever."

"It's my pleasure," the woman replies. "Isn't it beautiful up here? My wife and I love this hike. Speaking of which, she's over there and waiting to start the trek up to Iroquois, so I should get going." She smiles at us one more time before she walks away. "You two are a really cute couple."

For some strange reason, there's a blossoming in my chest. A sweet sensation that feels like a flower unfurling its soft, pink petals.

And for some strange reason, instead of correcting her, Jess just says, "Thanks."

With the woman gone, Jess takes my hand again. The touch of her fingers is different this time as she tugs me gently toward her. We're standing close enough that our faces almost touch. I can feel my heartbeat in every cell of my body. The tip of my nose tingles.

This isn't how I expected this day—our friendship . . . *anything*—to go. But I think I want to explore it.

I don't know who's leading and who's following. It's like we're reading each other's minds.

Jess gives me the smallest of nods.

I lean in.

Her mouth is the softest thing. Our lips together feel like

nothing and everything, the tingles spreading from the tip of my nose all the way down to my toes.

We press our foreheads together as we break apart from the kiss. "I was wrong before," Jess says.

"What do you mean?"

"*This* is the best surprise ever."

I stare into her eyes for a good, long minute, plumbing them for answers to the heap of new questions forming in my head. "Did you ever think . . . ?"

She shakes her head. "You?"

"No. The thought just kind of hit me, and then I . . ."

". . . really freakin' wanted to do it?"

"Yeah."

"Same."

We both laugh nervously. "Would you . . ." Jess bites her lip. "Would you maybe want to do it again?"

I've never kissed a girl before, let alone my best friend in the whole world. I have no idea what any of it means—for me or for us—but I do know how freeing it felt to kiss her simply because I wanted to kiss her. I push aside the rest of the unanswered questions and follow what my heart is telling me. Kissing Jess feels *right,* and maybe that's all I'll ever need to know. "Yeah," I answer. "I would."

So we do. We kiss for who knows how long on a mountaintop above the clouds. And I can't believe how lucky I am.

Wait, scratch that. I'm not having this romance-novel kiss because I'm *lucky.* Love isn't something you're picked for. It's something you make, together.

MONDAY, JULY 10

Jess Quigley @JQuigs11 · 5m

Beyond proud of my friend @Sam_h_young for walking the damn walk.

LINK:

> **The New York Times**
> *Student Calls Out "Toxic Competition for Sexual Prowess" at Sullivan-Stewart Prep School*
> Petition calls for headmaster's resignation after disturbing "King's Cup" details come to light.
> By Chris Collingwood, Staff Reporter

TUESDAY, SEPTEMBER 5

From: Marissa.Cole@sullivanstewart.edu
To: student-body@sullivanstewart.edu
Subject: Welcome back

Dear Sullivan-Stewart Student Body,

Welcome back to campus. I hope you all had a restful summer and feel energized as we start the school year.

After many years as a college advisor, I'm pleased to reintroduce myself as your new Head of School. In the spirit of transparency that I hope to promote across our campus, I wanted to share with you some of my top priorities for the coming semester.

- Revising our core curriculum to put a greater emphasis on systemic inequalities and social justice.

- Revising our sexual education curriculum to put a greater emphasis on enthusiastic consent.

- Establishing and implementing new protocols for reporting, investigating, and adjudicating cases of sexual harassment and misconduct.

Please feel free to drop by my office any time to discuss the above, or just to say hello. I look forward to beginning a new, brighter chapter in our school's history.

Sincerely,
Marissa Cole (she/her)
Head of School, Sullivan-Stewart Preparatory School

FRIDAY, DECEMBER 15

From: admissions@overbrooke.com
To: Alison.Benowitz@sullivanstewart.edu
Subject: Overbrooke College Early Admission Offer

Dear Alyson,

Congratulations! On behalf of the Overbrooke College, I am delighted to inform you . . .

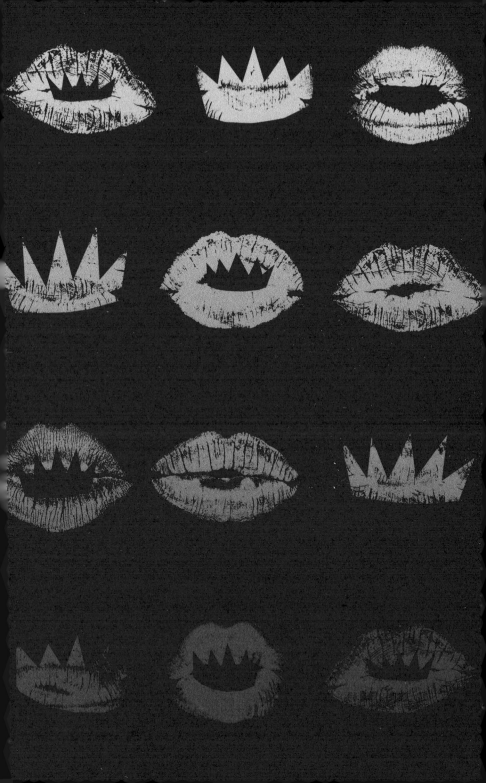

ACKNOWLEDGMENTS

It wasn't until I started writing *The Revenge Game* that I realized just how long I'd ached to tell this story. Thank you, reader, for picking up this book, and thank you to the incredible group of people who helped to make it a reality.

Wendy Loggia, your belief in this book from the very beginning has meant the world to me. Thank you, Wendy, and Ali Romig, for your genius ideas to take each draft to the next level. You helped me discover new depths to the Sullivan-Stewart crew, heighten the tension, and believe in myself the whole way through. You've made me a stronger storyteller, and you're both so wonderful to work with.

Danielle Burby, I'm proud to be a Mad Woman Literary Agency author, and proud to have a friend as bold, brilliant, and kind as you. *The Revenge Game* started as the B-plot for another book, and you helped me turn it into the star of the show. Thank you for being the world's best partner in social anxiety, feminist joy and rage, and sangrita-fueled story-plotting sessions that last until the restaurant closes.

Thank you to my wonderful author friends Jessica Goodman, Philip Ellis, Zachary Zane, and Marilyn La Jeunesse for the encouraging (and reassuring) texts and Slacks, and to my brilliant colleagues at *Men's Health* and Hearst for supporting my work in all its forms.

To the team at Sweetleaf Coffee & Cocktail Bar in Long Island City, Queens, my all-time favorite writing spot: thank you for the best caffeine, cocktails, and conversation. I'm probably sitting at the bar with my laptop as you read this.

Thank you to the Gray family for sharing your love of Lake Placid with me. With the exception of that time we froze and almost got blown off the top of Cascade, I've enjoyed every minute spent in the mountains with you. Special thanks to Hilary for teaching me all about high school lacrosse (fall ball!) and being the most supportive sister-in-law! I'm so lucky to have you all as family.

To my mom, Lisa; my dad, David; and my brother, Russell: I love you so much! Mom and Dad, thank you for instilling in me the confidence to tell stories that scare me. And thank you all for always sharing in my excitement and encouraging me as I navigate the highs and lows of writing life. I can't wait to finally—fingers crossed—get to hug you in person at a book launch.

And thank you, Tim, my love, for . . . everything. The mugs of tea you bring to my writing desk. The way you listen intently as I read you passages or work through plot holes while we go on walks. The countless times you've reassured me that I've done this before and I can do it again. We'll always be wing to wing. I love you.

ABOUT THE AUTHOR

Jordyn Taylor is the executive digital editor at *Men's Health* magazine and the award-winning author of the young adult novels *The Paper Girl of Paris* and *Don't Breathe a Word*. She is also an adjunct professor of journalism at New York University's Arthur L. Carter Journalism Institute. Jordyn was born and raised in Toronto and now lives in New York.

jordynhtaylor.com
@jordynhtaylor